UNDENIABLE

Eva & Deuce's Story

Madeline Sheehan

Cover by Meredith Blair

Interior designed by Jovana Shirley,
Unforeseen Editing

ISBN-13: 978-1481058131

Made in the USA
Charleston, SC
29 December 2015

DEDICATION

Dedicated to undeniable love.

TABLE OF CONTENTS

PROLOGUE

There will always be a reason why you meet people. Either you need them to change your life or you're the one that will change theirs.

—Angel Flonis Harefa

Mark Twain said, "The two most important days in your life are the day you were born and the day you find out why."

I don't remember the day I was born, but I remember the day I found out why.

His name was Deuce.

He was my "why."

And this is our story.

It is not a pretty one.

Some parts of it are downright ugly.

But it's ours.

And because I believe everything happens for a reason, I wouldn't change a thing.

Chapter ONE

I was five years old when I met Deuce. He was twenty-three, and it was visiting day at Rikers Island. My father, Damon Fox or "Preacher"—the president of the infamous Silver Demons motorcycle club (mother chapter) in East Village, New York City—was doing a five-year stint for aggravated assault and battery with a deadly weapon. It was not the first time my father had been in prison, and it wouldn't be the last. The Silver Demons MC was a notorious group of criminals who lived by the code of the road and gave modern society and all it entailed a great big fuck-you.

My father was a powerful and dangerous man who ruled over all Silver Demons worldwide and was highly respected but mostly feared by other MCs. He had government connections and ties to the mafia, but what made him the most dangerous and most feared was his many connections to average, everyday people. People who didn't run in his circle. People who were off the grid. People who could get things done quietly.

His way with words and his killer smile made him friends everywhere he went—and considering he'd been riding since he was in my grandmother's womb, when I say everywhere, I mean everywhere.

My father's shortcomings, the constant crime, and the club lifestyle weren't strange to me; it was all I knew.

I was holding my uncle "One-Eyed" Joe's hand as we walked through Rikers' family visiting room. Since my father was my only parent, my uncle Joe and aunt Sylvia had been given temporary custody of me. My mother, Deborah

"Darling" Reynolds, had split a few weeks after I was born. Many men would have crumpled under the responsibility of a newborn baby, especially a biker who couldn't handle more than a few weeks without needing the open road.

But not Preacher.

Aside from going to prison every once in a while, my father was a good dad, and I'd never wanted for a thing.

Dressed in an orange jumpsuit with his long brown hair pulled back in a ponytail at his nape, Preacher spotted us immediately and jumped up. He was hindered slightly by the handcuffs around his wrists, ankles looped together by a chain, and the prison guard standing behind him who shoved him back down.

"Eva," he said softly, smiling down at me as I climbed into an uncomfortable plastic chair. My sneaker-clad feet didn't reach the floor, and my chin barely cleared the table. Uncle Joe slid into the chair beside me and put his arm around me, pulling my chair close to his.

"Daddy," I whispered, trying so hard not to cry. "I want to hug you. Uncle Joe says I can't. Why can't I?"

My father blinked. Then he blinked again. I didn't know at the time, but my big, strong, rough-and-tough father was trying not to cry.

Uncle Joe squeezed my shoulder. "Baby girl," he said gruffly, "tell Daddy 'bout the spellin' bee."

Excitement battled my tears and won. "I won the spelling bee, Daddy! My teacher, Mrs. Fredericks, says even though I'm only in kindergarten, I can spell as good as a third grader!"

My father grinned.

Seeing this grin and not wanting to lose it, I kept going.

"Do you know how old third graders are, Daddy?"

"How old, baby?" my father asked, laughing.

"They are eight," I whispered excitedly. "Or sometimes nine!"

"Proud of you, baby girl," my father said, his eyes shining.

I beamed. When you are young, your parents are your entire world. My father was my world. If he was happy, I was happy.

Uncle Joe squeezed my shoulder again. "Eva, honey, why don't you go get somethin' from the snack machines so Daddy and I can have a word."

This was typical. At the club everyone was always "having a word"—words I wasn't allowed to hear. Most times, I didn't really care since all the boys loved me, gave me lots of hugs, let me ride on their shoulders, and bought me presents all the time. To a five-year-old biker brat, an MC full of surrogate big brothers and daddies is the equivalent to a normal child being able to celebrate Christmas every day.

I took my uncle Joe's money and skipped off to the snack machines. Two people were in line ahead of me, so I did what I always did when I was bored—I started singing. Unlike most children my age who were listening to New Kids on the Block or Debbie Gibson, I was listening to the music played around the club. A particular favorite of mine was "Summertime" by Janis Joplin. So there I was, shaking my butt and singing "Summertime" way, way out of tune, waiting in line for stale potato chips in the Rikers Island family visiting room, when I heard, "You like Hendrix, too, kid?"

I swiveled around and was met with a pair of denim-clad legs with the knees worn clean through. I looked up, and my eyes widened in delight. He was tall and tan. His arms and legs were thickly muscled, and his waist was trim. His forehead was wide, and his jaw was strong and square. His head was shaved, only a fuzz of blond hair showing, and his forearms were heavily tattooed with different depictions of elaborate dragons. I'd never seen a more beautiful man.

There are three different types of men in this world: There are weak men—men who run and hide when life slaps them in the ass. Then there are men—men who have a backbone, yet occasionally, when life slaps them in the ass, will rely on others. And then there are real men—men who don't cry or complain, who don't just have a backbone, they are the backbone. Men who make their own decisions and live with the consequences and who accept responsibility for their actions or words. Men who, when life slaps them in the ass, slap back and move on. Men who live hard and die even harder.

Men like my father and my uncles. Men I loved with all my heart.

Men like Deuce.

"I like Hendrix," I said. "But Janis rules. I listen to 'Rose' almost every single day!"

He grinned down at me and dimples popped out all over the place.

"I like you, kid," he said, still grinning. "You got good taste in tunes, and you've got a pair of Chucks on instead of those stupid fuckin' high-tops everyone's wearin'."

He liked me. This was hands down the best day ever.

"I hate high-tops," I said, wrinkling up my nose.

He winked. "Me, too."

I was so throwing out all my high-tops when I got home.

When it was my turn in line, I stood on my tiptoes and popped change into the machine. I took my time studying the selections, deciding on a small bag of salted peanuts. Moving out of the way, I watched as the man bought two bags of potato chips, three candy bars, and a big chocolate chip cookie.

"Wow," I said. "You're really hungry."

He laughed. "Not for me." He pointed across the room. "My old man."

I spared a quick glance at my father and Uncle Joe. Their heads were bowed over the table, still "having a word."

"Can I meet him?" I asked.

His eyebrows popped up. "Uh, he's kinda cranky."

I laughed. All the men I knew were kinda cranky.

I slipped my hand in his and looked up, ready to go meet his father. His hand was warm and comfortable, like my bed was after I'd slept in it all night.

He stared down at our joined hands, his expression confused.

"Ready," I told him, tugging on his hand. Shrugging, he led me to a nearby table where an older man with a long gray beard and a shaved head sat, cuffed the same way my father was. He released my hand to take his seat, and I climbed into the seat next to him.

"Hi," I said cheerfully.

"You got somethin' to tell me?" the old man asked his son.

"She likes Janis," he replied.

The old man studied me. "You like Janis, kid?"

I nodded. "And Steppenwolf and Three Dog Night and the Rolling Stones and Billie Holiday—"

"Billie Holiday?" he interrupted, sounding surprised.

I popped some peanuts in my mouth and nodded. "She rules."

The old man grinned and his entire face changed. I knew immediately; a long time ago, this cranky old man had been as beautiful as his son.

"I like Billie Holiday," he said gruffly.

"I like you," I said spontaneously because I always said stuff spontaneously. "Do you want some peanuts?"

"Sure, kid," he said, smiling. "I'd love some."

I poured the rest of my peanuts into his hand, and he popped them all into his mouth at the same time.

"Eva!"

I jumped at the sound of my uncle Joe's voice. He was walking briskly across the room toward me. Once he reached the table, not only did Uncle Joe looked pissed off, but so did my two new friends.

"You got a death wish?" Uncle Joe whispered to the old man. "Horsemen are in good with the Demons. Let's fuckin' keep it that way."

"Ah," the old man said, looking back at me. "You must be Preacher's little girl. He's talked 'bout you. Proud as fuck, he is."

I nodded proudly. "I am Preacher's little girl. And I'm gonna be just like him when I grow up. I'm gonna have a Fat Boy, but I want mine to be sparkly, and I want a pink helmet with skulls on it. And instead of being the club president, I'm gonna be the club queen 'cause I'm gonna marry the biggest, scariest biker in the whole world, and he's gonna let me do whatever I want because he's gonna love me like crazy."

My uncle Joe burst out laughing, and the old man shook his head, smiling. The beautiful man turned to face me and leaned forward.

"I'm gonna hold you to that," he whispered.

I didn't respond. I couldn't. I was captivated by the intensity I saw in his bright blue-and-white-flecked eyes. They reminded me of a frosted-over lake. He had beautiful icy blue eyes that sucked me in to a warm, safe place that I wanted to stay inside of forever.

He stuck out his hand, breaking the spell. "Name's Deuce, sweetheart. My old man here is Reaper. It was nice talkin' with ya."

I put my hand in his, and his big fingers closed around mine. "Eva," I whispered. "That's my name, and it was so, so great to meet you, too."

He smiled. And his eyes smiled, too. I got lost again in his pretty eyes.

Then Uncle Joe picked me up and threw me over his shoulder. "Isn't that fuckin' expensive-as-hell private school teachin' you 'bout talkin' to strangers?" he said. "Gonna have a talk with those prissy fuckers. Gonna have a talk with my fist."

"Bye," I yelled, waving frantically as I was marched away.

Reaper gave me a two-handed handcuffed wave and a big smile.

Deuce got to his feet grinning and gave me a two-finger salute. "Bye, darlin'."

Darlin'.

It was official. I was head over heels in love.

Deuce watched One-Eyed Joe, Silver Demon lifer, stalk off with Preacher's kid hanging over his shoulder, grinning and waving like a lunatic. He shook his head and smiled. When he could no longer see her, he lost his smile and turned back to his old man.

His old man had lost his smile, too.

"Cute kid," Reaper grumbled. "Shoulda had a girl instead of you two fucks."

He stared at his old man. He had a moment of longing, watching him smile at that kid and talk to her the way he should have talked to his own kids but never had. He'd been too busy beating on him and his brother.

Good times.

"Preacher's on the move," Reaper growled. "Takin' that fuckin' deal with the Russians right out from under you. Why the motherfuck didn't you snap that shit down when you had the chance?"

And there it was. He was VP, and that's all he was to his old man. Someone to pass the fucking gavel to when he finally—and it couldn't come fast enough—kicked it.

"Preacher's road chief beat me to it. Snagged that shit 'fore I even heard about it."

Reaper's expression went glacial. "You're such a fuckin' fuckup. Shoulda made Cas VP. Shoulda had that fuckin' cunt of a whore get ridda ya."

His mother had been a whore—not a streetwalker but a club whore. She was sixteen when his father knocked her up, his old man nearly thirty. After he was born, his old man kicked her to the curb with nothing but the clothes on her back. All he'd ever had of his mother was a gritty picture of a very young girl sitting on his old man's Harley; OLIVIA MARTIN was written on the back. He liked to think that she started a new life somewhere else with someone who was nothing like his old man. Found some peace and a family who loved her.

His younger brother, Cas, was the product of another knocked-up whore. Same story, different day.

For twenty-three years, he'd been putting up with his shit. He'd had enough. Pushing out of his chair he stood up, placed his palms on the table, and leaned forward.

"Nobody—and when I say nobody, I mean fuckin' everybody—gives two fucks about what happens to you, you miserable shit. The club respects their prez, but not one of your boys gives a fuck whether you live or die. You got life, old man, and I been runnin' shit in your absence. And seein' as I been runnin' shit a fuck of a lot better than you, I don't have to come here. But I do outta fuckin' respect, and I just lost the last shred of respect I had left."

"You little shit," Reaper hissed. "You're gonna pay—"

"No. You're gonna pay. Puttin' the cash up for bids the minute I walk outta here."

Fear flashed through his old man's eyes. He'd never seen anything sweeter.

"Remember, you piece-of-shit fuck, when you're bleedin' out, that it was me who fuckin' ordered it."

He turned away before his old man could say another word and strode through Rikers' visiting room breathing hard, his heart pounding in his chest, determined to end that man.

"Deuce!" a little voice squealed. He turned.

Eva was gunning for him. Just before she reached him, she came skidding to a stop, breathing heavy, and thrust her hand out. "Didn't get to share with you," she said breathlessly.

He bent down and closed his hand around a small bag of peanuts.

His throat closed up.

This kid, this little fucking kid who didn't know him at all, had just given him his first gift with nothing expected in return, no favors, no stipulations, no nothing. He'd been wrong. There was something sweeter than seeing fear in his old man's eyes. Eva was far sweeter. If he ever had a kid, he wanted a kid like this one.

"Thanks, darlin'," he said hoarsely.

"Will I ever see you again?" She cocked her head to the side, wide-eyed, waiting for his response.

He stared into her eyes, her phenomenal eyes that were too big for her face. Big and smoky gray like a thunderstorm. Fucking beautiful.

He smiled. "Hope so, sweetheart."

She gave him a killer cute grin and bounced back to her old man and uncle—who were staring daggers at him—shaking those pigtails.

After shoving the peanuts in his pocket, he left. First street pay phone he saw, he posted the hit. It took all of an hour, and he had a buyer. Three days later, his old man bled out in the showers.

Chapter TWO

Seven years passed before Deuce and I crossed paths again.

During those years, my father had been released from prison, and I had gained an older, pain-in-the-ass brother, Frankie.

Franklin Deluva, Senior was my dad's road chief. He died in a head-on collision with a Mack truck a few years back, and his old lady died several years earlier from breast cancer. As was the case with most biker brats, Frankie didn't have any other family willing to take him on. Since my father didn't have a son, he took Frankie under his wing and began mapping out his future as a Demon. If Frankie stayed the course, my father made it clear he'd be taking the gavel from him one day. Which was fine, great even, but there was just one big problem.

Frankie was angry.

All the time.

So much so that all he did was get into fights—at school, at the club, on the sidewalk, in the grocery store. Frankie would fight with a brick wall if it pissed him off. You wouldn't believe how many walls have pissed Frankie off.

His poor fifteen-year-old body was already covered in scars from street fights. Since he had come to live with us, he'd been hospitalized sixteen times for various broken bones, knife wounds, and numerous concussions.

Frankie also had serious abandonment issues.

When he first moved in with my father and me, he had violent nightmares. He would wake up terrified, covered in sweat, and screaming at the top of his lungs. The nightmares turned into night terrors, and Frankie began thrashing in his sleep, beating his head with his fists while screaming and crying uncontrollably. My father had to hold him down until he either calmed or regained full consciousness.

One night, when my father was out on a run, Frankie snuck into my room and slipped in bed with me. He slept soundly for the first time since he'd moved in with us, and he'd been in my bed ever since.

And life moved on.

Two weeks after my twelfth birthday, my father decided it was time for Frankie to tag along on an MC run. When he found out I wouldn't be going, he threw a violent fit until my father caved. When it came to Frankie, my father was a total pushover.

On the back of Frankie's bike, I left Manhattan headed for northern Illinois. Our first stop: a pumpkin farm. When your father and his cohorts were involved in illegal dealings and needed to meet privately, criminal gatherings at pumpkin farms were more frequent than one would think.

This sort of meeting usually lasted a couple of days; the adults stayed inside and the kids outside. There was always a lot of yelling, a lot of fighting, and a lot of drinking. And a lot of slutty women.

I started developing early and looked rather awkward, being as skinny and as tall as I was—all elbows and knees with a pair of C cups. Several boys, who had accompanied their fathers to the meet, had been following me around, snapping my bra strap, and calling me "stuffer"—which was how I found myself hiding in a tree, my headphones on, listening to the Rolling Stones, swinging my legs and bobbing my head while singing along.

I felt a tug on the toe of my Chucks, and I jerked my foot away.

"Go away, Frankie!" I yelled.

Frankie tugged my toe again, and I ripped off my headphones and glared down at him.

It wasn't Frankie.

Except for his hair, which was now thick and sandy blond and hung down to his shoulders, he looked exactly the same. Still devastatingly beautiful.

He grinned his multi-dimpled grin.

"Heard you were around here somewhere, darlin'. You remember me?"

"Deuce," I whispered, staring at him. "From Rikers."

He burst out laughing. "I'm not actually from there. Home sweet home is in Montana. I was just visitin' my old man, same as you. Remember?"

I nodded. "Reaper. I liked him."

His smile slipped. "He's gone now."

I never knew what to say to people who had lost their loved ones. Nothing ever sounded right. But seeing the faraway look in Deuce's icy blue eyes, I had to say something.

"He had a great smile," I said softly. "Just like yours."

His gaze shot to mine, and he smiled.

And I smiled.

"You know," he said as he pulled a thin gold chain out of his dirty white T-shirt and lifted it over his head, "you should have this."

He grabbed my hand and placed the chain in it.

"It was my old man's," he said. "Ain't no one ever said nothin' nice 'bout that bastard. Ever. Not even his own mother. Not until right now. Figure that makes it yours."

I held the chain up and studied the small round medallion hanging on it. The Hell's Horsemen's insignia was on the front. The words HELL'S HORSEMEN encircled a hooded Grim Reaper straddling a Harley and holding a scythe.

On the back, it read REAPER.

"That day seven years ago was the first time I'd seen that asshole smile. It was also the last."

I didn't know what to say. So I didn't say anything and just slipped the chain over my neck.

"Thanks," I said and tucked the medallion under my Jimi Hendrix T-shirt. "I like it."

Nodding, he looked off into the distance.

"Gonna take a walk through them pumpkins, darlin'. You wanna join?"

I hung my headphones around my neck, clipped my Walkman to my jeans pocket, and hopped down.

I didn't give it much thought and just slipped my hand into his, like I would with my father or Frankie. He glanced down but didn't pull away, and his thick, warm fingers curled around mine as we started walking.

As we walked, Deuce stared up at the cloudy gray sky, chain smoking, and not speaking.

"Are you sad?" I asked.

He glanced down at me, and his brows furrowed. I bit my lip. Had I said the wrong thing? Maybe he didn't wanted anyone to know he was sad. My heart started beating faster and faster. I felt my palm grow clammy, and because my hand was in Deuce's hand, I became embarrassed and started sweating even more.

"Little brother died, darlin'. Few days ago."

I stopped walking and threw my arms around his waist, squeezing as hard as I could. "I'm so, so sorry," I whispered.

Deuce sucked in a breath. "Darlin'."

Then he fell to his knees and squeezed me until I couldn't breathe, but I didn't care because it felt so nice, and I knew he needed it.

"You're a good kid, darlin'. A good, sweet kid," he whispered in my ear.

He pulled away and looked me in the eyes. "Promise me you'll stay that way, yeah? You and me, kid, we were fuckin' born in the life, reared by the road and the wheel. It's what we know and where we belong, but that don't mean it won't take its toll. So you promise me, no matter what you see, no matter what sort of fucked-up shit happens to you, don't let this life turn you bitter."

I stared into his icy blue eyes, entranced by the safety and comfort blanketing me, warming me. I couldn't look away. I wanted to tuck this feeling in my back pocket, take it home with me, and keep it safe under my pillow to have when I needed it most.

Eventually, when I remembered what he'd said, I nodded.

He brushed his knuckles down my cheek and stood. I slid my hand back into his, and we resumed walking. Deuce resumed smoking, and I began pointing out unusually large pumpkins.

"You ever watch *It's the Great Pumpkin Charlie Brown*?" Deuce asked. "Stupid fucker makes me laugh."

I decided I, too, really liked that stupid fucker Charlie Brown and made a mental note to watch everything featuring Charlie Brown as soon as I got home.

"You gonna dress up for Halloween, darlin'?"

"I haven't decided," I told him. "Halloween is very tricky. Once a year you get to dress up and pretend you're something or someone entirely different than you are. There's nothing else quite like it. You don't want to mess that up, you know? It's important to pick carefully—that way you have no regrets, only fabulous memories."

Deuce stopped walking and stared down at me.

"What are you thinkin' you might wanna be?"

"Maya Angelou," I replied immediately. "Or Eleanor Roosevelt."

He started choking.

"But," I hurriedly continued, "in order to dress up as Maya Angelou, I somehow have to make my skin black without insulting the African-American community. I'll probably end up as Eleanor Roosevelt. Not that I mind. She was an amazing woman."

"How old are you?" he asked roughly, pounding on his chest with his fist.

"Twelve."

"*Twelve?*" Looking bewildered, he shook his head. "Thought you were a pretty smart kid when I first met you. Now I know you are."

I blushed. Deuce—president, according to his cut, of the Hell's Horsemen—thought I was smart. How cool was that?

"How old are you?" I asked.

"Thirty, darlin'." He looked down at me and wrinkled his nose. "Old, yeah?"

I shrugged. "My dad's thirty-seven, and he's still pretty cool."

His eyes bugged out of his head. "Lemme get this straight. You're twelve years old. You're probably gonna dress up as Eleanor Roosevelt for Halloween. And you think your old man is cool?"

I nodded.

He shook his head again, smirking. "Damn."

My stomach dropped. He was making fun of me.

I ripped my hand out of his and crossed my arms over my chest. "I know I'm weird. Everyone at school always tells me that. Everyone except my best friend, Kami. They hate my music because it's old. They hate my clothes 'cause they're boy clothes. They think I'm a freak! So go ahead and say it! You think I'm a freak, don't you?"

Deuce knelt down in front of me. "Darlin', you ain't weird. You're twelve. And those kids don't hate you, not even close. The girls are jealous 'cause you're so damn pretty, and the boys are just bein' boys, tryin' to flirt but not havin' the first clue how to go about it."

You're so damn pretty.

"I'm pretty?"

His lips twitched. "Only twelve and already fishin'. Yeah, darlin', you're pretty. Gonna be beautiful someday. Gonna make some boy happier than a pig in shit."

I grinned. Who would have thought the words "pig" and "shit" used in the same sentence could make a girl blissfully happy?

"There it is," he said quietly. "That's what I like to see. Nothin' better than a pretty girl smilin'."

I stared up at him; he stared down at me. His hard eyes gentled, and I felt my body go butter soft. Something was happening to me—something important, monumental even.

The shift from child to teenager. Although I wouldn't understand this until I was much older, what had happened and why it had happened, standing there in the middle of a pumpkin field, I'd known I was irrevocably changed. And that I'd changed because of and for this man.

"EVA! WHAT THE FUCK!"

I swiveled around. Frankie was storming toward us, kicking poor, innocent pumpkins out of his way.

"Great," I groaned. "Frankie found me."

"Your man?" Deuce asked, watching Frankie's temper tantrum with marked interest.

My eyes bugged out of my head. "Ew! He's my fake brother!"

Frankie's long brown hair was flying all over the place, and his dark brown eyes had darkened further with burgeoning anger. Only fifteen and he was already six feet tall with the body of a quarterback. He wasn't as big as Deuce was, but he would be someday.

"I know you?" Frankie hissed, stopping only inches from Deuce.

Deuce's eyebrows popped up, and he smirked. "No, kid. 'Fraid we haven't had the pleasure."

Frankie hated being called a kid, especially in front of me. I watched as his hands clenched into fists.

Deuce wasn't smiling anymore. "You're gonna wanna reel that in. I don't take shit from grown men, and I'm sure as shit not gonna take shit from an asshole who's pretendin' he's grown 'cause he wants down a girl's pants."

I closed my eyes. Deuce didn't know Frankie, therefore he didn't know that Frankie wasn't trying to impress me. This was just the way he was all the time. Before he could throw a punch and get his butt kicked by Deuce, I pushed in between them and wrapped my arms around Frankie's middle.

"I missed you," I said hurriedly. "I've been looking everywhere for you and couldn't find you anywhere. I asked Deuce to help me look for you."

Frankie's arms wrapped around me, and his hard body sagged against mine. One of his hands fisted in my hair, and the other held tight to my waist.

"Sorry," he muttered. "I just thought…I don't know…you gotta stay close to me. I can't fuckin' protect you if I don't know where you are. If somethin' happened to you, baby, I would kill myself. Can't be in this world without you. Fuck, I can't even think 'bout you bein' gone. Makes me fuckin' crazy."

"Oh, Frankie," I whispered. "You gotta stop worrying. Nothing's gonna happen to me, and I'm never going to leave you."

Deuce hesitated leaving Eva alone with that crazy little shit, but it looked as if she was the only person who had any sort of control over him, so he left her to it. He knew kids like Frankie growing up—jacked in the head, no control, caught crazy at the drop of a hat, and usually ended up dead before they turned thirty. Preacher giving him a cut had been a big mistake. He didn't give a shit how much love Preacher had for the boy. When shit got intense—and it always did—you needed level-headed men on your crew.

"Dare you to touch her tits."

Deuce paused beside a run-down barn at the edge of the farm.

"Dare you to fuck her."

"Preacher finds out, he'll kill you."

He stiffened. Little shits were talking about Eva.

"I'm not scared of Preacher. 'Sides, she's the only bitch here old enough to fuck."

"She's fuckin' ugly. Except for her tits; bitch has nice tits. I'd fuck her just to see those tits."

Deuce saw red. Eva was twelve years old. Yeah, she had tits, twelve-year-old tits. And these fuckers were around sixteen and seventeen. He cracked his knuckles and stalked inside the barn.

Five little shits were leaning back against a row of empty horse stalls, smoking cigarettes, acting like they were grown.

"Deuce," one of the little shits said. "What's up, man?"

He didn't answer. Just walked up to the first little shit, kicked him in his face, and then moved on to the next. Yanking little shit number two up by his collar, he spit in his face, gave him a fist to the gut, and tossed him to the side.

The remaining three had scrambled behind stacked bales of hay.

"Get your fuckin' asses back here," he said, pulling his piece from the back of his jeans. "And take your fuckin' punishment like the men you ain't. If not, I got some bullets with your fuckin' names on 'em."

"What the fuck did we do?" a pimply-faced, gangly little shit screeched.

Using his gun, he gestured to where they had been sitting just moments ago. "Get. The. Fuck. Over. Here."

They got.

"I hear you talkin' 'bout Eva again. I see you lookin' at Eva. I see you within a hundred feet of Eva. You are all dead. You feel me?"

Wide-eyed, they nodded.

"Gonna go find your fathers next and tell them what kinda bastards they're raisin'. And I 'spect they'll be beatin' the shit outta you next, but first you're dealin' with me."

He took the third little shit by his greasy hair and brought the kid's head down on his knee. Out cold, he shoved him to the side.

The fourth little shit pissed himself the moment Deuce stepped to him. Laughing, he moved on to the last little shit. The one who had called Eva ugly. Grabbing his neck, he shoved the barrel of his gun in the boy's mouth.

"Know for a fact you got a couple of sisters. Know for a fact one of 'em is just a year older than Eva. How 'bout I go find your little sister and fuck her? How 'bout I get some of my boys to fuck her, too? Maybe we can all fuck her at the same time? Fuck her in her mouth, and her pussy, and her fuckin' asshole. Sound good?"

Crying, the kid shook his head.

"You respect women, you little fuckin' shit. It was a fuckin' woman who carried you around in her fuckin' body, fuckin' birthed you, and fuckin' loved you. It's gonna be a woman who keeps you warm at night, who lets you inside her body, and it's gonna be a woman who carries around your fuckin' children. You fuckin' respect that, you feel me? You fuckin' respect women—all of 'em—or I will end you."

He released him, and the kid fell to his knees retching.

"Fuckin' little shits," he muttered. Tucking his gun back in his jeans, he walked away.

Chapter
THREE

I was sixteen.

It was summer in Manhattan.

And it was the first Sunday of the month.

Smack dab between Morrissey's Bar and a Middle Eastern grocery store, up on the roof of the Demons' five-story Portland brownstone, the MC's monthly family barbeque was in full swing. Old ladies and girlfriends, children, cousins, friends of families, and business associates were talking and laughing, dancing and drinking, while dogs and burgers were being flipped on the grills as fast as the kegs were emptying.

On top of a picnic table, Frankie and I sat side by side sharing a pair of earbuds. My Discman was wedged between us, and our heads were pressed together while we rocked out to Led Zeppelin's "Dazed and Confused." I had my arm slung over Frankie's broad shoulders, and his hand slid up and down my thigh with his fingers tapping out the beat of the song.

"Heads up, brothers, the Horsemen are here!"

My head swiveled right.

Another yell. "Hide your women!"

This was followed by loud guffaws and a lot of feminine giggling.

I watched as a large group of leather-clad men joined the crowd on the roof. On the backs of their cuts was the Hell's Horsemen insignia.

Just like the insignia on my medallion.

My heart started pounding. Was Deuce here? I scanned the crowd, but the Horsemen had already dispersed throughout the sea of people.

Frankie squeezed my thigh to get my attention. I pulled out my earbud and slanted my eyes at him.

"Want me to hide some booze for later? Some smoke?"

Demon barbeques were infamous for becoming wild and reckless, and more often than not, every last biker would be passed out drunk before midnight. This was when their offspring partied with their leftover booze and green.

"Yeah," I said and smiled at him.

Frankie stood, ran his fingers through my long, dark hair, and pulled my head flush against his hard abdomen. "Be right back," he whispered.

"And Eva?"

I looked up.

"Don't fuckin' go anywhere until I get back."

Rolling my eyes, I put my earbuds in and resumed my head bobbing, foot tapping, and overly loud singing, happily ignoring the openmouthed stares my singing always caused.

Middle school had been rough for me, but I'd since grown into my awkwardness. I embraced my weirdness, and I was cool with my oddities. I was who I was, and I didn't care anymore about what anyone else thought. High school so far had been good to me. I was pretty, I was popular, and I had a ton of friends. I suspected most of my girlfriends used me to get near Frankie, trying to bag him. Frankie was a good-looking guy, big and broad, with finely chiseled features. He was a pureblood Italian with brown eyes, the color of dark chocolate, and thick brown hair he'd grown long.

The girls flocked, and bag them he did. In droves. Never did the same girl twice. So other than having to listen to all the girls at school whine and pine over Frankie, life was good. It was fun and uncomplicated, and I was happy.

My eyes trained on the blacktop beneath me as a shadow fell over me, and a pair of leather boots walked into my line of sight. I stared down at them. Full-grain black leather with a rubber sole. Detailed at the ankles with metal buckles, they looked edgy, sexy.

I looked up.

"Still wearin' Chucks and singin' out of tune I see."

Yep. Edgy and sexy. Just like the man wearing them.

Deuce was all dimples and smiles and icy blue eyes that matched perfectly with his long blond hair that he'd pulled back in a stubby ponytail. He was just as large as I remembered, broad and well-built; he towered over me and was at least half a body wider. He looked hot as hell in a tight white tee, his leather cut, and ratty, low-slung jeans. This time when I grinned at him, it wasn't with little-girl awe; it was with sixteen-year-old sexual fascination.

"Eva fuckin' Fox," he drawled. "You've grown."

"Deuce," I said, smiling impishly. "You've aged."

He threw his head back and laughed a deep, rumbling laugh that had my belly clenching and my nipples tightening. I wasn't the only female affected; several women on the roof were openly fawning over him.

Reaching inside his cut, Deuce pulled out a pack of cigarettes. He kept his eyes on me as he lit it. "How old are ya now, darlin'? Eighteen, nineteen?"

"Sixteen," Frankie hissed, appearing beside me. "Six-fuckin'-teen."

Deuce's eyes cut to Frankie, and I watched as recognition dawned. It wasn't happy recognition.

"Crazy fuckin' Frankie," Deuce said, smirking. "Got a pretty impressive rep for a brother so young."

Frankie had been nicknamed "Crazy Frankie" a few years ago because…well, he was crazy.

Hands clenched into fists, Frankie glared at Deuce. "You're gonna wanna back the fuck off Eva, Horseman."

I tugged on his cut. "Calm down. He's friends with Daddy."

Frankie turned his glare on me. "No, baby, he's not. He's in business with him. It's fuckin' different. You shouldn't be around him; he's fuckin' dangerous. If Preacher could, he'd take him to ground."

I gaped at Frankie.

He shrugged. "Way it is, babe."

Unaffected by Frankie's casual talk of his death, Deuce took a deep drag of his cigarette and blew a long stream of smoke right into Frankie's face. Frankie turned red with anger.

"Killed two of Bannon's boys last week in Pittsburg, yeah, Frankie? Whole circuit knows. Word is he's gunnin' for ya. You got Eva cuffed to your side all the time. Think that might be kinda fuckin' dangerous for her?"

My mouth fell open. "You killed someone?" I whispered, floored that Frankie was capable of killing. I knew it happened when MC business went bad, but no one ever talked to me directly about it, and I certainly hadn't thought my nineteen-year-old brother had been doing his fair share.

Frankie's nostrils flared; his dark eyes trained on Deuce. "You fuck," he hissed.

Deuce shrugged. "Way it is, brother," he said, throwing Frankie's words back at him.

"Frankie," I whispered. "Bannon's gonna kill you."

Mickey Bannon was a bad guy—Irish mafia kind of bad. He ran most of his business out of Pittsburgh, but he had ties all over the place, even overseas. I knew my father was having problems with him reneging on deals, but I didn't think it had gone so far as to result in murder.

With his eyes still on Deuce, Frankie gripped my shoulder. "No, babe. I already took care of it. Me and Trey. Nobody's fuckin' comin'."

Trey was my cousin, Uncle Joe's oldest son, and not a nice guy. Well…he was nice to me and his mother, but that was about it. Trey committing murder wasn't a surprise to me.

Deuce snorted. "Gonna need a new bedpost to keep countin' your notches. You're rackin' up bodies faster than the Germans took out the Jews."

Reflexively, I jerked away from Frankie. "What!"

His head whipped in my direction. "Ev—"

"No!" I snapped. "I need you to go away right now!"

"Be fuckin' pissed, Eva. I don't give a shit! But no way I'm leavin' you alone with this fuck!"

"How long you been followin' her around now, Frankie? Protectin' her from fuckin' nothin'?"

"Ten years," I helpfully supplied. Frankie glared down at me.

"You gonna follow her down the aisle, too? Move in with her and her man? Be their fuckin' nanny?"

Instead of looking at his face, Deuce was watching Frankie's hands, waiting for Frankie to make his move, so he could take him down. If he knew Frankie's rep, then he knew Frankie's fuse was nonexistent, and he was purposely baiting him.

"I'm. Her. Man," Frankie spat through clenched teeth. "Any fuckin' babies she'll be havin' will be mine."

Oh good Lord.

"Frankie," I said sternly. "First of all, you are not my man. I have no man. And I don't plan on having one anytime soon, especially not one who has fucked my entire high school! Second, I don't want to talk about hypothetical weddings or babies. Ever again. Third, if you get into another fight with one of Daddy's business partners that Daddy's cool with, he's gonna kill you this time. Not just put you in the hospital with minor brain swelling, but put you in the ground. So do me a favor, go get a beer, go take a walk, go get a blow job, whatever. Just calm the hell down. And lastly, I need some time to process all this new information. So please give me some space."

Frankie growled at me. An honest-to-God growl.

"I'm gonna tell Daddy," I warned.

"Do you have any idea how fuckin' dangerous this asshole is?"

I glanced up at Deuce. Our eyes locked, and those baby blues sucked me in. Sheesh, he was beautiful.

"I'm guessing he's about as dangerous as you," I said, still staring up at Deuce, unable to look away. "So go," I demanded.

"We're talkin' later, Eva," Frankie said, fuming. "Count on it."

He stalked off into the crowd.

"Boy's got it bad for you, darlin'," Deuce said, taking a seat beside me. I lifted my right leg onto the table and turned to face him. Suddenly, all my senses went on hyperalert. The proximity of him allowed me to smell the booze on his breath and a day's worth of summer sweat on his skin. It wasn't altogether a bad smell. It reminded me of…man.

"Not that I blame him. If I was his age and you were mine, I'd be jumpin' up and gettin' in faces, too."

If I was his age and you were mine. Wow. Just…wow.

"I'm nobody's," I shot back.

His eyebrow rose. "Not sure Frankie agrees with that."

I snorted. "Frankie's a whore."

"He fuckin' your friends?"

"Yep. All of them except Kami, my best friend. She would never touch him."

Kami and I had gone to prep school together since kindergarten. She was the daughter of a former senator and an heiress. She was raised by nannies, spent most of her time with me, and steered clear of Frankie. She'd didn't like him, and in all honesty, I think he scared her.

Smirking, Deuce shook his head. "He's tryin' to get you to notice him. Tryin' to make you jealous. A fuckin' blind man could see how bad that boy wants down your pants."

Grossed out, I scrunched up my nose. "Not gonna happen. He's like my brother. Besides, I'm not about having a boyfriend. I don't even like boys."

Except him. Only Deuce wasn't a boy; he was a man, full grown. It was ridiculous to feel this way, but I couldn't help it. Every fiber of my being felt drugged with his presence. I kept catching myself leaning into his space.

"Darlin', you just haven't met the right guy," he said, smiling. "If you were just a little bit older…"

He stopped talking and shook his head.

"If I was older?" I prompted, needing to hear what he'd been about to say.

He leaned sideways and bent his head to mine. His lips brushed against my cheek. "If you were older, darlin', I'd have you on the back of my bike and in my fuckin' bed. And you'd be not just likin' it, but lovin' it, beggin' me for more."

My lips parted, and my chest expanded as I sucked down much-needed air. Holy shit. I'd felt that statement all the way down to my toes and back up again. I wanted to feel it again. And again. Only naked and wrapped around Deuce's body.

"There it is, darlin'," he said softly, his lips curving slowly in a sexy grin. "Nothin' like seein' a pretty girl gettin' all fired up."

I. Just. Stared.

"Back of a bike is comin' for ya and soon, too. 'Cause, baby, the way you're lookin' at me is tellin' me you want it. And you want it bad."

Pushing himself off the bench, he winked once and disappeared into the crowd.

My heart pounding, I looked around feeling embarrassed and overexposed, but no one was paying me any attention at all.

I put my earbuds back in and started singing again, not quite as loud as usual since my voice was shaking.

Deuce stayed up on the roof long after everyone had moved inside the club to keep partying, start fucking, or pass the hell out.

He was having a hell of an internal battle and had already gone through half a bottle of Jäger and two packs of smokes while he was having it.

Eva. That fucking girl. She should have stayed awkward and skinny—all elbows and knees and legs too long for her body with insecurity blazing in those big gray eyes.

She was damn beautiful now. Her face had carved out nicely, baby fat gone, ivory skin as far as the eye could see, dark wavy hair hanging down her back, full fucking lips, and those damn big and beautiful eyes, the color of a rain cloud. Goddammit motherfucking shit. Her awful singing. Those damn Chucks. Those fucking tits—fat and heavy, nipples hard, pressing through her threadbare Harley tee. Jeans, big and baggy, hanging real low on her hips, low enough to see her hip bones.

He wanted inside of her. It was sick, and he knew it. His old man kinda sick. But there it was.

And he wasn't the only one. Frankie had it bad and not in a good way. Kid was fucked-up. Got crazy eyes every time he looked at her. He got the jealousy thing. Eva was a fine piece of ass; being as sweet as she was, as smart as she was, and not giving a shit about mainstream crap, only made her even hotter.

"Fuck," he muttered. He had to get out of there. Get on his bike and get the fuck out of Manhattan. Away from Eva fuckin' Fox and her soul-sucking eyes.

He made it down to the fourth-floor stairwell when he heard yelling coming from the floor below. Pausing, he leaned over the railing.

"What's wrong with me?" Frankie demanded.

"Nothing," Eva said. "It's not just you. I don't want to be involved with anyone…like that."

"You looked pretty fuckin' involved on the roof talkin' to that fuckin' Horseman! I watched you with that fuckin' asshole! You were fuckin' flirtin' with him! You let him touch your fuckin' face!"

"Yeah, Frankie, I was flirting with him, not shoving my tongue down his throat. He's hot, so what? It's not like he gives two shits about some sixteen-year-old girl he barely knows!"

She thought he was hot? Women didn't think he was hot. They thought he was scary as fuck. But this beautiful, young, sweet-as-fuck girl thought he was hot. His cock jerked.

Fuck.

Don't go there, asshole. Do not fucking go there.

"Not the fuckin' point, babe! What the fuck did I tell you?" he yelled. "What the fuck did I tell you about other fuckin' guys?"

Eva sighed noisily. "You said they'd hurt me. They'd use me and throw me away."

"Yeah, baby." Frankie's tone had gone soft and threatening. "What else did I say?"

"Sheesh, Frankie, what is up your butt tonight?"

"What. Else. Did. I. Say?"

"That they would never love me. That only you will love me."

Man, this kid was sick.

"Want you on my cock, Eva. Sick of waitin'."

Deuce's teeth clenched. If Frankie wasn't Preacher's golden boy, he'd fucking kill him.

"Then stop waiting!" she shot back. "Because it's not gonna happen! You're like my brother, Frankie! My brother!"

"You keep sayin' that," he growled. "But we're fuckin' sleepin' next to each other every night, and you're pressin' your tits on my arm and your ass on my cock, and I'm so fuckin' hard I can't see straight. You won't fuckin' do shit 'bout it. Makin' me go out and fuck other bitches when you know I only want you. When you know I'm not gonna let anyone else fuckin' near you. Ever. Never ever, Eva. You get me, or you get nothin'. Do you get that? You're not with me, you're never with no one."

Ass. Hole.

"Frankie," she said evenly. "Stop acting crazy. I do not press anything against you. You wrap yourself around me like a damn blanket, and it's you who is always rubbing against me and copping feels. And if you keep throwing this shit in my face, I'm going to tell Daddy you sleep in my bed every night. And I'll tell him you jerk off right next to me."

He heard Frankie's heavy boots pounding the wood floors, and then a door slammed. He waited a beat, and then continued down the stairs.

Eva was sitting in a corner on the third-floor landing, knees pulled up to her chest, smoking a cigarette. Her head turned in his direction, and she smiled. He smiled back.

"Hey," she said softly. "Thought you left."

He'd been trying to leave. He should still be trying to leave.

"I heard," he said gruffly, "you and that crazy fuck."

She pressed her lips together and looked away. "He's just overprotective."

"So your definition of overprotective is makin' sure no man gets anywhere near you, forcin' you into bein' with him?"

She shrugged. "My father's going to pass him the gavel someday, and Frankie and I together would give him peace of mind."

He got that. Preacher was looking out for his baby girl. Made sense. Put your VP and daughter together and you know the club is going to be there for her when you no longer can. What he didn't get was how Preacher could, in good conscience, hand off his girl to a fucking mess of a man.

"Doesn't sound to me like that's what you want."

He watched her suck her bottom lip in her mouth and roll it under her teeth. Damn. Fuck. Shit. He really needed to adjust his cock.

"It's not," she whispered, dipping her head down, looking up at him through her eyelashes.

Walk away, he told himself. Walk the fuck away.

He bent down in front of her. "What do you want, babe?"

She turned away from him and hid behind her hair, but not before he saw her turn bright red.

He filled with primal male satisfaction. She wanted him. Her, a fucking angel in a mess of demons, wanted him, one of the biggest fucking demons he knew.

"Say it," he said harshly.

Fuck. What the fuck was he doing?

She turned back to him and tucked her hair behind her ears. God, that face. That sweet, perfect face.

"You a virgin, Eva?" He already knew the answer.

"Yes," she whispered.

Christ.

He leaned in closer, close enough to smell the nicotine and beer on her breath. "You ever been kissed, darlin'?"

She sucked in a sharp breath. "No," she breathed.

Good. So fucking good.

He turned his head and rubbed his cheek up against hers, inhaling the fragrance of her strawberry-scented hair.

"You wanna be kissed?" he whispered in her ear.

He licked the skin just behind her ear, and she shivered. He sucked on her skin, bit down lightly, and rolled it between his teeth.

She was breathing hard, her pulse in her neck fluttering wildly against his mouth. He started sucking with vigor, and her legs fell open. He took advantage and shoved himself between them.

He spread kisses across her neck and under her chin, up to her cheek, kissing a line to her mouth. His lips met hers. She trembled.

"One more time, babe," he said low and raspy. "You wanna be kissed?"

"Yes," she whimpered.

He was instantly on his feet, yanking her up with him. Grabbing her waist, he hefted her up and pinned her against the wall. "Legs, babe," he rasped. She wrapped her legs around his waist as he jammed his erection between her thighs and shoved his tongue inside her willing mouth.

He'd lost his motherfucking mind. None of this should be happening.

But there it was.

The road to hell is paved with good intentions, and he'd just bought himself a one-way ticket.

Deuce's hand tangled in my hair while his other hand cupped my jaw and squeezed my cheeks, causing my mouth to open. His tongue plunged inside, slid along mine, and began exploring my mouth. No, exploring isn't the right word. He laid siege to my mouth. He plundered and pillaged until I had no reservations, no choice but to kiss him, and so I kissed him back with all the fervor and passion a sixteen-year-old who had never been kissed has when kissing the man of her dreams.

Which was a lot.

I have no idea how long we kissed. You tend to lose track of time when you're young and enthralled. But like all things sexual in nature, soon kissing was no longer enough.

I tried desperately to get closer. Burning hot, feeling ready to explode, I tore his hand from my hair and shoved it on my breast, whimpering needy little noises into his mouth. I needed more, so much more. I wanted his hands on me, touching me. I wanted skin against bare skin.

Shifting me in his arms, he lifted me higher and slid his hand down the back of my pants. One hand was squeezing my backside as the other slipped under my shirt and did the same to my breast. I was panting, and he was cursing. It was the most wonderful thing that had ever happened to me. If he would have asked me to, I would have jumped on the back of his bike and ridden to the ends of the earth with him.

"Deuce," I cried softly. "Oh my God, Deuce." His hips were between my thighs, and he was grinding his body into mine. The friction of our jeans, the feel of his hands on me, and his tongue in my mouth—something was happening, something that felt right and wrong and too much and not enough. Something I wanted more than my next breath.

He shifted me again and jammed his hand down the front of my jeans.

"Shhh," he growled into my mouth. "I got you. I fuckin' got you. Just let it go, baby girl, just fuckin' let go."

His fingers slipped inside of me, and my body locked up tight. My sex contracted and exploded, pulsing through the wonderful sensations.

He bent his head, pressing his forehead against mine.

"Wish I coulda felt that on my cock."

Oh. *God.*

He pulled his hand from my pants only to slide it back up my shirt to resume playing with my breasts. His hand moved from one to the other, and his fingers snagged on my necklace. Cupping the medallion in his palm, he looked up.

"Baby," he breathed. "What the fuck?"

"You gave it to me," I said lamely. I left out the part where I loved it, never took it off, and sometimes would hold it in my hand and stare at it for hours.

"Yeah," he whispered. He began thumbing my nipple, pinching and kneading the flesh around it. His groin pressed harder into mine. He started breathing faster. I started breathing faster.

"Kiss me," I said breathlessly, needing his mouth. "Please…"

Gently, he sucked my bottom lip into his mouth, pulling and lightly licking, and my head fell back against the wall. His mouth again found my neck, and my body lit up like a firecracker. I reached between us, reached for him, cupped him. Groaning, he pushed himself into my hand. The world ceased to exist. It was only Deuce and me and this beautiful, perfect moment.

It ended abruptly.

"Fuck," he muttered, running his hands through his hair, backing away from me. "Fuck, I fucked up."

I took a step toward him, reaching out, wanting him back, but he stumbled backward, putting more distance between us. I dropped my hand.

"I'm sorry," I whispered, not feeling sorry at all.

He shook his head. "No, darlin', you didn't do anything wrong. It's all on me 'cause I knew better, and I did it anyway."

We stared at each other. He still wanted me. I could tell by his eyes. Frankie looked at me like that, like he wanted to eat me alive.

"I'm married," he said quietly.

I knew that. My father kept tabs on everyone he considered even a mild threat to him, and the people he considered a major threat—people like Deuce—he had extensive amounts of information on.

"I know that," I said just as quietly.

"And you're sixteen…and I'm thirty-four."

I knew that, too.

"Fuck," he muttered, running his hands through his hair. "Fuck!"

He stared at me a moment longer; his indecision plain as day.

Next thing I knew the door to the stairwell was slamming behind him, and I was alone. I sat back down and lit up another cigarette. And grinned.

Deuce got away from Eva as fast as he could, took the stairs two at a time, burst out onto the sidewalk, and slumped against the clubhouse, breathing heavily. He fucked up. He fucked up big-time. He was so far beyond disgusted with himself, but his cock was hard as a rock, aching for sixteen-year-old pussy. Christ. Yeah, he was just like his old man. Rock fucking bottom.

He couldn't even blame his fucked-up marriage since he'd been solving that problem with club whores. This was different, so fucking different and so fucking confusing. He hadn't wanted a sixteen-year-old girl since he was sixteen, maybe eighteen. But he wanted Eva, and now that he'd gotten a taste, he wanted her something fierce.

Girl was about to give it up to him, too. And not because he was coercing her into it, but because she straight up wanted him. She didn't have the first clue how to kiss, but instead of being timid, like the teenagers he remembered from when he was a teenager, she threw everything she had into it. And when she came on his hand—fuck—that was beautiful.

Goddammit! What the fuck! How could he have lost control so completely? He was all about control. How could a sixteen-year-old have fucked him up?

"Holy fuck," he muttered, scrubbing his palms over his eyes. "Holy fuckin' fuck, I fucked up."

"Yeah, you did."

His hands fell to his side. Preacher stood a few feet away. Alone.

Not good. No witnesses to be seduced into ratting Preacher out if his body was ever found.

"Got cameras all over the club," he informed him. "Even in the stairwells."

He nodded. If he'd been thinking clearly, he would have known that and gotten the fuck out. He had cameras all over his club, too. Security in this business was necessary.

"You ready?" Preacher asked, pulling his piece. He watched him screw the silencer on.

Was he ready to die? No.

Did he deserve to die? Yeah. For a long time now.

Was he just going to turn tail and let Preacher kill him? Fuck no.

"Alleyway, Deuce. Now." Preacher pointed with his gun.

He faked a turn and went for his own piece. He wasn't fast enough, and Preacher's first bullet took out his right leg. He stumbled backward and fell on his side in a pile of garbage.

Preacher's boots pounded the concrete, and he braced himself for the killing blow. Fucking fitting that he was going to die in a pile of garbage. His old man had always said he was garbage. He sure as fuck felt like garbage.

His body jerked as pain exploded in his shoulder.

"Fuck," he groaned. He hated getting shot. Shit fucking hurt.

"I'll call your boys to come collect you," Preacher said, surprising him.

"Unfortunately, I need you alive. Our boys are in too deep together; got too much ridin' on shit you got a hand in. That said, you come anywhere near my girl again, first hit's gonna be in that sick dick of yours, the second in your brain. Next, you even try for retaliation, and I will gut every last boy in your Queens chapter."

"Understood," Deuce croaked. Since he liked both his dick and his brain just the way they were, and none of his boys deserved to go to ground for his fucking sins, he was never going to go near Eva Fox again.

But fate was one mean bitch.

And two years later, she slapped him in the face.

Chapter
FOUR

I loved dancing. I loved Club Red. And I loved my best friend, Kami.

She was loaded. I was loaded. She was spoiled. I was spoiled. She was bored out of her mind, and I was being suffocated to death.

Being the spoiled, bored, suffocated girls we were, with the help of another bored and spoiled rich kid we procured fake IDs and were able to escape to our happy place every Saturday night. Club Red.

The best part: Frankie had no idea where I was.

We were able to accomplish this with the help of Kami's sexy chauffeur, Jacob, who Kami had been giving it up to since she was thirteen and Jacob, eighteen. I'm fairly certain Jacob was head over heels in love with her, but he gave up trying for anything more than sex years ago.

Kami, being as starved for attention as she was, had convinced herself sleeping with a lot of different men was a good way to go about getting what she was lacking at home. It never worked, but she never stopped trying.

Anyway, this is how my Saturdays went. Frankie would drop me off at Kami's penthouse. If Kami's parents were home, we'd get prettied up, wait until they went to bed, and then sneak down the back stairwell. Jacob would meet us in Kami's underground parking garage, drive us out the back exit that was only used by the penthouse occupants—deftly evading the tails Frankie put on me—and off we went.

Freedom.

Deuce hated New York City something fierce. Always had and always would.

Even more than he hated New York City was the New Yorkers that resided in it. Even more than he hated New Yorkers was the New York City nightclubs filled with New Yorkers.

Two of his boys rode up with him on business. They wanted a party and some pussy, and since he sorta wanted to pick up some pussy for himself, he tagged along. He wished he hadn't.

He was standing against a wall in a packed nightclub with red satin hanging all over the place and red disco balls twirling on the ceiling, while surrounded by wall-to-wall drunk fuckwads grinding against each other to what he supposed was music, but sounded a lot like television static with a crappy beat.

He was a simple man. He liked kegs, country music, and down-home pussy. He didn't see the need to dress up the fact that he was getting drunk and laid. It was all the same in the end—sloppy kissing, skin slapping, and a nasty hangover. Why the fuck put a decorative umbrella on it?

His boys ditched him about an hour ago in favor of some slutty club bitches. He saw Cox disappear with two scantily clad Latinas, and Mick went off dancing with a woman he was pretty sure was packing a cock under her seriously short skirt. He was so fucking miserable he momentarily considered taking pictures of them with their whores and sending them to their wives as payback for making him endure this shit.

"Heeeyyy," a female voice slurred. He rolled his head left. Christ. Fucking skinny bitches everywhere in this city. No tits. No ass. All of them wearing skintight clothes that emphasized the fact that they had no tits and no ass. This particular bitch—tall and bleached blonde—was so fucking skinny her breastbone was on display through her skin. The napkin she was fronting as a dress was practically see-through, and he could see she wasn't wearing any underwear.

"Fuck off," he said.

Her eyes went wide. "What?"

"You deaf?" he asked. "I said fuck off."

Her mouth fell open. "What?" she whispered.

Christ.

"Bitch, I don't wanna fuck you, so I ain't gonna buy you drinks and tell you how fuckin' hot you are, hopin' you're gonna spread those bony-ass legs for me. 'Cause one, you're not hot. You might be someday if you start eatin', but as it is right now you're not. And two, I don't wanna fuck you, so I'm givin' it to you straight. Fuck off."

She blinked. Then she leaned forward and placed a bony hand on his chest. And smiled. He stared down at her hand, debating whether he should break her fingers.

"Wherever you want it, however you want it," she breathed. "Right here, in the bathroom, behind the club. Where. Ever. You. Want. It."

His eyebrows shot up. She had either major self-esteem problems, some serious daddy issues, or maybe she was just plain fucking crazy.

"Kami!" a female voice squealed. "Kami!"

The bitch beside him straightened up and looked around. "Evie?!" she yelled.

A giggling mass of dark brown hair surged forward through the crowd of people and barreled straight into the blonde. They were both shitfaced. Instead of hugging, they just kind of fell into each other, and then into him. Annoyed, he shoved them both backward, and the blonde's drink went flying. People scattered as the glass shattered.

Laughing hysterically and clinging to each other, they both stood up straight. He watched, frozen, as a Horsemen's tag slipped out from the brunette's shirt. Her imposter of a shirt.

Then she flipped her hair out of her face, and his blood ran cold. Then hot. Really fucking hot.

Last time he had seen Eva Fox, he'd been two seconds away from sinking balls-deep into all that sweetness, and he'd taken two bullets because of it.

"Kami!" Eva cried, oblivious to his presence. "Where have you been? I've been looking everywhere for you!"

Oblivious was the last thing he was. Bitch had on some kind of shirt that wasn't actually a shirt but a triangle of sequins that appeared to be staying on her only by a complicated-looking series of strings. The fucking thing barely covered her tits. Her fat, heavy, perfect tits. Her entire back and her midriff were exposed, her belly button pierced with some shiny bullshit, and the rest of her was encased in tight black leather pants. Tight as in he was damn positive she had to lube up her legs and juicy-as-hell ass to get those bad boys on.

On her feet, black Chucks.

His chest tightened.

Now standing, she tucked his old man's tag back inside her non-shirt and did a little wiggle as she straightened her top—that wasn't actually a top—causing her tits to bounce. He got hard. Just like that. Like he was seven-fucking-teen.

Still giggling, she surveyed her surroundings, finally catching sight of him. Her made-to-suck-cock lips parted, her stormy eyes went wide, and she swayed a little to her right.

"Deuce," she whispered.

He didn't know what the fuck to say, so he said the first thing that popped into his head.

"Babe."

Kami looked between them. "You know him?"

"Yeah," she said, her eyes on him. Jesus Christ, those eyes. She was damn beautiful.

"Introduce us!"

"Deuce, this is my friend Kami. Kami this is my…friend Deuce. But…"

She turned to her friend. "He's married. Got kids, too. So, hands off."

He stared at her, confused. He was married? He had kids? Oh, right. He was sorta married. And yeah, he had kids. He loved his kids. Their mother…not so much.

"Shame," Kami purred. "The whole scary-faced, badass biker thing is really working for you."

His lips curled in disgust. He just told this bitch he found her unattractive, that he in no uncertain terms wanted anything to do with her, and yet, she still wanted it. Fucking whore. Fucking fucked-in-the-head stupid fucking whore.

"He's not scary," Eva scolded. "He's beautiful."

Fuck him.

No one had ever called him beautiful, and he was pretty sure he never wanted to be called beautiful…until Eva Fox had called him beautiful, and now he wanted her to say it again. But this time, he wanted to be balls-deep inside of her while she said it.

"Do you want to dance?" Eva asked.

His eyes refocused. "What?"

"Dance. Do you want to?"

"No."

"No?"

"This isn't music, and I can't dance."

She bit her lip, and he knew she was trying not to laugh at him. Usually when people laughed at him or tried not to laugh at him—neither of which was often because he wasn't a funny guy—he punched them in their fucking face. Eva laughing at him made his cock twitch. This bitch did strange shit to him. His brain didn't work around her, and his balls fucking swelled, ready to repopulate the world as long as he was doing it inside her pussy.

"Everyone can dance." She giggled.

He shook his head. "I can't. I lumber. My wife says I lumber."

She wrinkled up her nose. "Your wife is a fucking cunt."

He choked. Coughed. Pounded on his chest. Took a long swallow of his beer. Cleared his throat. "Darlin', you have no idea."

Grinning, she sidled up next to him and leaned her shoulder against the wall, so the front of her body faced his and took a sip of her drink—her bright pink drink with a pink umbrella and lots of floating cherries that reeked of tequila.

He narrowed his eyes. How long had it been since he last saw her, since he'd taken two bullets because he was a fucking moron?

It hadn't been five years, so he knew she wasn't twenty-one.

"How old are you, darlin'?"

Her lips quirked. "My ID says I'm twenty-four."

He raised an eyebrow and smiled. "And what does your birth certificate say?"

She looked him dead in the eyes, and he felt himself leaning toward her.

"I'm eighteen," she said quietly, and her eyes went soft. He knew that look. Fucked a lot of women in his life—knew the signs and knew them well. Eighteen-year-old Eva Fox was handing him her pussy on a silver platter.

And he was fucking starving.

Fuck.

"Deuce?" She leaned into him, pressing her fat tits against his arm.

He stared down at her. "Yeah?"

Keeping her eyes locked with his, she wrapped her hand around as much of his bicep as her fingers could reach and started slowly sliding her hand down his inner arm. When she reached his palm, her fingers spread out and slid between his. Her hand folded closed. He closed his over hers.

"Let's dance," she whispered.

"OK," he whispered back because, fuck, he didn't know which way was up at the moment.

Those unfathomably plump lips split into a smile, and his cock freaked the fuck out. If she hadn't started leading him out into the club, he would have thrown her up against the wall and slammed his way home.

She took him dead center of the dance floor. It was packed with bodies—sweaty, writhing bodies. He felt completely out of his element.

Then Eva began to move, and he forgot all about elements and skinny bitches and stupid red disco balls. All he could see was Eva. Nothing else existed but Eva and what she did to him.

With her back to his front, she lifted her arms over her head and hooked her hands around his neck. He grabbed her, harder than he meant to, and dug his fingers deep into her hipbones. As her juicy ass hit his cock, he groaned.

"All you have to do is move with me!" she shouted over the music.

He didn't. He couldn't. He was far too busy trying to convince himself it would be a bad idea to take her right then and there on the dance floor.

Her ass was grinding into his rock-hard cock, her head fell back on his chest, and her hands…

She grabbed his hands, interlocked their fingers, and had him stroking across her bare stomach, her hips, the vee between her legs, and—fuck him—her tits. When he couldn't take much more, he slipped his hand down her pants and gave her what she was silently begging him for.

Her head on his chest, she looked up at him with unfocused gray eyes, her nostrils flaring with heavy breaths, and her wet lips parted.

He'd taken two bullets because of this bitch. If tonight ended the way he wanted it to, Preacher was going to bury him. He should care about that. His kids needed their father, and his MC needed their president. He had business that needed getting done, and he sure as fuck wasn't ready to kick it quite yet.

He should care about all that shit. But he didn't. And because he didn't—because he wanted her so fucking bad, he could taste the need and feel it in his gut like a live wire—he brought his mouth down on hers and kissed her hard and fast, still thrusting his fingers in and out of her, swallowing her cries as bodies pressed up against them, shoving them back and forth to the rhythm of the bass pounding in his ears.

It was pouring out, we were soaking wet, and the alleyway smelled like a month's worth of old garbage. Deuce was fumbling with his jeans, and I had completely lost my mind. I was frantic, crawling up his big, hard body like a sex-starved spider monkey in heat, and kissing him, giving as good as I was getting. Every kiss was full of hot, wet tongue—sometimes hit, sometimes miss. Teeth were clacking together, lips were bitten, and noses were getting in the way. I mauled him, not caring where his or my mouth was landing or what part of his face I was kissing, licking, or biting. His cheeks, his forehead, his chin, his neck—they were all fair game. His hands were full of my ass, my hands were full of his hair, and our mouths were full of each other. I had no idea where my clothing had gone. And I didn't care.

I wanted this man inside of me—so far inside of me that he wouldn't ever be able to leave.

"Gimme what I need, baby. Gimme that sweet pussy I been dreamin' 'bout."

Oh *God*.

I didn't think it was possible to want him any more than I already did. But he'd just proven me wrong.

"Please, please, just fucking take it," I mumbled, desperate for more of him.

Staring into each other's eyes—breathing heavily while rain sluiced down in sheets between us, over us, everywhere—he started pushing inside of me.

"Oh, fuck yeah," he breathed. "You're so fuckin' wet. You fuckin' want this bad, don't you?"

"Yes," I whimpered.

"Yeah, you do," he grunted and pushed harder. "Fuckin' tight, baby, you're so fuckin' tight."

There was a reason for that. A reason he was going to find out in about two-point-five seconds.

"Give it up, Eva, fuckin' open for me." Growing impatient, he gripped my backside and pulled me down as he slammed up into me. I cried out, and he froze. Just went statue still.

"Fuckin' shit!" he yelled. "Goddammit, Eva! God motherfuckin' dammit!"

Oh my God, he was pulling out.

"No! Please! I want this!" I dug my nails into his back and tightened my legs around his waist. "I wanted it to be you! I've been dreaming about this! About you and me! Ever since you kissed me! Even before then!"

He sagged against me. "Fuck," he whispered.

He was still inside of me, and I was so full of him. It felt so good, and when I tried to move—because I had to move, wanted, needed to move—he groaned. I liked hearing him groan almost as much as I liked the feel of him inside of me, and I wanted more. I wanted him to move. So

I told him this, told him everything I was feeling, and everything more that I wanted to feel. It just kept pouring rapidly out of me, feelings and needs, because I needed him to know how much this meant to me, that it was him I wanted to take this from me, him I wanted to give it to. That it was only him I ever wanted inside of me and only him I ever want to be inside of me.

His eyes met mine, arctic blue and beautiful.

"Please," I begged. "Deuce, please."

"I'm fuckin' married, Eva. Got two kids. This is fucked. It shouldn't have been me."

What? Here he was inside of me—because I wanted him inside of me, because he was the only man I have ever needed inside of me—and he had the nerve to tell me it shouldn't have been him. After making me beg him?

"Fuck you!" I snapped. "I don't give a shit about your wife and neither do you, or you wouldn't have been finger-fucking me in the club! And you definitely wouldn't have carried me out here with every intention of fucking me! You can't tell me it shouldn't have been you! You don't get to make that decision. I do! I did, and it's done! And I'm not giving it back!"

His eyes flashed with anger. "I can't give you shit!" he hissed. "All I've got to give you is my fuckin' cock, and that's not good enough! Not for you! Not even fuckin' close! You deserved better than this! Better than a fuckin' shit-filled alleyway and definitely better than me!"

There it was. The pain I glimpsed every time we crossed paths. The sadness that never seemed to leave him.

"You're better than you think," I whispered. "I didn't realize it when I was little—didn't understand that look in your eyes, why you always looked so sad—but I get it now. Someone got inside of you and messed you all up, made up down and left right, so now you think you're shit when you're not even close. So you need to listen to me when I tell you that you are better than you think. You're even better than that. To me, you're the best."

His nostrils flared. "Eva," he groaned.

"What?"

"Shut up." His mouth met mine, and we kissed slowly, deeply, deliciously lazy.

"Gonna fuck you now, baby," he muttered into my mouth.

Oh. *Good.* So good.

"OK," I breathed.

And he did. Up against a dirty brick wall, in a garbage-filled alleyway home to rats and feral cats, while warm summer rain poured down over us. And it was perfect. Better than I'd imagined. Better than anything. The best.

I spent the next four years in college, spent my days studying, shopping with Kami, trying to ditch Frankie, and enjoying my life. And I spent my nights reliving my moments with Deuce. All four of them.

The day after my graduation ceremony, I packed a backpack, grabbed Kami, wrote my father a note, and got on an airplane headed for Miles City, Montana.

Headed for Deuce.

Chapter
FIVE

If I needed any more proof that the Hell's Horsemen were into some seriously illegal shit—other than their alliance with my father—all I had to do was take one look at their clubhouse.

Smack dab in the middle of the Montana hills, down a barely there dirt road, enclosed with an electric fence topped with razor wire, sat their whitewashed warehouse, massive at around thirty thousand square feet, with their insignia painted huge on the front of the building. A line of Harleys was parked outside, along with some pickup trucks and a shiny red sports car.

I pulled our rental car up to the gate and peered into the camera. The intercom underneath crackled.

"Help you with somethin', darlin'?"

I cleared my throat. I was so nervous.

"I…um…wanted to…um…"

"Smooth, Evie," Kami whispered. "Really smooth."

I glared at her.

"You here to party?" the intercom crackled.

"Uh," I said and glanced at Kami. She bugged out her eyes. "Say yes, you idiot!"

"Uh, yes."

The gate clicked and slowly swung open, and Kami started jumping around excitedly.

I was parking when two guys came running outside. Kami grinned.

"H-O-T," she spelled out. "Me wanna lick."

I gave a shaky laugh. My stomach was in knots. I hadn't seen Deuce in four years—not since the night I gave him my virginity. I wasn't sure how he was going to react to me just showing up.

A well-built, good-looking Latino guy with a shaved head, lots of body piercings, and tattoos as far as the eye could see grinned at us.

"Name's Cox," he said, looking me up and down. "This is Ripper." He jerked his thumb at the man standing next to him. A drop-dead gorgeous man. He looked like a surfer straight out of Cali. Long, wavy blond hair and dark blue eyes. There was man candy to be had all around.

"Hey," Ripper said, his eyes on Kami. "You two been here before?"

I shook my head. "I'm looking for Deuce."

"I'm not," Kami said. "I'm looking for you."

I covered my mouth, stifling my laughter.

"Or you," she said to Cox, shrugging. "Doesn't matter."

Cox and Ripper looked at each other.

"Don't wanna fight you, brother," Ripper said. "But I fuckin' will."

"You'll lose," Cox growled.

"Boys?" Kami swept her long blonde hair over her shoulder and cocked her hip. "This is my last summer of freedom. My dad is a rich asshole who is making me marry another rich asshole. I have three months left before I become a proper little Jackie O and have to start fucking my staff just so I can get off. That being said, if you guys don't mind sharing, I've got a whole lot to give."

"I don't," Cox said quickly.

"Nope, me either," Ripper said.

"Awesome, now do you have any liquor in this big, scary building of yours?"

Ripper grabbed her elbow, Cox slung his arm over her shoulder, and they steered her toward the clubhouse.

Sheesh. It was like I was invisible.

Rolling my eyes, I followed them inside.

All around me were bikers ranging from age eighteen to eighty and the sluts who loved them. I realized that the Hell's Horsemen were having what my boys in New York called a "pussy party," which was undoubtedly the only reason Kami and I had been allowed inside. I scanned the room looking for Deuce.

The inside of the warehouse looked nothing like the outside. The entire place had been gutted, renovated, and remodeled. Running the length of the warehouse front was one giant man cave with fifteen-feet ceilings and modern skylights that gave it a cathedral-like appearance.

A fully stocked bar lined the entire right side of the room surrounded by several bar tables and stools, and beyond, five large pool tables took up a good portion of the room. The opposite side gave the impression of a high-class men's club, complete with dark leather furniture as far as the eye could see, flat-screen televisions, and a state-of-the-art stereo system. There were two hallway entrances on either side of the back wall and smack dab in the center were a set of doors surrounded by photographs of the members. Above the doors was a plank of wood nailed to the wall that read "Prez's Office." My heart started pounding, and my hands went clammy.

I willed my feet to move and headed toward his office. Taking a deep breath, I curled my hand into a fist and rapped on the door.

"WHAT?"

Oh God, that voice—that hard, rough, beautiful voice. I swallowed hard and turned the knob.

I saw a woman first. Tall, blonde, very tan, and curvy as hell. Beautiful. She was wearing a tight jean skirt, frayed at the bottom, and a hot pink tank top that showed off her copious amount of cleavage. I had large breasts, but I almost never put them on display unless I was going out. I just didn't see the point.

I glanced down at my Led Zeppelin cropped tee, way too baggy jeans that hung low, and my Chucks. The tee had once belonged to my mother, and I altered it to make it more my style to show off my belly ring and the circle of black and pink stars I had tattooed around my belly button. The jeans I'd had forever; I wasn't even sure where I'd gotten them. Frankie, maybe? That was a running theme during my teenage years, stealing his clothing. They were comfy, and so deliciously broken in, they felt like silk against my skin. Most importantly, they dragged when I walked. That was a thing for me; I liked to be able to hide my feet inside my pants at all costs. Weird, I know, but I was an only child—and a girl, no less—who grew up with a single MC president, his crew, and Crazy Frankie. I could have turned out a whole lot weirder.

But I felt like a homeless person next to this woman. This super-model-sort-of-beautiful woman who was more than likely his wife.

Deuce was seated behind a desk, turned away from me, cursing into a cell phone.

Whoever had decorated the office was either secretly gay or of the female variety. Although the dark oak desk, hutch, and meeting table were distinctly male, no man—correction, no biker—would have ever picked out these particular pieces to coordinate with each other. They were too perfect, each piece different yet worked fashionably together. A woman—I surmised, probably this woman—had a hand in decorating. Knowing this made me feel incredibly uncomfortable.

The blonde glanced over at me, gave me a once-over, and her pink-painted lips curled into a sneer. "Who the fuck are you?"

"I…um…was looking for Deuce."

"Well, you…um…fuckin' found him."

Sheesh. Attitude.

"Are you fuckin' kiddin' me?" Deuce growled into his phone. "You tell Street he gets his ass to the docks and picks up the shipment, or I will fuckin' bury your chapter! You feel me? I will scatter your boys and take you to ground! You don't fuckin' mess with the Buonarroti family! I made fuckin' promises, and I aim to keep them. A man's fuckin' word is a man's fuckin' word. You think this is a game? No? Good. Now get your fuckin' ass in gear!"

He swiveled around, his narrowed eyes swept over the blonde, across the room, and then finally to me. And stared.

He had let his beard grow out; there were signs of gray interspersed among the blond and a few lines around his eyes. I sucked in a breath. He'd grown even more beautiful with age.

"Gotta go," he said into his phone and tossed it on the desk.

I cleared my throat. "I was in the neighborhood," I said dumbly. "Thought I'd stop by."

"You were in the neighborhood," he repeated.

I nodded. Wow. I was such an idiot. If she'd heard this, Kami would have kicked my ass.

"Cole," the woman hissed. "Who the fuck is this girl?"

I have never heard anyone call Deuce anything but Deuce. I knew his real name, Cole West, but it didn't fit. Deuce, meaning "Devil," fit him.

Deuce blinked and looked back at the blonde. "Get the fuck outta here, Christine. You got your fuckin' money, now go."

He glanced back at me, and I watched his icy blues drink me in from head to toe and back up again, stopping on his father's medallion. His lips curved into a smile.

I felt my body go soft, warm, and needy. He did this to me just by looking at me. His power over me was incredible and indescribable, as it had always been. It didn't matter that I hadn't seen him in four years; I wanted him every bit as badly as the last time and the time before that. Even more because I had him and had craved him ever since.

He saw the change in me, noticed it instantly. His nostrils flared, and his eyes darkened with hunger. I knew this look. Deuce was hungry, and I was food.

I loved that look. It made me feel beautiful, powerful, and utterly feminine.

I sucked in air through my nose, willing myself to stay put when I wanted nothing more than to run to him, strip him naked, and fuck him blind.

"You here alone?" he asked roughly.

I shook my head. "Brought Kami with me."

His eyes narrowed, and I stifled a laugh. He obviously remembered her.

"Where is she?"

"Entertaining a few of your boys."

He smirked. "Cox?"

"And Ripper."

He rolled his eyes. "Nice."

"Cole! Who the fuck is this bitch, and why the fuck is she wearin' a Horsemen tag?"

His head swiveled back to Christine. "What the fuck did I say to you? Get the fuck outta here!"

Her face went arctic. Glacial. "No," she hissed. "Tell me why this little girl is standin' in your office wearin' a Horsemen tag! Old ladies don't get 'em. Kids don't get 'em unless they get a cut, and ain't no girl ever got a cut. And whores sure as fuck don't get 'em. So why the fuck does this bitch have one?!"

Deuce stood up. His Harley belt buckle sagged low on his low-rise, baggy jeans, jeans that were as equally holey as his white T-shirt. To quote Kami, H-O-T.

"Get out," he growled.

"TELL ME WHY SHE'S WEARIN' IT!"

Deuce's fists came slamming down on his desk, sending papers and file folders flying everywhere. "Because I fuckin' gave it to her!"

Christine's head snapped sideways. "You little fuckin' whore!" she screamed.

My mouth fell open, and I took a step backward. This was exactly why my father didn't allow his boys' old ladies in the club unless it was a planned visit or a Sunday barbeque.

"Christine!" Deuce bellowed. "Take the money you came for and get your fuckin' ass outta here!"

Ignoring Deuce, she kept her frightening gaze on me. "What the fuck did you have to do to get that?" she hissed. "You some kinda kinky fucked-up whore who takes on three brothers at a time? Was that your fuckin' prize for being such a goddamn slut, for fuckin' other women's men? You fuckin' proud of yourself, you stupid little skank bitch?"

Wow. Just…wow. How did one respond to that?

I looked to Deuce for help. I didn't know what to do or say or if I should do or say anything at all. This hadn't gone at all like I planned. Not that I actually planned on anything specific happening—only vague scenarios, all including Deuce without pants on and being really happy to see me. Being screamed at by Deuce's wife, I can honestly say, hadn't crossed my mind.

"Christine," he growled low. Scary low. "Only gonna say this one more time. Get your fuckin' ass outta my club."

"I'm gonna bleed you dry," she hissed. "Gonna take everything you fuckin' have. Gonna take your kids, your money, and when I tell the fuckin' cops what goes on 'round here, I'm gonna take your fuckin' freedom."

This had gone past uncomfortable and well into hazardous. I should have never come here. Since they were busy glaring at each other, I started backing out of the room and backed right into a hard body.

The biker standing behind me I recognized. His name was Mick, and I had seen him here and there growing up. His messy black hair hung long. He had pretty green eyes and a well-trimmed goatee. He was tall, leanly muscled, and looked extremely pissed off.

"Prez?" he asked. "You need help with this bitch?"

Deuce was rounding his desk and advancing on Christine. She met him head on, swinging her purse through the air. He ducked, grabbed her purse strap, and barreled into her. She went up and over his shoulder, screaming and flailing.

Deuce, with Christine, stalked across the room. Mick and I hurried out of the way. As soon as Deuce was gone, Mick turned to me.

"What the fuck are you doing here?" he growled.

My mouth opened, but no sound came out. What?

He shook his head, glaring at me. "Thought Deuce learned his lesson when Preacher put him in the hospital, but, Christ, the two of you just keep goin' back for more."

My heart stopped beating. "What did you say?" I whispered.

"Your old man, babe, capped him twice. He nearly bled out. He was in surgery for a *fuckin' minute*. Needed a transfusion. Was in the hospital for weeks."

I blinked rapidly, trying to process everything he just said. Shot him twice? Bled out. Surgery. Transfusion.

"Because of me?" I whispered. My voice caught, and my eyes filled with tears. I hadn't known. If I had, I would have stayed away from him. Never, ever, would I have put Deuce in danger. God, I was so stupid. Stupid to push him into having sex with me. Stupid to think my father wouldn't know. He always knew; he knew everything.

"Go," Deuce demanded, pushing his wife toward her car. "Now."

"Who is that?" she screeched. He squeezed his eyes shut, wincing. God, this fucking woman.

"She is none of your fuckin' business, bitch. Now fuckin' go."

"I fuckin' saw the way you were lookin' at her! You've never looked at me that way! Never!"

"Never looked at you like much of anything 'cause you're not much of anything 'cept a crazy fuckin' bitch."

She came at him, fake nails flying. Grabbing her shoulders, he threw her up against her car. "Get the fuck outta here!" he bellowed.

"What the fuck is wrong with me?" she demanded. "What's she got that I don't?"

He let her go and backed away from her. "What's wrong with you?" he sneered. "You're not her; that's what's wrong with you. What's she got that you don't? Bitch, she's got me, and you never fuckin' did."

He watched her suck in air. She blinked rapidly, trying to stop the tears he knew were coming. He wanted to care, he really did, but he didn't. Not anymore. Too much ugly shit had gone down between them for too many fucking years. Met her at twenty-five, married her when she got pregnant, and lived in misery with her ever since. There was only so much nagging, screaming, and crying a man can take. He had stopped fucking her years ago, and now he could barely stomach looking at her.

"Leavin' you, Christine, and gonna move to the cabin," he said quietly. "Can't do this shit no more. Haven't slept at home in over a year. You been showin' up here, demandin' money, spewin' attitude, and just plain pissin' me off with your fuckin' threats. Can't do it no more."

She put her hand on her throat, and her giant diamond engagement ring caught the sun. He had taken his ring off years ago, not to pick up women because that had never been a problem, but because looking at it made him sick.

"You gave her a tag," she whispered hoarsely. "You don't let any of your boys give their women tags."

He stared at her. "She doesn't belong to one of my boys. She's fuckin' mine."

It hit him then how right that sounded. Four years had gone by since he'd been inside her—four years of thinking about her, wondering what she was doing, and who she was doing.

Always thinking about her.

"Cole," she whispered. "Don't do this. We can make it work. We've done it before."

"Go!" he barked. "Don't fuckin' come back here."

He left her crying and stalked back inside. He had just reached his office when what he heard from inside made his blood boil.

"Yeah, babe. He almost died. Because of you. So I'm standin' here, lookin' at you, wonderin' why the fuck he thinks you're fuckin' worth gettin' shot for 'cause I sure as fuck ain't seein' it. You got a golden pussy or somethin'? Or was it the fuckin' innocent act he's likin'?"

"What the fuck?" he seethed.

Mick whirled around. A quick glance at Eva only enraged him further. She was shaking, trembling, tears pouring down her face.

Mick met him glare for glare. "She needed to know what the fuck you'd gone through just to get some underage Demon pussy who ain't all that anyway."

He saw red. He saw motherfucking red.

He swung his right fist, then his left, and then his right again. Mick blew backward with every hit until he ran out of room and hit wall. Grabbing Mick's shirt collar, he got up in his face.

"Take off your fuckin' cut and get the fuck outta my club."

Mick's eyes went wide. "You can't—"

He swung his fist into Mick's jaw, and the brother's face whipped right and hit brick. "I fuckin' can. You got no idea what you just messed with. No fuckin' clue. You think you know, but you fuckin' don't 'cause I didn't tell you shit about it 'cause it's none of your fuckin' business. So you take off your fuckin' cut and go the fuck home. When I fuckin' feel like it, I'll send Cox to bring you back."

Still holding Mick's shirt, he yanked him away from the wall and swung him out of his office. Mick hit the floor and went sliding across the room. Jase jumped out of the way, and Mick crashed into a pool table.

"Get him outta here," he growled to no one in particular. "Anyone else got somethin' to say to Eva, or somethin' to say about her, you're gonna answer to my fuckin' fist. We fuckin' clear?"

He received a series of grunts and nods during which he slammed the doors closed and locked them.

"Eva, babe, look at me."

She shook her head. "I should leave," she whispered brokenly. His chest went tight. No way was he letting her leave.

"Eva!" he said forcefully. "Fuckin' look at me!"

Hugging herself, she turned away from him. "I got you shot," she whispered.

Fuck.

"Eva!" he yelled. "Fuck! Look at me before I spank the fuckin' shit outta you!"

Her head jerked up, and her narrowed eyes zoomed in on him. He grinned.

"Babe, don't you fuckin' dare think any of that shit was your fault. It was mine, darlin', plain and simple. I shoulda left you alone, but I couldn't fuckin' help myself. Marriage had already gone bad, and I saw you sittin' there with a pair of great fuckin' tits, tappin' your Chucks, bobbin' your head, and singin' your heart out to fuckin'

Zeppelin. And you looked so damn innocent and fuckin' sweet as hell without a care in the fuckin' world except for right then, right there. I was so fuckin' jealous. I would've given an arm and a leg to have life be that simple again. Then that little shithead showed up, and I knew he fuckin' worshipped you. And then I heard that shit he said to you, and I knew nothin' was gonna make that boy back off until he got inside your sweet pussy. So I kissed you, babe, 'cause I was selfish. I wanted to taste that fuckin' sweetness before he took it all.

"And, babe, when I kissed you and you kissed me back, not knowing what the fuck you were doin' but doin' it anyway—not carin', just feelin'—I fuckin' lost myself in that kiss. Couldn't remember ever losin' myself in a kiss until then.

"That fuckin' kiss, Eva, has gotten me through some pretty bad nights. That fuckin' kiss reminds me that life ain't all bad.

"As for what happened in that alleyway, your old man never found out about it. But even if he had and he buried me, I wouldn't have fuckin' cared 'cause when it comes to you, darlin', I got no fuckin' sense. You fuckin' pull me in until you're all I can fuckin' see. Suddenly, I can't fuckin' breathe, but I don't care 'cause you, babe, you're you. I ain't ever met anyone as fuckin' perfect as you. Knowin' you gave me your first kiss, and then you gave me that sweet pussy first, knowin' that I got that and no one else can ever have it 'cause it's fuckin' mine—fuck, Eva—there ain't a day that goes by that I don't think 'bout that, 'bout you, and how much I fuckin' wish shit was different.

"And that's the God's honest truth, darlin'. I wouldn't change a fuckin' thing 'cept for you being in so deep with the Demons, me being a Horseman, me being fuckin' married to the biggest fuckin' cunt on the planet, and your old man being who he is. Take all that shit away and you'd be on the back of my bike and in my fuckin' bed. You wouldn't be leavin', and I wouldn't be walkin' away from you ever again.

"Now, woman, you need to start doin' what you came here to do, or I'm gonna do it for you."

I ran to him, wrapped my arms around his neck, and buried my face in his chest.

"Missed you," I whispered. "So, so much."

"Babe, yeah," he said softly. "Now you gonna give me that sweet fuck-me mouth, or do I need to take it?"

I went up on my tiptoes, and he bent down. I took his mouth, I took his tongue, and I ate him alive. Four years I had gone without him, without his mesmerizing eyes, and his devastating grin, and his perfect mouth, and his perfect hands, and his perfect body, and his perfect cock. Desire, slick and hot, heated my blood and pooled low in my belly. I had so much time to make up for, and it couldn't happen fast enough.

Frantically, I pushed his cut down his shoulders. Shrugging out of it, he tossed it aside.

Up went his T-shirt, over his head, and across the room. Mine was next; he yanked it up over my head and tossed it aside. Then my breasts were in his hands and then in his mouth, and I died a heavenly, happy death. We tasted, touched, grabbed, and gripped each other until it wasn't enough anymore, not even close.

I released him, slid down his perfect body, and onto my knees. After wrestling open his jeans, I took him in my mouth, all of him, and again I ate him alive. His breathing hitched, and his hands gripped a hold of my hair. I clung to the backs of his thighs, digging my nails in, keeping myself steady when I otherwise would have collapsed under the heady sensations rippling through me.

I made love to him with my mouth in the same frantic, desperate way I have always kissed him. I couldn't stop, didn't want to ever stop. I felt so alive, taking all I could as I gave all I had. My mouth loved Deuce, my hands loved Deuce, my body loved Deuce. Loved, loved, loved, loved...I loved Deuce.

Loved.

"Baby," he groaned, fisting my hair, pulling on it painfully. "Fuuuck...me..."

He exploded, and I took it all, whimpering desperate, greedy little whimpers, already wanting more. I wanted to own this man's body, this man's innate sexuality. I wanted to own this man.

I stared up at him through my wet lashes, trembling, my body quaking under the onslaught of need. For him.

"Eva, baby, fuck, do you know what you fuckin' do to me?" He bent down to cup my cheeks and ran the pads of his thumbs over my fluttering eyelids.

"You make me insane," I breathed. God, he so did.

"Babe," he rasped. "Yeah."

Scooping me up, he carried me to his black leather couch and stripped me naked, divested himself of his jeans, and bent me over the arm of the couch. He settled himself between my legs, lifted my hips, and leaned down over me. His chest pressed against my head, his stomach rubbed against my back, and his growing erection was pushing into me.

We were blessedly bared to each other. We were skin on skin.

Your mother holds you skin on skin when you enter this world and feeds you with her own body, skin on skin. Your father runs his fingers over your tear-streaked cheek, presses his lips to your forehead, skin on skin. You make love, skin on skin, with a man you love, a beautiful man. And then, if you're lucky, your own baby will enter this world, and you'll hold her, skin on skin. Feed her with your own body, skin on skin. It's a magical thing.

Nothing compares.

"Gonna fuck you now, baby."

"Yes, please," I whispered.

He pushed inside of me, and my breath caught. He withdrew and pushed back in, this time harder, this time going farther. I whimpered.

"Babe," he rasped. "So goddamn tight."

"Only you," I breathed. "No one else since you."

He sucked in a breath. "Christ, Eva. What the fuck did I do to deserve you?"

"You're you," I whimpered.

He pulled out and again pushed in. We both groaned.

"Goddamn your fuckin' body, so fuckin' hot, baby."

He pulled out again, and again he pushed in a little farther. I pushed back, trying to take him deeper.

"So fuckin' sweet and wantin' an asshole like me."

His hips swiveled, grinding into me, causing me to moan. He did this four more times before pulling away and thrusting roughly. It was all I needed. My body blossomed for him, stretched and spread, allowing him to seat himself fully inside of me.

"Not carin' that I got shit to give you. You just wantin' me for me and not the club and not the fuckin' money, just straight up wantin' me."

He pulled out and slammed back inside of me. I dug my fingernails deep into the leather and cried out.

"Fuck me," he rasped, his hips pumping back and forth, in and out of me, excruciatingly slow. "You fuckin' show up out of nowhere, lying, saying you were in the neighborhood and standin' in my office wearing my old man's tag, always wearing my old man's tag, and drop straight to your fuckin' knees."

He stilled, and I squirmed until his fingertips bit painfully into the skin on my hips and held me still. "You want it hard, baby?" he whispered. "Or you want it slow?"

"Hard," I breathed.

"Yeah," he said gruffly. "You want me to own you, don't you, baby? You been waitin' for me to own you for a long time now, haven't you?"

Oh my God, my heart was going to explode. I wanted this man so bad. I wanted him to own me. All of me. Every. Single. Inch.

I shuddered with need. "Yes, Deuce."

"Sweet fuckin' girl," he rasped and thrust hard and deep. "Sweet and beautiful." He thrust again, harder.

"Please," I moaned. "More."

He gripped my hips. "Anything you want, darlin'. Anything you fuckin' want."

"You," I whispered. "All I want is you."

"Fuck," he muttered. "Fuck."

Then he gave me everything I wanted, and he gave it to me hard.

Cradled in Deuce's arms, I stared up at him with unfocused eyes, my sated body limp and heavy. He ran his hand down the side of my face, down my neck, across my collarbone, and over my breasts.

I arched my back, pushing more of me into his hand.

"Fuck me," he muttered, thumbing my nipples, making them hard. His other hand slid down my stomach and in between my hipbones where his fingers traced my indented abdomen.

"Know I don't deserve nothin' as sweet as you," he whispered darkly as his hand dipped in between my legs. "Anything a man's gotta steal to have he don't deserve."

"You didn't steal this," I breathed, writhing against his hand. "I gave it."

His blue eyes glittered with amusement. "Naive, darlin'," he murmured. "I stole you a long time ago. 'Round the time you fuckin' stole me."

You fuckin' stole me.

He just said that. He really, really said that.

"I love you," I breathed into his mouth, overcome by sheer sensation and the larger-than-life force that was Deuce.

He went rigid and the pleasure-induced fog I was floating around inside of instantly cleared. Oh no. Ohnononono. I did not just say that. There was no way he was going to understand what he meant to me. I barely understood it; I just accepted that it just was.

"Wait…that's not what I meant," I stammered. "I didn't… I don't…"

Deuce wasn't listening to me; he was moving me off of him, laying me down on my back, settling his hips between my thighs and pushing back inside of me.

"Say it again, Eva," he growled.

I bit my lip.

"Babe. Say it again."

I didn't. Mostly because he was inside of me again—so full, so big—and he was fucking me deliciously slow. I went soft beneath him, staring up into his eyes. Eyes that I could never look away from. Eyes that pulled me inside of him where it was warm and safe. Eyes that I loved. And that's when I realized he wasn't fucking me. He was making love to me.

"Say it," he demanded, his expression fierce. Dominant. Possessive.

"I…didn't mean…"

He pulled his hips back and slammed inside of me. "You love me. Say it."

"No, I meant…"

"You love me."

I gave up. "Yes," I cried. "I love you! I've loved you forever!"

His eyes closed, and his head dropped to my chest. "Fuck," he whispered.

"Deuce," I whispered.

He looked up at me. "Yeah, baby," he asked hoarsely. His eyes were hooded, his mouth slightly parted, and his breath coming in short, hard pants. Beads of sweat dotted his brow. He wasn't Deuce, badass biker, and I wasn't Eva, his rival badass biker's daughter. He was a dangerously beautiful man, I was a woman he wanted, and it was so fucking beautiful. I wanted to freeze time and stay in this moment with him forever—touching, fucking, and loving.

"Come on me," I said, driven only by need. "I want you to come all over me."

His body went stiff; his nostrils flared. He barely had enough time to pull out of me before his body let go.

"God, baby...fuck...*fucking good*."

Watching Deuce orgasm was absolutely beautiful, an aurora borealis kind of beautiful. His face drew in tightly, and then loosened as his release began. For a moment, he looked younger than he was, young and vulnerable like I remembered him looking the day I met him. His eyes were glazed over, his lids at half-mast. A small, noisy breath passed through his lips and swept warmly over my breasts. Wet warmth shot up over my stomach and chest, and suddenly, Deuce's fingers were inside of me, pumping. My sex clenched and clenched again, throwing me into orgasm.

Taking his fingers away, he slid his hand over my body, rubbing his liquid heat into the skin on my stomach and breasts, down between my thighs, and up into my sex, staring into my eyes the entire time.

He was marking me.

Claiming me.

Owning me.

"Say it again," he demanded.
"I love you, Deuce," I whispered.

Chapter SIX

My eyelids fluttered open, and I blinked sleepily. The thick, steely arm around my stomach tightened.

I lifted my arm behind me and encircled Deuce's neck, pulling his head down until I could see his eyes. "Morning," I breathed.

His hand left my belly and moved lower, cupping me. I lifted my leg and hooked my foot behind his knee. He made a hungry noise in the back of his throat that I felt all the way to my toes.

"You sore?" he asked roughly.

"Uh-huh," I whispered. "In a really, really good way."

He chuckled. "You want it?"

"Please," I breathed.

"You want it hard?"

"Please…"

"Bitch is gonna kill me," he laughed. "Keep wantin' it raw."

Oh God, he was teasing me. Here we were lying in his bed, and he was teasing me. It was so…domestic. I loved it.

He groaned as he entered me. I whimpered as I stretched for him, molded around him, drenching him, and then finally, eagerly accepting him. All of him.

I came, and I came hard.

Shaking his head, he let out an amused grunt. "Fuck. Never seen a woman catch fire the way you do, darlin'. The way you squeeze my cock and that body of yours shakin' so hard while you scream in my ear, pull my fuckin' hair, and claw up my fuckin' back. When I let you outta my bed, darlin', I'm gonna be spendin' the rest of my life thinkin' 'bout that pussy and not findin' anything that comes close. And, babe, my balls are gonna fuckin' explode."

We switched positions, and he started moving again, this time with vigor, hard and fast, skin slapping skin. Then, slow and sweet, our sweat-slicked bodies sliding against each other.

There was nothing else quite like it. And there was no one else quite like Deuce.

"Oh fuck!" I cried out, cursing and clawing through my second orgasm. "Holy fucking shit!"

He grinned down at me, all beautiful blue eyes, laugh lines, and dimples.

"There it is," he rumbled appreciatively. "There's my fuckin' girl."

His girl.

How long had I been waiting to hear him say that?

After fucking Eva all morning, she had fallen asleep again. It was late afternoon now, and Deuce and a few of his boys were drinking brews and grilling steaks out back of the clubhouse.

"Where's the hottie?" Tap asked around the neck of his beer bottle.

"Which one?" Jase asked. "The blonde or the brunette? They're both badass."

ZZ laughed. "The blonde's been in a Ripper/Cox sandwich since she got here."

Hawk made a face. "Shit's not fair. If it'd been me that walked out there first, bitch would be in my bed."

Deuce shrugged. "Kami's a fuckin' whore. Doubt she'll be opposed to you joinin' the party."

"Naw," Chips said. "I already tried. They don't wanna share. Not that I blame 'em. Not many holes left available when they're both hittin' that shit at the same time. So how's 'bout yours, Prez? You wanna pass her on yet?"

ZZ spit out his beer.

"Asshat," Jase muttered. "That's not a whore. That's Eva Fox, Preacher's fuckin' daughter. The bitch our prez can't seem to think straight around. The bitch who got him shot."

Chips eyes went wide.

"I got myself shot," he muttered. "Wasn't her fuckin' fault. She was sixteen. I had my hand down her fuckin' pants, and my tongue down her throat. He's her old man; do you really fuckin' blame him?"

"You die," Marsh said, his expression hard, "then, yeah, I would fuckin' blame him."

"Sixteen, huh?" Danny D. grinned. "Nice."

Tap frowned at Danny. "You're fuckin' sick, dude. I got a fifteen-year-old daughter. Some fuckin' old asshole like Prez gets anywhere near her pants, and I'm gonna put him to ground. I'm puttin' a one-year age difference on her datin' life." Tap turned to him. "Not a fuckin' eighteen-year difference."

"It's not like that," Deuce muttered, feeling strangely embarrassed. "Got nothin' to do with her age. Never has. Been likin' her since she was just a kid, and now her bein' a woman, my cock likes her, too. But it's never been 'bout her age. Straight up, it's always been just 'bout her."

His boys were staring at him as if he had grown a second head.

"Damn, Prez," Jase muttered. "Just…damn."

Chapter
SEVEN

Aside from Cox, Ripper, and Mick—who hadn't returned—I met Blue, ZZ, Chip, Bucket, Worm, Freebird, Hawk, Marsh, Danny D., Danny L., Tramp, Dimebag, Tap, Dirty, and Jase. And those were just the names I remembered.

Out of everyone I met, I liked Cox, ZZ, and Freebird the most. ZZ was an eighteen-year-old novitiate who, like me, had been born into the life. He also reminded me of Frankie with his chocolate brown eyes and shoulder-length brown hair that he kept in a ponytail midskull. He was tall and lean with an overall innocence that I knew would soon be wiped right out of him.

Figuring out how Freebird got his name wasn't hard. Long gray-and-black hair hung greasy and stringy halfway down his back. He was balding on top, but he hid it well using Bret Michaels' bandana-balding solution. His gray beard was braided in one long braid that reached his chest, and he still wore bell-bottom jeans that had been patched over so many times I wasn't sure if any of the original denim remained. His arms were covered in tattoos: peace signs, yin and yang, and words like freedom, peace, and the open road. Kinda hypocritical for a biker belonging to the Hell's Horsemen MC, but whatever, he told dirty jokes and made me laugh.

The clubhouse whores weren't half as bad as the ones constantly camped out at the Demons NYC MC, half of which were actual whores. That's not saying these girls didn't have their problems. The biggest being they desperately wanted to become an old lady and early on had made the mistake of sleeping with half the club. Now they were stuck. No biker was going to put a woman on the back of his bike who's slept with half his brothers.

My least favorite was a bleached blonde named Miranda. She was twenty-five, a high school dropout, and a mom of two, fathers unknown. When I asked her where her kids were, what she did with them while she was here— which apparently was all the time—she told me her mother had custody. This disgusted me. I had no love for deadbeat moms.

I asked Deuce if he'd been with her, and he gave me a cocked eyebrow, lazy-eyed look.

Then he said, "Babe," in such a way that made me feel like I just asked the most ridiculous question ever asked.

I stormed off, and he burst out laughing. Next thing I knew, he was tossing me up over his shoulder and taking me back to bed.

As for the rest of the regulars, they varied in ages and sizes, same as the bikers they catered to. Some were young; others were middle-aged. Some were thin and shapeless; others were plump with a little too many curves in all the wrong places. Most were average women who wore too much makeup and not enough clothing. All of them were pathetic.

All except Dorothy, a petite redhead with lots of adorable freckles. She was twenty-four and married with a seven-year-old daughter. Her husband was a scumbag truck driver who was gone three weeks out of every month. She would wake up in the morning, drive her daughter to school, and then come straight to the club. Aside from participating in her exclusive relationship with Jase—who wasn't exclusive to her and was married, to boot—she was paid to clean the club, make breakfast and lunch for the brothers, and do their laundry before she left for the day. Jase was there every day she was; they would spend an hour or two in his room, and then he would leave and she'd get back to work. Around three, she'd leave to pick up her daughter and wouldn't return until the next morning. Every now and then, she would drop her daughter off at her sister's on a Friday or Saturday, so she and Jase could spend the night together. All this I knew because she had made lunch for Kami and me, and we spent the afternoon talking.

At twenty-five, Jase was a fairly gorgeous man in the Marine Reserve with a high-and-tight haircut and a kick-ass body. The club whores flocked to him like flies to shit, and Dorothy—pretty, but in a girl-next-door sort of way—knew this and simply accepted it. She was prime old-lady material. She was a good woman who obviously loved him, put up with his shit, and had no problem with having to put up with more. Only, she would never be his old lady because Jase already had one.

I wasn't sure how to feel about Jase, knowing what I knew. From what I saw, he treated her well enough. I watched him slip money in her wallet when she wasn't looking, and most important, he didn't carouse in front of her, but still…

He was married to a girl he knocked up in high school (information also gleaned from Dorothy), and while I could understand that he was unhappy with his situation, he should have rectified it before he involved himself in someone else's life.

But this was typical. And I was used to it. I was also used to keeping my opinions to myself.

"Earth to Eva," Dorothy said in a singsong voice while waving her tiny hand in front of my face.

I jerked my head up, and she started laughing.

"Did you hear anything I just said?"

"No," I said honestly. "I was lost inside my head."

"She's always lost inside her head," Kami announced.

I cut my eyes at her. "Speaking of head…where are Cox and Ripper?"

It was lunchtime, and I hadn't seen either of them since they dragged Kami off again last night.

"Sleeping me off," she stated proudly. Both Dorothy and I burst out laughing.

"Speaking of which," she continued, popping her last bite of ham sandwich into her mouth. "I should go wake them up." She slipped off the barstool and sauntered through the kitchen, looking graceful and beautiful despite her lack of sleep and vigorous exercise.

"Hey, Deuce," she purred.

I spun around. Deuce was standing in the doorway, arms above his head, his hands grasping the top of the door frame, causing his muscles to bulge and his black T-shirt to ride up, revealing a fabulous abdomen. He was also covered in grease. Head to toe.

Kami was looking up at him like he was a hot fudge sundae.

"Go easy on my boys, woman; they got shit to do today."

He moved aside to let her pass and slipped onto the stool she had just vacated.

"You're gonna kill me, babe."

I took a sip of my coffee. "What?"

"That fuckin' dress, babe. Killin' me."

I glanced down at my strapless sundress. It was dark green, virtually shapeless, soft cotton that hung just slightly above mid-thigh. It was simple, comfortable, and very me. And not at all sexy, not compared to the clothing women like Kami wore.

"Um…seriously? It's like a big green bag."

He narrowed his eyes. "No, babe, it's not."

Jase chose that moment to barrel into the kitchen. He crossed the room and literally swept Dorothy off her feet into a passionate embrace, like the ones you see in movies.

"Missed you, baby," he groaned into her mouth.

She giggled. "You saw me yesterday."

With her legs wrapped around his waist and her arms around his neck, he strode back through the kitchen.

"Eva!" Dorothy yelled. "Are you going to be here for the barbeque?"

"Twenty-four hours," Jase growled. "Babe, it's been twenty-four horrible fuckin' hours, and you're talkin' 'bout barbeques. This is me time, and you need to focus. You gotta let me get you your own place; you gotta leave that man, so I can see you whenever the fuck I want, and you'll be fuckin' focused. On me. You gotta let me take care of—"

The doors closed behind them, leaving Deuce and me alone.

"Speakin' of the barbeque, how long you stayin', babe?"

My gaze slid back to Deuce. I couldn't tell by his expression if he wanted me to stay or not.

"Babe?"

"Um…"

Laughing, he reached out and pulled me into his lap. His hands wrapped around my middle, and he buried his face in my neck.

"How long you got?" he murmured.

"All summer," I whispered.

"Then you're stayin' at my cabin."

Oh God. He wanted me to stay all summer. At *his* cabin.

"The clubhouse is fine with me," I whispered, reeling from this new development.

"No, babe. I know you're used to it, but I don't want you seein' all the fucked-up shit the boys are always doin'."

"It doesn't bother me."

He snorted. "Me fuckin' Miranda bothers you."

"Not if it's in the past tense." I narrowed my eyes. "It is in the past tense, right?"

He snorted. "You're here; it's in the past tense."

Huh. I wasn't sure I liked that answer.

"OK," I said slowly, "then it doesn't bother me."

"Babe. Old ladies don't hang at the club. And they sure as shit don't sleep here. You know that."

What?

What!

I twisted around in his lap, so we were face-to-face. "What did you just call me?"

His eyebrows drew together. "Babe?"

"No!" I yelled. "You called me an old lady! I am not an old lady; I'm a Demon! I was born and raised in the life, and I'm not going to be locked up in some cabin in the middle of nowhere waiting for you to hang out with me!"

"You done?" he asked evenly.

"Are you going to let me hang out here?"

"No."

I scrambled off his lap. "No?" I whispered.

"Yeah, babe. No. You're goin' to my place, and I'll be there with you when I'm not here."

I gaped at him. "You won't let me stay here, but you'll let Kami?"

His expression hardened. "Kami's a fuckin' whore," he said flatly. "Locked in a room with two of my boys right now."

"Fuck. You," I spat. "If I wanted to be treated like this, I'd be in a Demon's bed, not yours!"

In the blink of an eye, Deuce was off the stool, gripping my shoulders.

"First," he growled, "don't run your fuckin' mouth at me. Ever. Second, ain't no way I'm lettin' you hang here, so stop fuckin' askin'. Third, bitch, you throw shit 'bout bein' in someone else's bed at me again, and I'm puttin' you on a plane back to New York, so you can climb right the fuck in someone else's bed. And you can fuckin' stay there."

Staring up at him, watching the lines around his eyes tightening, his nostrils flaring, his lips pressing together in a thin white line, and hearing the raw anger in his voice made my stomach drop. This wasn't the Deuce I knew glaring down at me; this was Deuce—badass biker, cold-blooded killer—furious with me. Me.

What had I done?

My lip began to tremble, and I bit down on it.

"You feel me, Eva?"

I nodded.

"Say it," he growled.

Sheesh. My own father, even when mad at me, had never spoken to me like this.

"I feel you," I whispered.

He shoved me toward the doors. "Go to my fuckin' room if you're gonna cry. Last thing I need is weepin' females in my fuckin' club."

My tears spilled over as I pushed blindly through the swinging doors, down the back hallway, past the hall of bedrooms, and to the very end to Deuce's suite. Digging through my backpack, I pulled out my credit card and called the airline. I was going home.

Deuce ran his hands through his air. Fuck, she pissed him off.

She had called herself a Demon! What the fuck was Preacher thinking raising her inside the club? The entire fucking circuit knew Eva Fox. Why the fuck had Preacher done that shit?

Christ. He would not rearrange his whole fucking life for some bitch just because he had some fucked-up obsession with her.

"Hey, you."

He turned and found Miranda pushing through the kitchen doors.

"You want somethin' to eat, baby? I was gonna make myself a salad."

"Yeah," he said roughly. "I want somethin' to fuckin' eat."

Miranda was his bitch. He didn't share her. He gave her a room at the club, so he had access to her when he wanted it. Since Eva's arrival, he'd considered sending her to the apartment he paid for.

He was seriously reconsidering that now.

Gripping Miranda's tiny waist, he swung her up on the counter in front of him and pushed down the straps of her tank top revealing the double-Ds he bought a few years back.

"You done with that little girl?" she purred.

"Shut up," he muttered and took her mouth in his.

After booking a flight home for the next afternoon, I dried my eyes and set out to find Kami. I found her in Cox's bedroom in a seriously compromising position with Cox and Ripper that I was pretty sure would be giving me nightmares for the rest of my life. I told her I would talk to her later and slammed the door. Then I headed toward the front of the warehouse to tell Deuce I was leaving. He wasn't in the main room or his office, which left the kitchen or the bathrooms. I checked the kitchen first.

Miranda's back was facing me, but I could see Deuce just fine.

I was not going to cry. Nope. Just because he wasn't the man I thought he was didn't mean I was going to cry. It was my own fault, putting him on some kind of pedestal; when in reality, he was just another biker who lies, cheats, steals, and can't resist slutty club ass.

He looked up and saw me standing in the doorway. If he was surprised to see me, or felt any sort of guilt at all, he didn't show it. For this, I was grateful. My threatening tears were replaced by anger—anger that allowed me to meet him stare for stare.

I was still standing there staring when the gate alarm went off.

ZZ came flying down the hallway past me. "RAID!" he bellowed. Several more brothers followed him, looking panicked. Cox and Ripper were next, shirtless and pulling on jeans as they ran.

I moved out of the way of the stampede and into the kitchen. Miranda had since jumped off Deuce and was pulling up her tank top. Deuce walked by without even looking at me.

Miranda and I caught eyes. "Eva," she said softly. "I'm gonna tell you this because you're a sweet girl. Deuce is not a one-woman man. He never will be. You'd do well to find yourself a nice guy who will worship all that beautiful you've got goin' on—not just once in a while, but all the time."

She was being sincere; she even looked apologetic.

I shrugged. "It's really not a big deal. I was on summer vacation and wanted to have some fun without my daddy and brother breathing down my neck, you know?"

Lie. Biggest lie I had ever told. But the last thing I wanted was a club whore feeling sorry for me. She bought it and took off down the hallway to hide in her bedroom. I was still standing there staring at nothing when Deuce walked back in.

"ATF's outside; we got 'bout two minutes before they blow the gate," he said. "Figured Preacher might have used you before, yeah?"

"Yes," I said.

He handed me a ring full of keys. "Those are for the doors. Code to the gate is 009673."

I nodded. "009673," I repeated.

He stared at me.

"Go," I said. "Do what you need to do. I'll stall them."

Outside the gate stood white-collar special agents wearing bulletproof vests over their button-downs. Behind them, SWAT was pouring out of several large paddy wagons dressed in military-issued boots and BDUs. They, too, wore bulletproof vests, but unlike the agents, they had Glocks strapped to their thighs and assault rifles slung over their shoulders.

"ATF," an older, seasoned agent said in greeting. "You mind opening the gate?"

I smiled. "What's this about?"

Another agent—young, clean-cut, and good-looking—waved a piece of paper around angrily. "Warrant," he barked. "Open the fucking gate!"

"Can I see that?" I asked sweetly.

He shoved the piece of paper through the gate, and I scanned it quickly. It was a search and seizure, dated correctly, and signed by a judge. In order and legit.

I handed it back but took my time punching in wrong code after wrong code after wrong code until a good fifteen minutes had passed by, and the agents were getting angry with me.

As soon as the electricity running through the gates was disarmed, they clicked open, and the tarmac flooded with SWAT headed straight for the club.

"Front door's locked!"

"Side door's locked!"

I rolled my eyes. Of course, they were locked. I wasn't stupid.

"Get the ram!"

"Wait!" I yelled. "Don't break it down! I have the keys!"

The younger, good-looking agent turned to glare at me. "Get over here!" he barked.

I hurried to the door, and the good-looking agent leaned down over me. "Open it," he hissed.

I tried the first key, and it didn't work. Truth be told, I didn't know which one would. Deuce didn't tell me.

By the third key, I had two agents screaming at me. By the sixth key, the good-looking agent grabbed a fistful of my hair and yanked me roughly aside.

"Give me the keys," he growled and snatched them from my shaking hands.

When the doors were open, I was shoved aside as the crowd poured in. Aside from ATF, no one else was in the front of the warehouse. I took shelter in a corner near the bar and watched the room being torn apart. Leather couches were sliced open, televisions were smashed, and cupboard doors were ripped off their hinges. Crashes, the sounds of wood splintering, and plastic cracking came from inside Deuce's office and the kitchen.

There was so much activity going on around me that I didn't see the good-looking agent until he was standing right in front of me, breathing hard, his face red with rage. "Where are they?" he bellowed, sending spittle flying in my face.

Wiping off my cheek, I shook my head. "I don't know," I whispered because really I didn't know.

He grabbed my arm and shook me hard. "Where. Are. They?"

Tears burned in my eyes. The Horsemen must not have any Feds on their payroll, or this wouldn't be happening.

"Please," I begged. "I really don't know."

Pain exploded throughout my face. My mouth flooded with blood. His punch had landed on the left side of my jaw, the force of which had me stumbling backward into the wall. He closed the distance between us, and I turned my head into the wall, bracing myself for another punch. His fist barreled into my stomach, and my lungs exploded. I doubled over, clutching my midsection, gagging and gasping for air.

"GOT 'EM!" a voice boomed. "Trap door! Basement!"

The brothers were led single file into the room, their hands zip-tied behind their backs. Individually, they were shoved up against the far wall.

Deuce was directly in the middle of the lineup, nonchalantly scanning the room full of people. His gaze landed on me—lying on my side, holding my stomach, trying to breathe—and he went ramrod straight, his eyes blazing with fury. More tears flooded my eyes, and the room went blurry.

I recognized the good-looking agent's voice.

"I have witnesses placing your L.A. boys meeting with Curtis's boys in Vegas. I know for a fact you're distributing for them. I also know you haven't moved it yet. So let's make this easy. You tell me where the fuck you stashed the weapons, you blow in Curtis, and I'll go easy on you."

"No fuckin' clue whatcha talkin' 'bout."

I thought that sounded like Cox, but I couldn't be sure.

"Really?" the agent sneered. "AK-47 rifles, AK-47 pistols, FN 5.7x28 millimeter pistols, and .50 caliber point rifles—twenty-five hundred in all and all from fucking Curtis—isn't ringing any fucking bells?"

"Nope." That was Deuce.

"How about the twenty thousand grams of cocaine, a thousand grams of crack, and a pound of methamphetamine? All intercepted yesterday. Got your handiwork written all over it, West."

Holy crap. That was going to come straight out of Deuce's pocket. I didn't know the Horsemen's finances, but that would hurt anyone.

"You got any proof of that?"

Several heartbeats passed. "We will," came the biting reply.

"Good fuckin' luck with that, asshole." Definitely ZZ. This was followed by a large whoosh of air and familiar gagging and coughing. ZZ had just gotten slammed in the gut.

"Where's Davis's team?" an unknown voice bellowed.

"Still searching," was the answer.

"Tell me someone found something!"

"Aside from a few females hiding in bedrooms, the place is clean. The assholes have permits for all the weapons found. There's nothing here. Not a goddamn thing. Not even a dime bag of weed."

If I wasn't in so much pain, I would have laughed. Who called weed "weed"? Too funny.

"You run IDs on the girls?"

"All of 'em except the one on the floor over there. But check this shit, one of them is the daughter of a senator and the heir to the Carlson Food fortune."

I swallowed. They were talking about Kami. If her parents found out about this…things would not be good for her.

A pair of dress shoes stopped in front of my face, and the toe of one poked me in the leg. "Name?" a man's voice demanded.

"Eva…Fox," I croaked.

The man's legs bent. His pudgy, blotchy red face came into my field of vision. "Eva Fox?" he repeated slowly. "Who's your father?"

This was either going to go very bad for me or very good. I didn't know which, so when I answered, it was very timid and terrified sounding. "Damon Fox."

"Shit," he muttered. His arm slipped around my back and under my armpit, and then I was being lifted and settled onto a barstool. Still clutching my stomach, feeling like at any moment I was going to puke, I slumped forward and put my forehead on the counter.

"Who the fuck beat the shit out of Damon Fox's kid?" Pudgy Face demanded.

The entire place had gone silent.

"I did." I recognized the good-looking agent's voice. "She was playing us, stalling."

"You fucking moron!" someone else yelled.

OK, so it was going good. Either they were on my father's payroll, or they were scared shitless of him.

A gentle hand came down on my shoulder. "Ms. Fox?"

I turned my head slightly. Pudgy Face bent his head to mine.

"I've written down the name of the asshole who hit you on the back of my card. You give it to Preacher; you tell him what he did. And I'd appreciate it if you'd tell him that no one else touched you."

Definitely on his payroll. Probably getting a hefty percentage of the sales from the weapons they were supposed to be confiscating. Probably sending half the weapons they did confiscate straight to my father for redistribution.

"OK," I whispered, knowing I wasn't going to tell my father anything. Me disappearing only to show back up beaten by the ATF...

That would not go over well. For me or the ATF.

The hand patted my back. "OK," he whispered. He slid his card across the bar and walked away.

Deuce carried Eva down the hall to his bedroom. Kicking the door shut behind them, he laid her out on his bed and stared at the growing bruise on the side of her face. Since she told him her old man didn't have a clue where she was, he knew she wasn't going to tell him what happened. That meant it was up to him to take out the agent, which was fine with him. This fucking girl had just taken a beating for him and his club.

"I'm OK," she whispered. "He punched like a girl."

Fuck him. She was perfect. Perfect old-lady material. Perfect heart-shaped face, big gray eyes, smooth skin, and fuck-me lips. Perfect tits, long legs, and a flat stomach. Perfect curves to run his hands over and long hair to grab hold of.

And he'd gotten angry, let his temper get the better of him, and completely fucked everything up.

Sighing, he sat down on the bed beside her. "'Bout earlier," he started. "I—"

"Don't," she whispered. "I get it. I was stupid for expecting anything from you. I'm leaving tomorrow anyway."

His chest went tight. He'd been too hard on her. He had a horrible temper and couldn't think straight when he was angry. Add Eva Fox to the mix and his brain was just a big lump of idiot.

"No, babe. You're not leavin'."

There. Now she wasn't leaving.

Fire flashed in her eyes. "Yeah, Deuce, I am. You made it clear that I couldn't hang at the club, that you didn't want me around your boys, and I refuse to be locked in some cabin for an entire summer. Besides, Kami and I had planned on going to Hawaii after this."

She was lying. He could see it in her eyes.

"Babe, calm down. You can come to the club with me when I don't have to work."

She snorted, and then winced in pain. "Sorry, *babe*. I've already made up my mind. You pretty much sealed the deal when you decided I had to share you. My daddy's going to be angry enough when I return; I'm pretty sure bringing back an STD as a souvenir would result in me being locked up in a nunnery."

Fucking shit. She was running her mouth again, and he was getting pissed.

"Woman, if you think I'm gonna let you walk outta here, you're fuckin' crazy. You showed up outta nowhere 'cause you fuckin' wanted me, so you fuckin' got me. And I'm gonna tell you straight up that a few fuckin' days of you hasn't been enough. So you reel that fuckin' attitude in 'cause you're fuckin' stayin'!"

Her face wiped clean, no expression whatsoever. "Get the fuck away from me," she said evenly. "Now."

He curled his hands into fists. "Eva," he growled. "Stop it."

She rolled to her side, facing away from him.

Stiffly, he got off the bed and stalked to the door. He shot one last look at her. She was staring off to the side at nothing.

I woke up in darkness as the bed dipped, and Deuce slid in beside me. Instead of curling up next to me, he stayed on the opposite side of the bed. I couldn't let it end like this. Not with him. My stomach was sore, but nothing like my face and nothing I couldn't handle, so I rolled over and crawled on top of him.

"Hey," I whispered.

His arms wrapped around me. "You still mad, darlin'?"

Instead of answering, I kissed him. When I pulled away, we were both breathing heavily.

I rubbed my lips across his and whispered, "You want it hard, or you want it slow?"

"Babe," he said thickly. "I want it fuckin' slow."

So I gave it to him slow.

He woke up alone.

Deuce rolled over and hit air. He patted around for a moment looking for Eva and came up empty. He clicked on his bedside lamp. No Eva. No iPod on his nightstand. No Chucks by the door. No backpack on the floor. His stomach clenched.

Pulling on a pair of jeans, he headed straight for Cox's room and kicked open the door. Ripper was snoring loudly, his long body draped over an armchair. Cox, lying belly-down in bed, jerked his head up.

"Prez?"

He scanned the room. No Kami.

The vice around his chest went painfully tight.

"Where's your fuckin' bitch?"

Cox looked right, then left. "Shit," he muttered. "I thought I heard something earlier. Figured she was fuckin' Ripper again. Fuckin' hell. I was gonna ask her to marry me."

"You're already married, shithead. This ain't fuckin' Utah." He slammed the door shut and took off down the hall.

He found Blue sitting alone at the bar in the dark. Seventy-two years old, two-pack-a-day smoker, and a raging alcoholic, yet healthy as a twenty-year-old.

"Eva?" he asked.

Blue swallowed down a shot of Patrón. "Gone."

His chest went so fucking tight he had to slap his palm over his heart and rub before he could breathe again.

"When?"

Blue poured, and then threw back another shot.
"'Bout two hours ago."

Fuck.

FUCK.

"Sorry, Prez, I woulda woken you up, told you what she was doin', but she was cryin' her fuckin' eyes out. Hysterical. Beggin' me to open the gate. Beggin' me not to wake you up. Can't deal with hysterical women myself. Makes me want to drink."

"Right," he said numbly.

"Left you this." Blue held out his hand.

He took the small, folded piece of paper and opened it.

Deuce,
I'm sorry.
I shouldn't have come and imposed on your life.
<3, Eva
P.S. Take care of yourself.

"Prez?"

"What?"

"She's a good girl," Blue said. "Sweet, too. Knows her way 'round a club, took two fuckin' fists for it. Fuckin' adores you, too. Woulda thought you were the king of fuckin' England the way she looks at you, and she's good to the boys, not givin' 'em shit 'bout the girls, bringin' them beers, talkin' and jokin' with 'em, makin' friends with Jase's piece of ass. Didn't much like Miranda…"

Blue tossed back another shot and chuckled.

"But I don't much blame her. I were you, I woulda done everything I coulda to keep a girl like that in my bed."

What else could he have done short of tying her to the bed or drugging her?

"Yeah," Deuce muttered. "Too late now."

His hand fisted around the note, crushing it.

"Pour me one of those," he muttered, taking a seat beside Blue.

Fuck Eva Fox and her perfect face and her perfect tits. He had a life to get back to.

So he got back to it.

For three long years, he lived his fucking life.

His miserable fucking life.

And then he saw her again.

And miserable got a fuck of a lot worse.

Chapter
EIGHT

Groaning, Frankie collapsed on top of me.

"Off," I demanded, pushing at him. "I can't breathe."

He lifted his head, grinning. "Like you where you are, babe. Fuckin' naked and underneath me."

Frankie was insatiable. I almost wished he would start whoring around at the club and give me a break.

"Frankie! I can't breathe! Get off!"

Grunting, he pushed himself up a few inches. "I'm tryin', babe, but you're not lettin' me back in."

"Ahhh!" I yelled, shoving him as hard as I could—which wasn't very hard, but I did manage to shove him off to the side, so I was able to roll away.

Frankie rolled, too, reaching for me. I jumped backward and slapped his hands away. Glaring at him, I headed into the bathroom to dress.

"Remind me why we had to sleep at the club?" I asked, stepping into my underwear, and then slipping my jersey cotton sheath dress over my head.

"Got a meetin' this mornin'."

I pulled my hair up and turned on the faucet. Scooping water in my hands, I started washing my face. "So why did I have to stay at the club?"

"Can't sleep without you, babe."

Grabbing Frankie's toothbrush, I loaded it with toothpaste and shoved it in my mouth.

"What's the meeting about?" I mumbled around the toothbrush.

"Bunch of MCs havin' trouble with Angelo Buonarroti. Seems the douchebag put out a coupla bids for the same jobs. Things got messy; brothers got buried. Need to get this shit straightened out. Maybe Buonarroti needs to go to ground. We'll see."

I spit, rinsed the toothbrush, and put it back in its holder. Then I grabbed my makeup bag and set to work making myself look presentable.

"Gonna go have breakfast with Kami while you're working."

"At her place?"

I leaned forward, dotting some cover-up underneath my eyes. "Probably."

"Don't like that fucker she married," Frankie muttered.

I grinned. "Who does?"

Chase Henderson was a high-paid lawyer for a very successful leading law firm and had made partner by the age of twenty-five. We all went to prep school together, but he went to Harvard, whereas Kami and I stayed in Manhattan to attend NYU. Their parents had arranged their marriage a long time ago. It was ridiculously old-school, but it wasn't unheard of in their circle. There were many wealthy political families that still practiced arranged marriages.

Chase was extraordinarily good-looking in an all-American Calvin Klein underwear model kind of way. Never once had I seen him not clean-shaven and without one of many designer outfits on. He never had a single gelled hair out of place and always wore a pissed-off, haughty expression. There was nothing simple or comfortable about him. He reminded me of a house that was too expensive, too new, too clean, and too perfect to feel comfortable in.

Kami despised him.

She had been cheating on him with her personal trainer since they got home from their honeymoon. He cheated on her with a variety of women, none of whom lasted longer than a few weeks, if that.

It was ridiculous.

"Don't like the way he looks at you, babe."

I snorted. "Frankie, you don't like anyone looking at me. Period. You didn't like my college professors looking at me when I raised my hand. Remember Professor Reynolds? Daddy had to pay him off big-time for the beating you gave him. Besides, Chase thinks I'm biker trash."

"Bitch, get a fuckin' clue!" Frankie yelled. "Asshole looks at you like he's fuckin' starvin', and you're a goddamn steak!"

Letting my hair down, I rolled my eyes. Men. Always hungry.

"Don't you have a meeting to get to?"

"Waitin' for your sweet ass, so I can walk you out."

I shook my head and smiled at him.

Frankie was a great-looking man. Long brown hair, a scruffy beard, a body made for sex, and covered in tattoos and sexy scars. He was good in bed, too. A good combination of attentive and demanding, and he didn't stray. This I knew because wherever I was—at home, at the clubhouse, in the supermarket, in the shower—Frankie was there, too. Or somewhere nearby. Or on his way there. Or Skyping me. Or tracking me through my cell phone with his cell phone.

Three years ago, I came home from Montana and was met with insanity the likes of which I'd never seen before. The club was in an uproar—first, because I was missing and second, because Frankie completely flipped his shit and was beating on anyone who got near him, beating himself with the butt of his gun, bashing his head and fists into walls until they bled, and screaming, swearing, and cursing me to hell.

Ignoring my father's temper tantrum and responsibility speech, I went straight to Frankie's room and found him curled up in a corner covered in blood.

"Shit," I muttered, getting to my knees beside him.

"Frankie," I whispered. "Baby, look at me."

He moved fast. His hands shot out and gripped both my forearms. Dragging me down to the floor, he rolled over on top of me. Blood-encrusted eyelids blinked down at me.

"Eva," he croaked. "Where the fuck have you been?"

"I just needed some breathing room, baby. I'm sorry I left you."

He cupped my cheeks, ran his fingers through my hair, then down to my shoulders, and up and down my arms. Before I knew it, his hands were all over me, pulling the top of my sundress down, baring my breasts. He took one in his hand and the other in his mouth.

"Fuck," I breathed. "Frankie, no…"

"Not waitin' anymore, babe," he muttered around my breast. Lifting his hips, he pulled the hem of my dress up.

I tried to push him off me. "I'm not going to leave you again!" I promised. "We don't need to do this!"

Frankie dug his fingers in between my knees and wrenched my legs open. His hips surged forward, forcing them to stay open, and he yanked on his belt. I started to panic.

"Please!" I cried. "Please don't do this!"

"No, baby," he growled. "I'm not gonna fuckin' let you say no to me anymore. You get me? You're not fuckin' runnin' from me anymore. Told you a long time ago you were mine, and it's 'bout time you got that shit through your thick fuckin' skull."

This was all said while he was opening his belt and unzipping his jeans. Now he was yanking my underwear to one side, and I could feel him trying to enter me.

"Wait!" I cried, shoving at his chest. "Don't!"

"Fuck," he muttered. He spit in his palm, rubbed his hand over me, wetting me, and then he was back, pushing inside.

"Frankie!" I screamed, trying to wiggle backward to prevent him from fully seating himself.

"STOP!"

His hand slapped down over my mouth. I kept screaming, but the sound was muffled and hoarse, and no one heard but Frankie and me.

"Been waitin' too fuckin' long for this," he groaned, pushing harder, his heavy chest crushing my attempts at moving him. "You're not fuckin' stoppin' me anymore. You're never fuckin' stoppin' me again."

He thrust. Hard. And found purchase. I stilled, tears in my eyes, staring up at him. Frankie had just forced himself on me, inside of me. My Frankie. It was surreal, confusing, like a dream or a movie you remember from a long time ago.

"Lock your ankles around my back," he rasped. Dazed, I did as he asked. He released my mouth to grip my backside and pump harder. Numb, I listened to his skin slapping against mine, his heavy breathing, and my head knocking against the wall.

"How the fuck could you leave me?" he rasped. "I can't fuckin' sleep without you, haven't fuckin' slept in days. You fuckin' did that to me, bitch. You fuckin' let that happen."

I had. I'd known he was going to freak, and I'd left him anyway. I should have realized this was going to happen—that he would completely lose it and need to bind me to him in a way he thought was permanent.

God, this was all my fault.

"I'm sorry," I whispered brokenly. "God, Frankie, I'm so sorry. It won't happen again, I promise."

"No shit," he hissed. "You won't fuckin' like what happens if you do…Eva…fuck, baby…I'm gonna come…fuck…"

His hips slammed into me, banging my head harder into the wall. "I'm coming, baby, I'm fuckin' coming…"

I stared up at the ceiling. I wasn't on birth control. I would need to get the morning after pill. I blinked. Did all of our bedroom ceilings look like that? I wasn't sure. I made a mental note to check.

"Fuckin' love you, Eva," Frankie breathed.

I wiped my tears away and wrapped my arms around his neck. "I love you, too, baby," I whispered, holding him tight, rubbing his back and murmuring apologies.

It wasn't a lie. I did love Frankie. With all my heart. But it was the wrong kind of love. I loved him like a best friend or a big brother—and not at all like a lover. But he forced his way into the lover category, and there was nothing I could do. He needed me. He wasn't going to let me go, so I gave him what he needed and tried to make the best of it.

That was three years ago.

Three years of being on the back of Frankie's bike and in Frankie's bed—which was actually mine. My room at the clubhouse was bigger and better.

"Who do you love, babe?"

I finished brushing my hair and walked out of the bathroom. "You," I said.

"Fuck yeah, you do."

Frankie finished dressing and sat down on the bed to pull his boots on. He looked me over and frowned. "Lot of leg you're showin', babe."

I snorted. "Hardly."

Suddenly, Frankie was on his feet, unbuckling his belt and reaching for me.

"Jesus!" I screamed, scrambling away from him. "Focus, you horny bastard! You have a meeting! I have a breakfast date!"

He had my belly pressed up against the wall in two seconds flat. His tongue shot across my neck.

"Don't care, babe. You can't fuckin' walk around half-naked and expect me to keep my hands off."

"You don't play fair," I whispered.

"When it comes to you, Eva, I don't fuckin' play at all."

It was nearly an hour before Frankie decided it was time to go to his meeting, and even then, he did so reluctantly.

Deuce frowned at Preacher. "Don't know whatcha talkin' 'bout, old man. I got no connections with Angelo Buonarroti. His old man, yeah. Couple of his cousins, too, but not him. If you lost your deal with them, it ain't on me."

"You're full of it," Preacher growled. "My boys seen yours on the fuckin' docks."

"Can't help it if my boys in Queens got business on the side. They got families to take care of."

Preacher's dark eyes narrowed and cut to his right where Dog, One-Eyed Joe, and Tiny sat. Next to Joe were his boys: Mick, Cox, and Jase. He was seated at the end of the table directly across from Preacher. Next to him, on the other side of the table were Kickass Charlie, president of the Notorious MC, and two of his boys. Shit was tense. Not one brother in this room wanted to be here—he and Preacher for their own personal reasons involving sixteen-year-old Eva and a gun, and Charlie because Frankie had buried his old man a few years back. It was one of the crazy fuck's few caps that had been on the grid. Charlie's old man had been a tried-and-true dirty bastard.

Yeah, shit was real tense—even without Frankie in attendance.

The meeting room door burst open with a loud bang. Startled, several brothers shot out of their chairs, pulling their pieces.

Frankie sauntered in, grinning. He was zipping up his jeans, buckling his belt, and completely oblivious to the firearms pointed at his head.

"Sorry I'm late," he said to no one in particular and slid into his chair at Preacher's left.

Preacher glared at him. "Where the fuck you been?"

Frankie started to open his mouth when an empty coffee cup sailed across the table, hitting him in the chest.

One-Eyed Joe scowled at Preacher. "He's walkin' in here grinnin' like a dirty dog, zippin' up his pants, and you're askin' him where he was! You know where he was, you fuckin' idiot, and you know what he was doin' and who he was doin' it with 'cause that's all the two of them ever do! Spankin' each other day and night, not carin' that we all gotta hear it! And you're gonna ask him stupid questions 'bout where he's been, knowin' he's gonna start talkin' 'bout fuckin' my niece! I just can't fuckin' stomach that shit. He says one more word about hot pussy or titty-fuckin' in relation to my girl, I'm puttin' him back in the hospital!"

Frankie grinned.

His stomach dropped.

Preacher sighed. "You tryin' to say I should keep my own baby from the club? Not sure I could handle not seein' her all the time."

Dog gasped. An honest-to-God gasp. Like a little fucking girl. "Nobody's keepin' Eva from the club!"

"No fuckin' way!" Tiny bellowed. "She keeps my old lady off my back and does my laundry!"

"Damn straight!" Joe's fist came down on the table. "That's our girl! We didn't have Eva here, who would keep the books straight? Who would cook us fuckin' breakfast? If anyone's gonna go, it's gonna be Frankie!"

Frankie was still grinning. "Can't kick me out. Your baby girl loves me. Case you haven't noticed, that's her room I'm sleepin' in upstairs."

Deuce blew out a breath. He hadn't wanted to come to New York, he really hadn't wanted to meet with Preacher or Charlie, he especially hadn't wanted to meet them at the Demons MC, and he fervently hadn't wanted to lay eyes on Frankie.

And now that he knew Eva was giving it up to him…he wanted to blow holes into the skull of every asshole in the room.

That wasn't even the worst of it. These men—her father, her uncles, even three-hundred-pound, sweat-drenched Tiny—all of them looked horrified at the thought of Eva being kept out of the club like their old ladies were. Not caring that she was well aware of the debauchery that went on, probably having seen most of it, helped hide it, and cleaned up after it.

She even had her own room. *Her own room.* At a fucking MC. What. The. Fuck.

His mistake slammed into him like a fucking freight train. He had thought she was being bratty and obstinate when she'd only been reacting to him wanting to push her away from what she'd always known. She hadn't been running from him; she'd been running from the cage he'd wanted to lock her in.

"Ya think you can save the fuckin' drama for later?" Charlie asked. "Maybe we can get back to fuckin' business?"

Frankie turned his head and gave Charlie a crazy-eyed, vicious smile. "Sure thing, Chuck," he said pleasantly. "I fuckin' loved doin' business with your old man, gonna love doin' it with you, too."

Charlie's nostrils flared, but he wisely kept his mouth shut. The whole circuit knew Frankie was bad news, trigger-happy, and more than willing to throw down at the drop of a hat.

"All right," Preacher growled. "If we're not playin' each other, then it's the fuckin' Buonarroti family that's playin' us. Someone needs to pay Sal a visit, ask him if he knows what his fuckin' kid is up to. You get the sense that he does—"

The door burst open, and again guns were drawn as Eva tore through the room. Frankie slid down his chair and disappeared under the table.

"I see you!" she screamed. "Get out from under there and give me my purse and my Chucks! I was supposed to meet Kami a half an hour ago!"

Cox sat up straight in his chair. "Kami? Where's Kami?"

"Don't know what you're talkin' 'bout, babe," came the muffled, laughing reply from under the table.

"Oh, Christ," Preacher muttered, pinching the bridge of his nose.

"DADDY!"

"Busy, Eva, baby," he sighed. "Can we do this later?"

"NO!"

Fucking hell. She was beautiful. Hair, dark and long, falling in soft waves over her shoulders and past her breasts. She was wearing makeup, more than he ever saw her wear; it looked good, made her appear polished, but he didn't like it. He couldn't see the freckles on her nose or the natural pink of her cheeks. Her dress was thin cotton, off the shoulder and shapeless, showing off a lot of leg, giving her a casual and sexy appearance. She looked hot as fuck, but he liked her better in baggy jeans, hanging low on her hips, and tiny T-shirts that showed her belly. His gaze traveled to her neck, to the gold chain still on it, and his old man's tag that he knew was hanging in between her breasts underneath her dress.

She was so mad, so focused on Frankie, that she hadn't even noticed him. He was staring at her, boring holes through her head, and still nothing.

"Frankie, tell Eva where her shit is 'fore I kick the fuckin' shit outta you!"

Preacher's body jerked and a shout came from under the table. Frankie crawled out, holding his side, and glaring at Preacher.

"Franklin Salvatore Deluva," Eva snapped. "I am waiting."

Jumping to his feet, Frankie pulled a cell phone out of his back pocket and tossed it to her. She caught it one-handed.

"Where's the rest?" she demanded, not quite as angry as she'd been a moment ago.

"Chucks are in the freezer, babe," Frankie said, grinning.

"You put her Chucks in the freezer? With our food?" Dog asked.

"Yup."

"Huh."

Eva started tapping her bare foot. "Purse, Frankie. Where's my purse?"

"Purse?" Joe snorted. "Don't cha mean that fuckin' potato sack you could fit a family of midgets in?"

Preacher, Dog, Joe, Tiny, and Frankie all burst out laughing.

Pissed off, Eva spun around, ready to march out of the room. Her eyes found his, and she froze in midspin and lost her footing. He shot out of his seat, but Cox was closer and grabbed her waist, hoisting her up from midfall and what would have been a nasty spill.

"Hey, Foxy," Cox whispered, grinning. She blinked up at him.

He helped her straighten up, and she quickly stepped away, glancing warily back at Frankie.

Frankie's face was bright red, his hands were clenched into fists, and his veins were bulging out of his neck and arms. He looked like the madman everyone thought he was.

Preacher rolled his eyes. "Frankie, he was just helpin' her. You bury your bullshit right fuckin' now."

He didn't. His crazy eyes stayed focused on Cox. Cox, who had never backed down from a challenge in his life, held Frankie's stare and didn't back down.

"FRANKLIN!" Preacher roared.

Pouting like a five-year-old, Frankie sat down hard in his chair and crossed his arms over his chest.

Swallowing hard and avoiding any eye contact with him, Eva turned back to Frankie. "Purse, baby," she said softly. "I need it."

Some of the crazy faded from Frankie's eyes, and he smiled at her. "Microwave, babe."

Tiny guffawed loudly, and Preacher shook his head.

"Sorry I interrupted," she said, turning to Preacher. "Love you, Daddy; love you, Uncle Joe; love you, Uncle Dog; and love you, too, Tiny, with extra sugar."

Every single one of those men went liquid. She wasn't just another biker brat; she was *the* biker brat. The glue that held these men together. Eva Fox was the princess of the Silver Demons MC.

Even Charlie looked affected. Girl was sweet and bright. She blinded every man in the room.

"Love you, baby," she whispered to Frankie.

His heart seized.

"Fuck yeah, baby," Frankie whispered back. "Always."

Preacher looked back and forth between them and smiled proudly.

Since Deuce was pretty sure he was five seconds from pulling his piece, he excused himself.

"Is Mrs. Henderson expecting you?"

I glared at the snotty woman. "Yes."

"You're not on her list for the day, Ms. Fox, and I'm afraid I can't let you go up. The Hendersons do not like being disturbed on the weekends."

I slammed my fists down on the desk. "CALL HER!"

Scowling, the woman turned away and dialed Kami's apartment. Or rather, her two-story sky-rise penthouse with a bird's-eye view of Manhattan.

"Mrs. Henderson, I have a Ms. Fox here to—"

The woman's jaw went slack, and I knew Kami was laying into her. I could hear her screaming through the phone from where I stood.

The woman hung up. "Go on up," she said crisply, avoiding eye contact.

"Thanks," I sneered.

I burst into Kami's cathedral foyer complete with Romanesque pillars, shoved past a bewildered Chase—who was surprisingly wearing flannel pajamas—and ran through a series of white rooms, furnished with either white or gray furniture and colorless abstract art that didn't resemble anything I'd ever seen before in my life—except maybe an ink stain after a pen explodes—and burst into Kami's bedroom.

She was lying in her king-sized canopy princess bed in a pale pink teddy and a pale pink silk robe, her long blonde hair fanned out around her head, flipping through a fashion magazine.

"Kami!" I screamed, throwing myself at her. "Kill me!"

"Oh God, Evie, what's the matter, baby? Is Frankie acting crazy again?"

"No," I whispered, rolling off her and onto her bed. "Well, yes…when isn't Frankie acting crazy?"

"I don't like that guy," Chase muttered, appearing in the doorway holding a decanter of whiskey and two glasses.

He held the decanter up in offering.

"Yes, please," I whispered.

I gulped it down quickly and held out my glass for a refill that I drank just as quickly. The burn of the whiskey subsided and soothing warmth spread in my stomach. I took a deep breath.

"I walked into Daddy's office this morning, and I was yelling at Frankie, and then I saw Deuce, and I tripped, and Cox caught me, and—"

"COX!" Kami screamed, sitting up straight. "Cox is here?"

"Who's Cox?" Chase asked.

"None of your business," Kami snapped. "Oh my God, Evie, did he ask about me?"

"Um…" I glanced up at Chase. I knew he was aware of Kami's affairs, just as she was of his, but they didn't talk about them, at least not to each other. I wasn't sure how Chase would feel having to hear about it.

He shrugged. "Go right ahead, Eva. I don't give a shit who she fucks."

"OK," Kami breathed, looking wildly around the room at nothing in particular. "I'm going to get changed, and then we are going straight to the club."

"Uh, Kami…"

"What?"

"Did you not hear what I just said to you?"

"You said Cox was here."

I backhanded her bicep. "Bitch! I said *Deuce* and Cox were here!"

"Who's Deuce?" Chase asked, taking a sip of whiskey.

"None of your business!" Kami snapped. "Oh my God, Evie, what did you do?"

"Nothing!" I cried, doing a face-plant into my palms. "What was I supposed to do? Frankie was right there! You know—my crazy, overprotective, homicidal boyfriend—Frankie? I had a silent freak-out and left! Now I'm having a loud freak-out because Frankie isn't here!"

"I don't like that guy," Chase muttered.

"Go away," Kami hissed.

Ignoring her, he sat down on the foot of her bed. Kami gaped at him.

"Seriously, Chase, don't you have anything better to do?"

He took another sip of whiskey. "Nope. It's Saturday morning. What the fuck should I be doing?"

"Your eighteen-year-old assistant?" I said helpfully.

Kami started laughing.

Chase, clearly not bothered by this, shook his head. "She got clingy. Fired her."

Kami snorted. "She's eighteen, Chase. What did you expect?"

"To have some fucking sense and realize it wasn't going anywhere," he muttered. "It wasn't as if she could have forgotten I was married, not with the five million pictures of you that you annoyingly wallpapered my office with. Pictures she saw up close and personal when I was bending her over my desk."

"Gross!" Kami cried out. "You should have at least moved the pictures!"

"Nah," he said. "I like to look at you while I'm fucking other women."

"Hmm," Kami said thoughtfully. "I don't like to look at you ever."

"Ahh," he replied. "So that's why you always have a pillow over your face when I'm fucking you."

"Pretty much," she said cheerfully.

"You guys are so weird," I informed them.

"You'd be weird, too, if your dad forced you to marry a douchebag."

Chase raised his glass in the air. "Cheers to that," he murmured.

Kami rolled to her side and brushed my hair out of my face. "Let's go shopping," she said softly. "Retail therapy. It's on Chase."

I giggled. "Not exactly hurting for cash, Kam."

"My cash is legally earned," Chase stated. "Not a drop of blood on it."

I glared at him. "You're a lawyer, Chase. There's blood all over you."

"Kinky, Eva," he murmured silkily. "I like it."

I wrinkled up my nose. "Maybe you should have a cup of coffee."

He raised an eyebrow. "If I accept my drinking problem and turn to God, does that mean you'll finally accept my offer and become my mistress?"

This was exactly why Frankie hated Chase.

"God, Chase, you're so pathetic. Eva would never fuck you. Hell, the only reason I fuck you is because I have to."

"Eva will fuck me eventually," Chase said lazily. "Everyone has their price; I just haven't found hers yet."

Any normal person would have found this insulting, but this was Chase, and I was used to it. So I decided to give him a taste of his own medicine.

"Chase," I purred. "You wanna know why you'll never get this?" I swept my hand down the length of my body.

"Do tell," Chase said, staring at my chest.

"Because, baby, I'm wild pussy, and wild pussy can't be bought. Wild pussy doesn't like having pretty things thrown at it and being expected to do the samba on someone's cock in return. Wild pussy doesn't do deals. Wild pussy lives free and for itself and takes it however it likes it—on a bed, on a couch, on the hood of a car, in a bathroom stall, or up against a wall in an alleyway—and it laughs the entire time. I've known you for a while now, Chase. I know you've never had wild pussy, and I know you never will. Wild pussy doesn't fuck uptight cock. And it sure as hell doesn't like silk boxers."

Chase's mouth fell open.

Kami's high-pitched laughter echoed throughout the large room.

"Time to go shopping," she said in a singsong voice.

"Pick me up some cotton boxers while you're out," Chase muttered.

"Pick them up yourself!"

"Can't. I'm going to be jerking off all day to the beautiful imagery of Eva's pussy that she has so graciously provided me with."

Courtesy of Chase, Kami and I spent the entire day shopping—Kami, because she can shop for weeks without tiring, and me, because I wanted to be nowhere near the club.

Around eleven and after a few drinks at a neighborhood bar, Kami's driver took us to the clubhouse. Three Harleys with Montana plates were still parked out front, and Kami was beside herself with excitement.

I was beside myself with anxiety.

We found them in the club's spacious living room with several of my Demon boys and their girls. Mick had a whore on his lap, and Cox was in the middle of a heated debate with my cousin Trey. No Deuce. I didn't know whether to be relieved or upset.

The second we entered the room, Cox locked on Kami.

"Babe," he groaned. "You up and left me in the middle of the fuckin' night. Haven't slept good since."

Kami grinned. "You need me to tire you out?"

Cox bolted across the room, scooped her up over his shoulder, and headed for the stairwell.

"Christ," Mick muttered.

"Second floor," I called after them. "Empty beds!"

"Frankie?" I asked a Demon named Split.

He grinned. "Passed out cold awhile ago. Took three of us to lug him upstairs."

I gave Split a kiss on the cheek, waved to Trey, and turned to go.

I was halfway to the stairwell when a large hand came down on my shoulder. I quickly shrugged out of Mick's grasp. "Don't ever touch me," I said evenly.

His eyebrows shot to his hairline. "Didn't mean nothin' by it, darlin'. Just wanted to apologize for how shit went down last time we crossed paths. Deuce is my prez and my brother, and I got love for him, you feel me?"

"I feel you," I snapped. "But none of that changes how you treated me when you didn't know shit about me! So keep in mind you're in my club, these are my boys, and if you fuck with anyone, I will bury you myself."

He stared down at me. "You've gotten harder, babe. Fire's burnin' brighter; life's takin' its toll on you, ain't it?"

I blinked, and it was Deuce's face I saw.

You're a good kid, darlin'. A good, sweet kid. Promise me you'll stay that way, yeah? No matter what you see, no matter what sort of fucked-up shit happens to you, don't let this life turn you bitter.

I wasn't hard, was I? I definitely wasn't bitter. Right? Why did I suddenly feel like crying?

"Whatever, Mick. Just stay out of my way and don't fuck with my club."

He smiled. "I feel you, babe. You got love for the club, I get that, and I admire that in an old lady. Been hearing 'bout how fuckin' awesome you are all day."

I glared at him. "I am not an old lady."

"You in Frankie's bed?"

"Nope," I shot back. "Frankie's in mine."

Turning on my heel, I left him to stew on that.

After dumping my purchases in my room and divesting Frankie of his boots and jeans, I made my way downstairs. Yawning, I pushed open the door to the kitchen and felt around for the light. It switched on.

Rubbing my eyes with the heels of my palms, I trudged to the fridge, grabbed a bottle of purple Gatorade, and turned to go.

I dropped the Gatorade.

There was Deuce, leaning back against the opposite wall—mere inches from the light switch—with his pants around his ankles and his hands full of badly bleached-blonde biker babe hair. The space of three years closed, and I was back in Deuce's kitchen watching Miranda bounce in his lap.

"What the fuck?" I whispered hoarsely.

The girl jerked her head up; Deuce shoved her back and laughed bitterly.

"What the fuck? You sneak out of my bed in the middle of the fuckin' night and hop straight into Frankie's and have the fuckin' nerve to ask me what the fuck!"

The girl jerked again, and again he pushed her back. "Bitch, you stop suckin' one more time, and I'm gonna slap you," he threatened.

I gaped at him. "You're a pig," I choked out.

"Yeah."

"No, *really*, you're a sick pig."

"Yeah, darlin', I know."

Furious, disgusted, feeling oddly betrayed and heartbroken—and a whole bunch of other emotions I couldn't pinpoint because my mind was spinning wildly, trying to comprehend and deal with what I'd just walked in on and couldn't—I ran for the door. Deuce's hand shot out and hooked around my forearm, his grip as tight as a vice.

Tears burned in my eyes. "Let me go!"

"No."

"This is sick," I whispered.

"Yeah, babe," he whispered back. "I just don't give a fuck."

He yanked me sideways, and I tripped over the girl's feet. Deuce pulled me forward, and I fell into his chest, right on top of the girl.

My stomach was pushed against the girl's head, and I was straddling her back. Back and forth, I went with her as she continued sucking him off.

Our lips were nearly touching; Deuce was breathing hard, his hot breath smelling strongly of rum. Actually, his entire self smelled like rum, like he had taken a bath in it.

"I'll scream," I hissed.

"Go ahead," he shot back. "I really don't give a fuck."

God, he really didn't. His beautiful eyes looked empty. But I wouldn't resort to screaming. Screaming would result in Deuce's death. And I loved him far too much to be the bearer of that blow.

"Just let me go," I whispered. "You're shitfaced!"

"Yeah. Your fault, babe. Want you so bad I fuckin' ache."

Oh God. Pain and regret so violent gripped my insides, and my knees buckled under the onslaught. Deuce caught me under my arms and hauled me back up.

He pressed his mouth against mine and breathed into it. "One fuckin' kiss, baby," he whispered.

I choked on a sob. "Deuce," I whispered through my tears. "Please don't do this. This is really, really fucked-up."

"That's the thing, darlin', I've always been really, really fucked up. For some fuckin' reason, you weren't seein' it. But you get it now, so shut the fuck up and lemme fuckin' kiss you and pretend that hot mouth around my cock is your sweet pussy."

"Deuce, please…"

"Yeah," he breathed into my mouth. "Keep beggin'."

"Fuck you," I whispered.

"No, babe," he gritted out. He released me, and his hands shot into my hair, gripping handfuls. "Fuck you."

He shoved his tongue in my mouth and tightened his grip on my hair to keep me in place. He came moments later, groaning, and I burst into tears.

"Please, please," I begged. "Please let me go."

His nostrils flared. "Let you go?" he hissed. "Let you fuckin' go?"

He pushed me backward, and I tripped over the girl's legs and landed hard on my backside. Deuce shoved the girl away from him and hiked up his jeans. He glared down at me.

"Been tryin' to let you go, been tryin' for fuckin' years," he said roughly. "Haven't figured out how yet."

Speechless, I watched him stalk out of the kitchen.

The girl, who I had just realized was Lynn—my uncle Joe's favorite girl—wiped the back of her hand across her mouth and looked over at me. "Bikers, Eva," she huffed. "Fuckin' crazy."

"Don't say anything to Joe," I whispered.

"No worries, baby."

I heard the telltale sounds of Harley pipes growling loudly, and then fading off into the distance. I wondered if this was the last I would ever see of Deuce. For five years, I wondered.

Then one summer night I didn't have to wonder anymore.

Chapter NINE

Deuce cut his engine, toed his kickstand down, and studied the farmhouse in front of him. Mick pulled up beside him. Five more of his boys followed suit.

"You sure 'bout this, Prez?" Ripper asked, leaning forward on his handlebars. Even in the dark, Deuce could see the ugly-looking slashes that marred the entire right side of Ripper's face. Right eye gone, right side of his mouth slashed, frozen in an ugly-looking frown. His chest was worse. This was all courtesy of Crazy Frankie, who had done him over real good about two years back. Frankie was all about the torture before the killing. Luckily, Ripper had gotten away before the fucker could do him in.

"How can you ask that?" Mick said. "After what he fuckin' did to you?"

Ripper shrugged. "Don't get me wrong, Mickey. I want the fucker dead more than any of you."

He wasn't so sure about that.

"I'm just lookin' out for the club. We do this, we do Frankie, and we're at war with Preacher. Full-out war. Shit won't be easy; it will be downright fuckin' ugly."

He looked back at the house. Loud music was blaring; bikes and a few pickups covered the lawn. Through the lit windows, he could see people dancing with beers in their hands. It was a typical MC party.

But he wasn't here to party; he was here to kill the Silver Demons' VP.

He looked back at his brothers. "We all agree, or we all leave."

Tag, ZZ, Cox, Mick, and Jase all gave him the thumbs-up. He looked at Ripper.

Ripper stared at the house. "We got the manpower to go up against Preacher. We got the connections, we got the money, we got the Russians, fuck, we even got some of Preacher's connections ready to go up against Preacher for the right price—so what the fuck? Let's do it. 'Bout time someone put that rabid dog down."

Deuce nodded to Cox. "You and me are goin' in. Tag and ZZ take back. Mick and Jase take front, and Ripper…you just fuckin' wait. I'll bring the fucker right to you, and you can gut him like the fuckin' pig he is."

Ripper grinned his deformed half grin. "You sure do know how to turn a guy on, Prez."

He shoved an extra clip in the back of his leathers. "I try," he said dryly.

He grabbed Cox's arm before they entered. "Remember, we need to be cool. Frankie knows we got a beef. Look like you're here to party. Start drinking, just don't get shitfaced or grab some pussy, but keep your eye on your phone."

"You got it."

It wasn't hard to grab pussy at an MC party; it was usually a free-for-all. But Cox being Cox—shaved head, pierced every-fucking-where, and covered from neck to ankle in tats—the women fucking flocked. Boy didn't even have to crook his finger. They just magically appeared on their knees in front of him.

They walked in and split up. The place was packed solid with Demons. He saw a few Red Devil cuts wandering around and a healthy mix of nomads, but fuck, there was a crapload of Demons. He went straight to the kitchen, nabbed a blue, pushed off a crack whore who'd grabbed at him, and started walking around, getting the lay of the place.

"Horseman!" a familiar voice shouted. A meaty hand hit his shoulder.

He turned around and faced the three-hundred-pound, sweat-covered asshole.

"Tiny," he said evenly.

"Whatcha doin' in Virginia?"

"Passin' through."

"Lucked out, brother. Mad fuckin' pussy here. Got sugar, too."

Fucking morons. Snorting what they're supposed to be selling. Fuck-ing mor-ons.

"Gonna get some pussy first. Been on the road for weeks. You gonna be around?"

Tiny slapped his bicep. "Blow your load and come find me. Got some side business goin' on that you might be interested in."

Rolling his eyes, he resumed walking, stepping over drunk fucks and drunks fucking. When he reached the back, a closed-in porch that ran the length of the house, he stopped walking and started staring.

Leaning casually against the wall, smack dab in the middle of a long line of Demons, was motherfucking Frankie. And no, his eyes hadn't gotten any less crazy. But he had gotten a fuck of a lot bigger.

His long brown hair was pulled back in a man bun, displaying his spiderweb neck tattoos interspersed with extensive, thick scars. His beard was long and ratty, and the brother's muscles were bulging out of the skintight Van Halen tee he had on.

He might have half an inch on Frankie, but bodily, they were evenly matched. And with the asshole being as crazy as he was, Deuce wasn't too sure he'd come out on top.

Frankie and his crazy eyes were fixated on something across the room. He followed his line of sight.

Fuck.

Black Harley tee with the collar cut off, causing it to fall off her shoulder, exposing a new tat of a colorful collage of flowers. Her tight pants were leather, and on her feet, sparkly silver Chucks. Her dark, wavy hair had grown even longer, nearly reaching her ass. She'd gained a little weight, none of it bad. How long had it been since he'd seen her last and acted like a fucking asshole? Four years? Five? She had to be around thirty now. She didn't look it. If he didn't know her, he'd think she was in her early twenties.

He wanted her still. *Fucking. Bad.*

He looked back at Frankie whose gaze hadn't moved, whose body hadn't moved. Every inch of him was solidly trained on Eva.

Crazy. Fucking scary crazy.

Eva looked up from her conversation with another woman—older, battered-looking, wearing stripper heels, definitely an MC whore—and her gaze caught Frankie's. Frankie's eyes fucking blazed with possession and…insanity.

Eva handed her beer to the woman next to her and started for Frankie. Crazy fuck never took his eyes off her, watched her like a vulture does when it's waiting for something to die.

When she reached him, his arm wrapped around her wrist, and he pulled her up against him. His head lowered, his mouth covered hers, and he just fucking ate at her. Eva's arms went up around his neck; she pressed her body into his and kissed him back just as hard.

He stared at them, his fists clenched and his chest aching something fierce.

Frankie pushed Eva off him. "Got business, babe," he yelled over the music. "Stay right fuckin' here until I get back, or you're gonna catch a lot of fuckin' shit from me that you know you don't fuckin' want. And I don't wanna give it to you, but I fuckin' will if you don't fuckin' listen."

She nodded. *She just fucking nodded.* Frankie walked off and disappeared out the back door.

Turning around, he dug his phone out of his pocket and dialed Cox. Brother answered on the first ring, breathing hard. The sound of skin slapping against skin came through the phone loud and clear.

"Yeah?"

"Got a problem."

"Fuck. What is it?"

"Eva."

"She here?"

"Yeah."

"Fuck."

"Yeah."

"Is Kami here?"

Deuce closed his eyes. What. The. Fuck.

"No, asshole. Kami is not here."

"Damn."

"Cox, call the fuckin' boys. Have 'em stick with Ripper 'til I figure this shit out."

"Got it."

He shoved his phone back in his pocket and headed back the way he came. After grabbing another beer, he headed out the kitchen door. The door had just barely shut behind him when he felt the barrel of a gun pressed against his temple. Startled, he dropped his beer.

"What's up, fucker? Think I didn't see you standin' there watchin' me? Think I don't know you're here for me? Been waitin' on you assholes for a grip now. Figured you didn't give a fuck I carved your boy up, but here you are givin' a fuck. Took you long enough."

He didn't say anything. There wasn't anything he could say that would make a man like Frankie back down. He had to think fast, or he was going to die. Frankie didn't fuck around. So he played the only card he had. Eva.

"Saw your old lady in there, Frankie; she's lookin' fuckin' good."

The barrel pressed in harder. "She's my fuckin' wife, and you shouldn't be lookin'. People who look get fuckin' dead real fuckin' quick."

Wife? *Christ.*

He shrugged. "She ever tell you 'bout us?"

Frankie went stiff. "There ain't shit to tell," he growled.

Perfect. So perfect. Asshole walked himself right into it.

"First taste wasn't yours, kid. That was all fuckin' mine. Demon barbeque 'bout fourteen years ago. Right after she fuckin' denied you, I had your bitch up against a wall, a hand on her tit, two fingers up inside, and my tongue shoved so far down her throat I could taste her heart beatin'. Bitch loved it, was ready to give it up right fuckin' there. Didn't even remember your fuckin' name 'cause she's pantin' mine. Her first fuck, got that, too. Stripped her naked and fucked her in an alleyway in the pourin' rain. Had her fuckin' beggin' me for it."

Frankie sucked in so much air Deuce felt the world go dry. Time to sucker punch. He slammed his elbow into Frankie's chest, simultaneously grabbing the barrel of the gun, and then he grabbed Frankie's arm and twisted, wrenching him to the ground. With one hand gripping Frankie's forearm, he put his boot on the fucker's shoulder and fucking yanked. Crazy fucker didn't even scream when his shoulder dislocated. Didn't even flinch.

Crazy. So fucking crazy.

Pressing Frankie's own gun into his forehead, he leaned down over him.

"Know how I know I had her first? Aside from her being tighter than a motherfuckin' vice? Bitch fell to her knees after she caught fire and sucked her own pussy blood off my cock. Didn't even know what she was doin', but bitch fuckin' licked my shit clean and let me blow in her mouth. So it don't matter how many times you been takin' that ride 'cause I fuckin' own that shit. You can choke on that while your brains are leakin' all over the place."

"If you kill me," Frankie said quietly, eerily calm, "you'll kill Eva."

He blinked.

"What?"

"Eva. I die, she dies."

"How do you fuckin' figure?"

He grinned. "As a weddin' present, I put a fuckin' hit on her. I die, she dies. Bitch by my side in life, bitch by my side in death. Way it should be."

He. Just. Stared.

Stared.

There wasn't a whole lot in this fucked-up world that could shock him. He'd seen so much shit in the forty-eight years he'd been alive, most of which had all happened to him personally. And it had happened so often that when he came across some pretty fucked-up shit, he wasn't surprised. But this—Frankie telling him in all seriousness that he'd put a hit on Eva, his lifelong obsession, his motherfucking wife—had shocked the fucking shit out of him.

It also told him that Frankie needed to die. He just didn't know how to take care of that with Eva's life on the line. Yet.

With Frankie's gun still trained on Frankie, he pulled out his cell phone and called Mick. Two by two, his boys began appearing at his side, forming a circle around Frankie. He held his palm up, silently telling them not to take Frankie out.

"Get up, you sick fuck," Ripper growled.

Frankie got to his feet, his arm hanging limply at his side. He turned his back on them and positioned the side of his body against the house. With a heave and a shove, his shoulder popped back in its socket. Everyone stared. Fucker had balls of steel.

Rubbing his shoulder, he focused on Ripper. "Nice face, fuckwad. I were you I woulda just let me finish you off. Now you gotta go 'round life lookin' like Freddy fuckin' Krueger."

Ripper's gun hand started shaking. Jase grabbed his wrist and lowered his arm.

Frankie shook his head, smirking. "Fuckin' bitches, the lot of you. Cryin' 'bout scars and missin' eyes like little fuckin' girls."

Frankie turned to him. "So I've been gettin' Horsemen sloppy seconds all these years. Whore coulda least picked an MC prez worth fuckin'."

Furious, he took a step forward.

Mick's hand came down on his shoulder and squeezed. "He's baitin' us, Prez," he whispered. "Crazy fuck wants one of us to step to him."

Frankie grabbed a cigarette from behind his ear and dug out a Zippo from his front pocket, oblivious as all seven men tensed, ready to shoot.

He took a few long drags before he spoke again.

"Knew she wasn't a virgin when I took her the first time. She cried like one, but she wasn't. Never would tell me who broke her in. Been tryin' to get her to give it up for fuckin' years. She won't 'cause she knows I'd kill 'im."

His chest went tight. She was protecting him from fucking Frankie. He didn't know whether to be insulted that she thought he needed protection from this fuck or to do a motherfucking jig because the woman obviously still cared about him.

"You're fuckin' twisted," ZZ spat.

"Don't matter anymore how fuckin' twisted he is," Jase hissed. "'Cause he's done."

Frankie ignored them. "Knowin' it was you, shit makes sense now. Bitch cries in her sleep, says shit I don't catch, but she's always grabbin' that fucking Horsemen tag 'round her neck and holdin' tight when it happens. Never did think much of it, seein' as she's had it nearly her whole fuckin' life, but you gave it to her, yeah?"

He didn't say a word, but he didn't need to. Frankie knew.

"Yeah," Frankie said. "You got to know, Deuce, that shit ain't sittin' well with me."

Tap laughed. "Why the fuck should he care if shit's sittin' well with you, you fuckin' asshat? He's not the cocksucker with seven fuckin' cannons pointed at his fuckin' head."

Frankie, as usual, never seemed to care about anything other than Eva.

"Figure he's gonna care when I'm rippin' out his insides and makin' Eva string 'em up on our Christmas tree."

"Yeah, dude," Tap muttered. "You're fuckin' normal."

Frankie's head whipped left, and he stared his crazy-eyed stare until Tap took a step back.

"Prez, what the fuck we waitin' for?" Tap said warily. "Just fuckin' kill him."

Frankie grinned—an evil, sadistic grin that sent chills up his spine.

"Prez isn't gonna let you kill me," Frankie drawled. "Are you, Prez?"

"No," he said flatly. "I'm not."

"What the fuck?" Tap yelled. "Look at your boy's face!"

He stared at Frankie, feeling nothing but hate. "He dies, Eva dies. Asshole put some fucked-up death pact hit on her."

"Fuck," Jase breathed.

"Then we can't kill him," Ripper said, pulling out his cell phone. "But we're not lettin' him go, so he can start decoratin' Christmas trees either."

"Yo, Gina, babe, it's Ripper...yeah, babe, I know...babe...wait, I...no, I fuckin' apologized for that shit...BABE...yeah, through a fuckin' text message, what the fuck you want? A singing telegram? Would you just shut the fuck up and listen to me? I need you to run a Franklin Deluva and tell me what you got."

Frankie, looking bored, was leaning up against the side of the house, smirking at nothing.

Ripper held the phone away from his ear and glared at it. When Gina stopped screaming, he put the phone back to his ear. "Deluva, D-E-L-U-V-A...right."

There was a long pause during which Ripper started to smile. "Fuckin' sweet...bitch, I fuckin' love you right now..." Another long pause. "Aw, Christ, Gina, don't fuckin' start up again..."

Deuce grabbed the phone and tapped END. "Care to share?" he growled.

"Bitch said he's got four outstandin' warrants for assault, and he's wanted for questionin' in two murder cases. She's 'bout six hours out, so she's passin' the bid to some dude named Crank nearby. Should be 'bout five minutes."

Never in a million years would he have ever thought he'd be happy that Ripper was fucking a bounty hunter, seeing as his entire crew was swimming in illegal shit. But there it was.

"Tap, man the front door. Jase, the back. Make sure shit is tight until we get this wrapped." Last thing they needed was a Demon-Horsemen standoff.

"And, Ripper, get rid of Nikki and put that fuckin' kick-ass bitch on the back of your bike."

"Yeah, dude," Mick said. "Nikki's a cunt."

Ripper shrugged. "Yeah, but she's got great tits."

ZZ choked on his laughter. "'Cause you fuckin' paid for 'em to be great."

Ripper flipped ZZ off. "Gina's a drive-by. Never fuckin' around. What the fuck would I be fuckin' in the meantime?"

He laughed. "Are you really gonna stand there and tell us you ain't got shit to fuck 'sides Gina and Nikki? What a fuckin' crock. Ever since your face got all fucked-up, bitches been fallen to their feet wantin' to make your boo-boos all better. I see your dick so fuckin' much you'd think I'm fuckin' you."

"Yeah, dude, you never put that fuckin' thing away."

Ripper glared at ZZ, and ZZ shrugged. "What? You don't. And personally, I'm sick of seein' it."

"Tap!"

"Prez?"

"Find out who bought Eva's hit from Frankie. Use whoever you got to—the fuckin' Russians, the fuckin' Japs, cash in all my fuckin' favors, I don't give a shit—just find 'em and end 'em."

"On it." Tap pulled out his cell and walked off.

"Prez?"

He turned around and found Jase standing beside Eva. She was staring at Frankie with tears in her eyes.

Shit.

"She came outside," Jase explained. "Lookin' for Frankie. She heard you, Prez."

"You put a hit on me?" she whispered.

Frankie wasn't smiling anymore. Eva took a step toward him, and Cox stepped between them and pressed the barrel of his gun into Frankie's throat. "Don't come near him, Foxy."

"Why, baby?" she whispered. "What haven't I given you that you needed?"

Frankie blinked. "Don't fuckin' cry, baby," he said quietly. "Wasn't tryin' to hurt you, just wanted you with me always. Can't fuckin' sleep without you, and dyin' is sleepin' forever. Can't sleep forever without you."

Eva's tears spilled over, and Frankie went stiff.

"I love you so much, baby," Frankie whispered. "I thought you'd want to be with me forever."

Letting out a strangled cry, Eva reached for him. He lunged forward to grab her, but ZZ was faster. Catching her around her middle, he started dragging her backward.

"No!" she screamed, thrashing. "Let me go to him!"

Seeing Eva upset and struggling, Frankie's face went ice cold, and his eyes cut to Cox. Shit was about to go bad.

"Cox!" he bellowed. The crazy fuck grabbed the gun, headbutted Cox, then dropped to his knees. One swift punch to Cox's balls, and then Frankie was jumping to his feet, aiming, not at Cox, but at him.

He didn't think, just reacted, barreled straight into Frankie, and they went rolling. By punching Frankie in his newly set shoulder, Deuce was able to gain the upper hand and managed to pin him facedown in the dirt.

Cox was lying on the ground, cupping himself, groaning about never being able to fuck again. Eva was screaming hysterically and struggling violently, and ZZ was having a hard time keeping a good hold on her. It was a fucking mess.

"Gonna find a way to end you, asshole," he hissed in Frankie's ear.

Frankie laughed.

Frankie was still laughing when a pair of headlights turned off the street and headed up the driveway.

Crank was a big guy. An ex-Marine who had no trouble taking Frankie off his hands and chaining him up in the back of his ride. It wasn't the preferred ending, but it was better than nothing, and it would keep Eva safe until he could figure out Frankie's tangled web of crazy.

And speaking of crazy…

"No!" I screamed, struggling to get free as Frankie was taken away. "God, no! You can't do this! He won't make it!"

Frankie couldn't go to jail. He wouldn't last. He couldn't sleep. He couldn't play nice with others. It was a recipe for disaster.

"Good," Mick sneered. "Let's hope he doesn't make it five fuckin' seconds."

I jerked my head in Mick's direction. "You piece of shit!" I screamed. "Can't ever keep your big fucking mouth shut! Always butting into business you have nothing to do with!"

"Reel it in, Eva," Deuce growled.

I stopped struggling and stared at him. Had he lost his mind? My husband was being sent to his death, and he was telling me to reel it in. Oh, hell no.

I let out a bloodcurdling scream, twisted out of ZZ's grasp, and headed straight for Deuce.

"You fuck!" I screamed, slapping, punching, clawing at any part of him I came into contact with. "You stupid piece of shit!"

It didn't take him long to bring me down. Straddling my hips and pinning my wrists above my head, he glared at me. I happily noted his fat lip, bloody nose, and scratched cheek.

"What the fuck, Eva?" he roared. "You find out your man's got a fuckin' hit on you, and you're attacking me?"

I was so beyond upset, beyond angry, beyond hurt. I felt so helpless, destroyed, ripped apart by my seams and everywhere in between. I'd been taking care of Frankie for so long now, and I was so tired, but it wasn't his fault he was sick and couldn't see things the way other people did.

As for Deuce. Who the fuck did he think he was?

"Who the fuck do you think you are?" I screamed.

"I'm pretty sure I'm the asshole who's trying to save your fuckin' life, you stupid bitch!"

"Stupid bitch? *Stupid bitch!* Don't do me any favors, you fuck! I've never needed your help, and I sure as fuck don't need it now!"

Blue eyes blazing, he lowered his face to mine. "Bitch," he growled, "we came here to bury your fuckin' man. What the fuck woulda happened if he wouldn't have told us 'bout the hit? Huh? What, bitch? You fuckin' tell me!"

I gathered as much saliva as I could and spit in his face. "Fuck you!" I yelled and bashed my forehead into his. My vision swam. That was definitely not as cool as it looked in the movies. Deuce shifted both my wrists into one of his hands and slapped his palm down on my forehead, holding my head down.

"You fuckin' done?" he roared.

I was so far from done.

"The last time I saw you, you were getting your dick sucked by a club whore and trying to make out with me at the same time! The time before that I found you in the kitchen with a half-naked whore on your lap only a few hours after you fucked me! You're fucking trash, Deuce! Fucking garbage! What the fuck makes you think I would be grateful to you for fucking anything?"

Deuce's eyes were bugging out of his head; his body was shaking with fury. Having a cold-blooded killer boring down on you with a murderous expression might have made any normal person feel fear, but I was so far gone. Pure adrenaline was more powerful than any street drug, and I was flying over the fucking mountain.

Not even the cold steel of Mick's gun pressed into my cheek could cool me off.

"Reel it in, you fuckin' cunt," Mick growled.

"Fucking do it," I hissed. "I fucking dare you, you stupid motherfucking piece of shit. Bring down every Demon in the fucking country on your stupid piece-of-shit ass!"

"Reel it the fuck in, Eva!" Deuce bellowed.

I looked back at Deuce. "Tell him to do it," I hissed. "But let me close my eyes first. I don't want your ugly fucking face to be the last thing I ever see."

Deuce's nostrils flared.

Mick's hand jerked.

And that was the last thing I saw... for a little while.

Chapter TEN

Deuce stalked out of a no-tell motel office with three keys. He tossed one at Mick and another at Jase.

"What the fuck?" ZZ complained. "There are only two beds in a room."

"You're on the floor," Ripper said.

"Fuck you," he shot back. "You and Cox should share; it's not like you don't share everything else."

Ripper grinned. "Best couple days of my life."

"Speaking of Kami…" Cox looked down at Eva, who was passed out cold in his arms. "Prez?"

He shook his head. "She wakes up, and she's with me, shit's gonna get ugly. I'm the last fuckin' asshole she wants to see."

Mick cursed. "Why the fuck didn't we just leave her there?"

"Dude," Jase said, "you'd leave a hot piece of unconscious ass at a fuckin' club party without her man? Might as well put a fuckin' sign on her that says 'Free fucks for all.'"

"Who fuckin' cares?" Mick growled. "Bitch wasn't even grateful that we're tryin' to save her ass! I shoulda knocked her harder, and then we wouldn't be havin' this discussion at all!"

He knew his boys were arguing, but he wasn't listening. He was staring at Eva, hanging limply in Cox's arms, replaying in his mind everything she'd said to him over and over and over again.

You're fucking trash! Fucking garbage! What the fuck makes you think I would be grateful to you for FUCKING ANYTHING?

It was Eva he'd been looking at, but it was his old man's voice he was hearing.

What a fucking coincidence. The last time he'd seen his old man was the first time he'd ever seen Eva. His blood ran cold. It was his old man's tag around Eva's neck.

The asshole was still here, ruining his fucking life. Fucking shit up with the only woman he'd ever given a shit about.

They'd spent only moments together here and there— some good, most painful. It didn't make any sense. They didn't make any sense. He should have let her go a long time ago. But he couldn't. And he still couldn't. Because he didn't want to. Because he fucking loved her.

He dialed Preacher.

"Yeah?"

"It's Deuce."

"What the fuck you want?"

"Frankie's up the river. Got him a one-way ticket tonight. Woulda buried him, but it turns out your boy put a hit on your girl. If he gets buried, she goes down with him. You know 'bout that?"

Silence.

"Fuck," Preacher rasped.

"Yeah. Got my boys workin' my connections tryin' to find who bought it. Not gonna be easy; doubt Frankie left a fuckin' paper trail, and gravediggers ain't exactly forthcomin'."

"Fuck!" Preacher roared. He took the phone away from his ear and looked at it while Preacher cursed and yelled nonsense and broke everything, it sounded like, within a mile radius of him. Turned out temper tantrums ran in the family.

"Horseman," Preacher rasped into the phone. "Where the fuck is my baby girl?"

"Got her with me. Got six of my boys. She's safe."

"Good," he barked. "Lemme talk to her."

Deuce glanced at Eva. She was still out cold.

"She's sleepin'. Don't really wanna wake her. She's not too fuckin' happy 'bout what went down."

Mick snorted.

"Understatement," Cox added.

"Yeah," Preacher muttered. "I bet."

"Preacher, we cancel Eva's hit, and Frankie's not buried within a week, I'm takin' him down."

"We'll talk. For now, Frankie's locked up, and I got a hit to find. Right now, you just take care of my girl."

"Preacher," he growled. "Frankie's gotta go to ground."

"That's my fuckin' son-in-law you're talkin' 'bout! This is family business, and I aim to keep it that way! Now shut the fuck up and get my girl home, or I'll fuckin' take you to ground!"

Preacher hung up.

Jesus. Crazy. All around.

Groaning, I rolled over, gripping my head. Where the hell was I? Why did my head feel like the Incredible Hulk had been Irish step dancing on top of it?

I had…three beers? Not nearly enough to merit a hangover of this magnitude.

With one hand holding my forehead, I reached around in the dark. Okaaay. I was on a bed with cheap, scratchy sheets and a nylon comforter.

Had Frankie and I gotten a motel? Why would Frankie and I get a motel while on a run when there were MCs we could stay at?

"Frankie?" I croaked, wincing as my own voice reverberated painfully inside my skull.

No answer.

I felt my way around the bed until I found the edge. Carefully, so as not to jar my head, I swung my legs over the side and met with floor. I cracked an eyelid. To my left, a small clock read 2:43 a.m. I edged my way over and felt around until I found a lamp.

I switched it on.

Yep. Motel. Crappy one, too. Burnt orange walls and floral pattern comforters. A carpet that had probably been new in the seventies and furniture that had seen better days.

Shielding my eyes, I headed for the door. The chain lock wasn't on, so I grabbed the wobbly knob, turned, and pulled open the door.

Deuce and Cox swiveled around.

I gaped at them. Deuce took a step toward me.

I slammed the door closed and put the chain lock on.

Shit.

Shit.

That asshole got Frankie arrested and kidnapped me. No, he knocked me out, and then kidnapped me!

The door slammed open a total of five inches, hindered by the chain lock. "Eva!"

"Fuck off!" I yelled, and then crumpled to the floor, grabbing my head.

I heard the chain lock snap, and the door hit the wall. I heard heavy footsteps, and then I felt myself being lifted against a large, warm body and gently set back down on top of the uncomfortable bed.

"I need to go to the hospital," I whimpered.

"Do you?" Deuce asked. "Or are you just tryin' to get the fuck away from me?"

"Yes and yes!" I snapped. "I don't often associate with fuckwads who steal my husband, and allow their friends to pistol-whip me!"

"Eva," he said evenly. "I get you're fuckin' pissed. But I didn't have much of a choice."

I snorted. It hurt to do, but I did it anyway.

"Showed up at the party plannin' to take him out for what he did to Ripper, saw you there, and didn't know what the fuck I was gonna do. Frankie blindsided me outside, put a fuckin' gun to my head, and started spoutin' crazy. Only way I could get the drop on him was to tell him the one fuckin' thing in the world that would distract him from a kill. You know what I had to tell him, don't cha?"

Oh God.

"No," I whispered.

"Yeah," he bit off. "That's when he decided to tell me about his hit on you. Didn't know what the fuck to do at that point. Thought if I let him go, he was gonna fuck you up for fuckin' me, and I knew if I buried him, you were gonna be next. Didn't want either to happen, so here we fuckin' are."

"Go away," I hissed.

"Sorry, darlin'. Paid for this room, and I plan on gettin' my money's worth."

"Go fuck yourself," I shot back.

"Later," he said. "Right now I gotta get a girl outta her muddy clothes."

He took my Chucks off first, then pulled my pants down my legs, and lastly, he lifted my shirt over my head, leaving me in only my underwear. His eyes dropped to my breasts. I watched as he leaned forward and lifted up his father's medallion. He stared at it, his nostrils flaring.

"It's all his fuckin' fault," he growled. Then he gave the chain a sharp tug, and it broke.

I sat up too fast and gripped my head. "What are you doing?" I cried.

Deuce stormed across the room. He threw open the door and tossed the necklace outside. "Get rid of that," he barked to someone I couldn't see, and then slammed the door closed.

"Shoulda never given it to you," he said roughly.

My mouth fell open. "What?" I whispered.

"You heard me. You been wearin' that piece of shit's tag for eighteen years now. For eighteen years, that fuckin' bastard has been hangin' 'round your neck, and I'm fuckin' sick of it."

Tears burned in my eyes. "But that was mine. You gave it to me, and I loved it and I—"

"Shut up," he growled. "Reaper was a dirty fuckin' bastard who didn't care who he had to fuck, beat, or kill to get his way. No way in hell should I have ever given you somethin' that belonged to him."

My chin began to tremble. What was he trying to say? That everything that happened between us had been a mistake? I couldn't handle this right now. Not after today.

Frankie had always had problems, but to do this...to put a hit on me. Me. I'd given him everything—me, my love, my body, my life.

I couldn't comprehend it. Or didn't want to comprehend it. Or couldn't. I didn't know.

I knew Frankie's feelings for me had surpassed love a long time ago, if love was ever what he'd felt. Frankie had convinced himself at a very young age that he needed me to breathe. It was unhealthy for him, for me, for our relationship, but I thought I'd gotten him relatively under control. I'd been dead wrong.

It hurt like hell.

And now this. From Deuce.

I rolled away from him and hugged my knees to my chest. My tears started out small, leaking out of the corners of my eyes and running slowly down my nose and cheek, but once I let myself go—released the pent-up anger, pain, regret, and guilt—my tears turned into a torrential downpour. I sobbed uncontrollably, hiccupping, gasping for air as I rocked back and forth and cried and cried until my tears ran dry.

When I woke it was light out. I didn't remember falling asleep, and I certainly didn't remember falling asleep in Deuce's arms. I untangled myself from him and headed for the bathroom. I was covered in dirt, my hair was a rat's nest, and I had blood splattered all over me. Not mine, Deuce's. Tentatively, I felt the side of my head. I had a good-sized goose egg; it was tender and hurt to touch, but otherwise, I felt fine.

After a long shower, feeling numb, I wrapped myself up in a towel and headed back to the bedroom. Deuce had thrown the sheet off him and rolled on his side. Wearing nothing but his boxers, the Hell's Horsemen insignia tattooed on his back gleamed black against his tan skin.

He had to be nearing fifty now. His short shadow of a beard was mostly gray; the gray in his hair wasn't as easily noticeable, but it was there. His body was every bit as impressive as it had always been, lined and cut in all the right places, his muscles still large and toned. He was still beautiful. The most beautiful man I'd ever seen and still the biggest asshole I'd ever met.

And I loved him still. That had never changed.

I made a quick phone call to the motel office, and then another to Tiny, telling him when and where to pick me up. Then I climbed back into bed beside Deuce. Lying on our sides, face-to-face, I stared at him. God, I missed him. Especially lying awake at night, thinking about all that could have been but would never be. It all revolved around him. If I could go back in time and take back what I had said about being his old lady, I would. I would have become his old lady, stayed away from the club, and done whatever he wanted. Been happy because I would have had him.

But it hadn't gone down that way. And there was no going back from the decisions I'd made over the years.

Without thinking, just feeling, I pushed him gently until he rolled onto his back. Then I pulled down his boxers, touching him gently at first, holding him, stroking him, once again familiarizing myself with his body.

When it came to Deuce, my body took control—my body and my heart. My brain was always on a permanent vacation in his presence.

I took him in my mouth and he groaned in his sleep, shifted a little, but kept on snoring.

When he was full and ready, I straddled him and slowly took him inside my body. I trembled as he stretched me and let out a shuddering moan.

His hands went to my hips, and his eyes flew open.

"Hey," I whispered.

"Fuck," he said hoarsely.

I bit my lip. "Do you want me to stop?"

"Fuck no."

"I'm so, so sorry about last night," I whispered.

"Eva?"

"What?"

"We're good, babe. Don't need to explain."

"Deuce?"

"Yeah?"

I clenched my sex around his. "Gonna fuck you now."

He inhaled sharply. "Babe. Yeah."

Deuce stared down at Eva. Lying on her back, naked, sleeping beside him. He ran his hand from her neck to the dark curls between her thighs and back up again.

"Not lettin' you go this time, darlin'," he whispered. "Chain you up, fuckin' drug you if I have to."

It was crazy, and he knew it; he just didn't care anymore. He was sick of thinking about her all the time, wondering what she was doing and if she was thinking about him. He was sick of aching for her. He was sick of this fucking game they played, running into each other, fucking or fighting, and then taking off. He wanted more. He needed more.

He pulled his Horsemen chain over his head and, trying not to disturb her, slid it over hers. She should have never had his old man's tag; she should have had his. She should have had him.

Then he pulled her close, tucked her head under his chin, tossed his leg over hers, and fell asleep.

When he woke up, she was gone. Again.

Chapter  ELEVEN

For three weeks, I had been home. For three weeks, I had been meeting with the club's lawyers and lawyers all over the city, none of whom could get anything done as quickly as I needed it done. For three weeks, I had been begging Chase to take a look at Frankie's case, to use the dirty connections I knew he had, that his family had, that they'd all used to worm their way into the positions of power they were in. For three weeks, Kami had been trying to threaten Chase into looking into Frankie's case. So for three weeks, I'd been going out of my mind.

My nerves were shot. Frankie was losing it. Every visit to Queensboro to see him left me reeling. His grip on reality had become nonexistent; I had never seen him this bad before, and I couldn't do a damn thing without legal help. I needed Chase, and I needed him badly.

The morning Kami called me informing me that Chase had finally agreed to meet with me, I practically fell out of bed and nearly killed myself dodging Manhattan traffic getting to the thirty-fifth floor of Martello Tower, where the law offices of Fredericks, Henderson, and Stonewall were housed.

"Mrs. Fox-Deluva?"

I stopped my anxious foot tapping to Janis's "Me and Bobby McGee" and yanked my earbuds out. "Yeah?"

"Mr. Henderson will see you now."

I had only been inside Chase's office once before when he first made partner and wanted to show it off. It was every bit as opulent and extravagant as his home was. The office itself was huge with plush carpeting, wall-to-wall bookshelves, a cozy seating area, a minibar, and a private bathroom complete with a shower. His desk was dead center—solid oak, large and imposing—with two leather wingbacks for clients.

When I walked in, Chase was standing by his minibar pouring two tall glasses of whiskey. He turned when I walked in and paused to smooth out nonexistent wrinkles in his pinstriped suit that I knew cost more money than most people spend on cars.

"Eva," he drawled, gesturing to a wingback. "Please have a seat."

I narrowed my eyes. "Cut the shit, Chase. Why the fuck did you make me wait so long?"

His brow rose. "I'm sorry. Were you in the waiting room long?"

Sheesh. He needed a good kick in the balls.

"No, Chase. You made me wait three weeks just to talk to you! What. The. Fuck?"

He smiled, and I wrinkled up my nose. If a shark could smile, it would look just like Chase.

Chase gestured for me to take a seat. When I did, he handed me a glass of whiskey. I took it and gaped at him.

"You do realize it's nine in the morning, right? And this is an eight-ounce glass of booze?"

He took a seat behind his desk. "Eva, you do not refer to Macallan single malt as booze. For $75,000 a bottle, I think it deserves some respect."

I wrinkled up my nose again. "You paid $75,000 for a bottle of booze?"

He raised an eyebrow. "I've paid more for better."

I raised both my eyebrows. "Um…cool?"

He smirked. "Yes, I can tell you're impressed as usual with the finer things in life."

I rolled my eyes. "Whatever, Chase. Frankie?"

He drummed his fingers on his desk. "I've already gone over Frankie's extremely large file with a fine-toothed comb."

I perked up. "And? Can you help him?"

He smiled his wide, bleached-white smile, and again I thought of sharks.

"I can," he said smoothly. "I'm fairly certain that with the aid of some business associates of mine, I can have him on the medication he's obviously needed for some time now. I believe the introduction to psychiatric drugs will not only improve his prison stay, but also allow him to speak with law enforcement without trying to kill them. When his mental health has improved, we can start looking into the charges against him."

"Oh my God," I breathed. "Thank you."

"Ah, ah, ah." He waved his index finger at me. "Here's where the *booze* comes in. I figured you would need it when I tell you how much my services will cost you."

"Money isn't an issue; you can have whatever you want."

His malicious smile spread to his eyes. "As you are well aware, I have more money than I can spend in ten lifetimes."

I narrowed my eyes. "What are you doing, Chase?"

"Frankie attacked a guard last night, almost killed him," he continued, "which is why I agreed to meet with you today."

Oh God.

Oh no.

Eva will fuck me eventually. Everyone has their price; I just haven't found hers yet.

"Chase," I whispered, feeling sick. "Please don't do—"

He held his hand up. "Frankie's in solitary, Eva. In. The. Hole."

I bit my lip to keep from crying. Frankie would not survive the hole.

"God, Eva, you poor thing. You must be feeling pretty desperate right about now and willing to do anything to save your psychopath of a husband."

I blinked, and two tears slipped out. "Everyone has a price. Right, Chase?"

He grinned. Then he pointed to my abnormally tall glass of whiskey. "I figured you would need it."

"You're sick," I choked out. "You fucking planned this; you purposely waited until Frankie didn't have any more time."

Unperturbed, he took a sip of his drink and nodded. "I did."

"Fuck you," I rasped. "I thought you were my friend."

He had the nerve to look offended. "We are friends, Eva. In fact, we are such good friends that I want to be the one to save the homicidal maniac you married."

"Why?" I demanded. "I'm biker trash, right? You've said it a million times. I come from dirty money, and my family—the club—is a stain on society. So why are you so hell-bent on fucking me?"

He took another swallow of whiskey. "Since you were oblivious to my attempts at bedding you all throughout high school, during, and after college, I thought maybe you were one of those women who responded to being put down. I was wrong. Nothing works with you. Unless you're with Frankie, you've got a chastity belt on."

"You've been engaged to Kami since you guys were in diapers!"

His upper lip curled in disgust. "I know," he sneered. "And I would have told my father to go fuck himself when he ordered me to marry that vile woman if I didn't have my eye on her closest, most beloved friend."

"Are you serious?" I whispered.

"Quite," he said. "You see, when it came to who I was to marry, I knew it would never be about anything other than politics and family ties; meaning I would be free to fuck whomever I wished. I realized my mistake too late. You aren't the sort of woman to have an affair with a married man, nor will you cheat on your husband."

I knew true rage then. Chase backed me into a corner; he made sure to cover every angle, leaving me no choice to make but the choice he wanted.

For the first time in my life, I wanted to kill someone.

"You're wrong, Chase," I hissed. "On both counts. I have cheated on Frankie; in fact, I've been fucking a married man for twelve years now."

His eyebrows popped up.

"So you see," I continued, "your perception of me is seriously misconstrued. It's only you I do not want to fuck."

His jaw clenched. "What's it going to be, Eva?" he bit out. "Will you be lowering yourself to fuck me, or will Frankie be left to his own devices?"

I raised my ridiculously overpriced glass of whiskey. "Fuck you, Chase."

While I drank, Chase pulled his cell phone from his suit pocket.

"It's Henderson," he said. "Get Deluva out of solitary now…yes, I am aware of how violent he is…I'm also aware of how much I'm paying you…then make sure he's out cold and restrained before removing him…I'm not interested in how many men it will take to sedate him. I'm only interested in it getting done and it getting done now…good. Make sure he is taken directly to the med center, and you are to call me when he's awake and somewhat in control of himself. I will send both a physician and a team of psychologists to complete a full psychological profile. You and your staff are to concur with their findings, sign and date where it is required, and await my next instructions."

I finished my whiskey and set the glass down hard.

"Very good," Chase continued, eyeing me. "Am I to assume said guard has been taken care of?"

I took a deep breath that did nothing to calm me. Although my belly had warmed from the whiskey and my body had loosened, my heart was firmly lodged in my throat. I might need the entire bottle. All $75,000 of it.

As if he read my mind, Chase pushed his half-empty glass across the desk.

"Wonderful," he said into the phone. "I will be in touch."

He hung up, and then pressed a button on his desk phone.

"Yes, Mr. Henderson?" came through the speaker.

"Cancel the rest of my day."

"Pardon? You have two meetings, one with Judge—"

"Cancel the rest of my day."

"But—"

"If you want to keep your job, cancel the rest of my day."

"Yes, sir."

The intercom clicked off, and Chase looked up at me. Shuddering, I turned away and chugged the rest of his whiskey.

"Eva," Chase said. "I don't need to tell you that this will not be a one-time occurrence, correct?"

"Isn't that what you just did?" I asked sarcastically.

He glared at me. "It's not going to work if you're going to view this as a chore."

"Oh," I sneered. "What should I view it as? A workout? A date?"

"We could go somewhere," he said quietly. "Have lunch first. I have standing reservations at everywhere worth anything in the city."

I snorted. "We're not dating, Chase. I just agreed to spread my legs for you. You don't need to woo me."

Chase's already dead eyes went cold. Chase was a beautiful man, but someone—probably his parents—had repeatedly broken him until there was nothing left to fix.

"Fine," he said callously. "Strip."

We glared at each other.

"Strip," he bit out. "Now, Eva."

Gritting my teeth, I yanked my T-shirt over my head and tossed it aside. I kicked off my green Chucks, and then stood to unbutton my oversized jeans. They fell to my feet, and I kicked them away. Hooking my thumbs in my underwear, I shoved them down and stepped out of them.

Chase looked his fill, his face tightening and his eyes darkening with hunger.

"Where do you want me?" I said sarcastically.

"Where do you want it?" he asked just as sarcastically.

I leaned over his desk, causing my breasts to swing forward. Chase's eyes followed their movements. I was so angry, furious, and crazy with hate for this man—a man I had considered somewhat of a friend.

And, to my astonishment, I was furious with Frankie.

Something happened to me while I glared at Chase—something both terrifying and profound. I wasn't just furious with Frankie; I hated Frankie. He had fucked me up so badly that I didn't know who the fuck I was.

All I'd ever known was Frankie. What Frankie wanted.

My entire life had been about him…and a few secret longings that I had so rarely given in to.

Realizing all of this shit only made me even angrier.

Fuck Frankie.

Fuck everything.

With a hard sweep of my hand, I sent everything within my reach on Chase's giant desk flying across the room. His laptop smashed into his bookshelf. Framed photos of his wedding, others of just Kami, and a few of Kami and Devin—their four-year-old son—flew across the room and shattered. Papers went flying into the air. I wasn't sure where his phone ended up.

I jumped up on his desk and slid myself to the edge directly in front of him. I placed my feet on his thighs and spread my legs wide open.

Chase sucked in air through his teeth.

"This is what you want, isn't it?" I growled. "You want wild pussy, don't you, Chase?"

He gripped my calves and looked up at my face. "Yes," he hissed.

And I wanted to give it to him. I had only ever been wild with Deuce. I wanted wild. I wanted free. I wanted my secret longings to become my reality.

"Then kiss me," I whispered, leaning forward. Just before his mouth met mine, I reared back and slapped him as hard as I could. His head whipped to the right.

When he turned back to me, his cold eyes were blazing with fury.

And it turned me on.

I moved my foot from his thigh onto his bulging erection and gave him a nasty grin. Stroking him, I crooked a finger. "I thought you wanted wild pussy, Chase. You want it; you gotta work for it."

His eyes widened with understanding.

"Fuck...me," he whispered. "I knew it."

I leaned forward and hooked several fingers in between the buttons on his dress shirt. "You know nothing," I hissed and yanked. Buttons flew every which way, and I jumped into his lap.

Chase and I didn't have sex, and we certainly didn't make love. Chase and I fought. I made him work for every kiss and for every touch. This turned out to be perversely exciting for me, but what really threw me over the edge was how much I loved that final moment when he managed to pin me on my back long enough to pry my legs open and force himself inside of me.

I felt like screaming at the top of my lungs, "FUCK YOU, FRANKIE!"

I stopped fighting then.

That's when we fucked—sick, depraved fucking.

Chase got off on things that would turn the stomachs of most people. He had me doing things I'd never done before, things I hadn't thought myself capable of doing, let alone capable of enjoying.

And I begged for more.

Exhausted and sore, I left Chase's office on shaking legs with a key to his suite at the Waldorf and an invitation to use his personal driver whenever I wanted.

I had just hit rock bottom, and I didn't care. In fact, I didn't give a shit about anything at all.

Lying on his bed, Deuce stared down his naked body at the bobbing head between his legs, shuddered, and took another long swallow of Jack. He wasn't going to come; he desperately wanted to come, but it wasn't going to happen. He was drunk, he was pissed, and he wanted the release too fucking badly.

Fucking Eva. He should have left her at that party. Bitch wasn't his, never was. She'd always been Frankie's, and he'd been...what? A once-in-a-while distraction? A fucking joke?

Cursing, he pushed Miranda off him, positioned her on her knees, and sank inside of her. He fucked her until he had fucked himself into oblivion and passed out unsatisfied.

And he dreamt of Eva. He always dreamt of Eva.

Chapter

TWELVE

It wasn't long before my meetings with Chase had become more and more frequent. He was calling me four times a week, making me stay overnight with him at the Waldorf, and buying me shit I didn't want but kept asking him for, raising the price of the items each time. He started taking me out to dinner at exclusive restaurants and raunchy nightclubs—the existence of which the general population in Manhattan knew nothing about. He began making me dress up for him in the sort of clothing I never would have looked twice at—clothing even more ridiculous than what Kami wore. That was for our dinners. What he had me wearing to go clubbing was far, far worse. As were the clubs—sex clubs, weekend-long partying from Friday night to Monday morning. Booze, drugs, free sex, kinky sex, violent sex, every kind of sex imaginable, and all of it public.

Any inhibition I'd ever had quickly diminished after being fucked in front of a club full of people—some watching, some touching, and others involved in their own public fucking.

I stopped talking to Kami. I stopped going to the MC. I was constantly canceling my lunch or dinner dates with my father unless Chase was with me to discuss Frankie's case.

And Frankie…Frankie was gone. I didn't visit him, I didn't write him, and I refused to accept his calls. Gone. I didn't care. And I did care. Half the time I didn't know what I cared about or what I was feeling—maybe because Frankie wasn't here to tell me how I felt and what I should care about, and Chase couldn't care less about anything other than what he was feeling.

My already precariously tilting world had gone and spiraled out of control, and shit was dropping from the surface and being sucked into outer space. I didn't try to stop it; I didn't do much of anything really, except what Chase wanted me to do, which usually involved his cock and an orifice on my body. Or several of them.

Then one day my world stopped spinning, and I fell flat on my face.

It was a Thursday in late August. I was sitting on my bed at the club, and I was glaring at my cell phone. It kept ringing and ringing and ringing. I was supposed to have met Chase over an hour ago for lunch at his office, but I couldn't stop staring at the pregnancy test in my hand. The freshly peed-on, undeniably positive pregnancy test.

My phone started ringing again. Knowing he wasn't going to stop, I answered it.

"Where are you?" Chase demanded.

"The club."

He didn't say anything. He knew I didn't go to the club anymore. I could practically hear the wheels in his head working overtime at this new development.

"Listen, Chase. I, uh, can't—"

"You can't what?" he ground out.

"I can't meet you today," I whispered. "I don't, um, feel good."

"What's going on, Eva? You felt fine yesterday."

No. I felt nauseated yesterday; I just didn't tell him.

"I think I have the flu," I continued in a whisper. "I just want to stay in bed, OK?"

"Eva, what the fuck is really going on?"

I took a deep breath. "Nothing, Chase. I just don't feel good. I'm not up to cage fighting with you today."

He hung up.

I stared at the phone. I should tell him. If he was the father, he had a right to know. Only, I wasn't sure if he was the father. Early June, I slept with Deuce. I closed my eyes, remembering rocking back and forth overtop his large, powerful body, watching every change in his hard face as my body worked his, and that beautiful moment at the end when he tensed, our eyes locked, and I felt him spill himself inside of me. It was greedy; I knew that even in my haze of need, but we both had been greedy. For that one moment, we were done pretending. I wanted it, he wanted to give it, and then I ran back to Frankie when it was over.

I choked back a sob. I was such an idiot. And I desperately needed Kami.

Grabbing my purse—my $400 Poppy Coach purse that Chase's personal shopper had picked out for me last week because it was designer but edgy and not overly expensive, and Chase had decided it worked for me—I headed for Kami's. I was going to tell her what was going on, and I would deal with whatever she threw at me.

The cab ride was uncomfortable, but the elevator ride up to her penthouse was downright awful. My nerves were jumping out of my skin, add that to my constant nausea, and I was headed for a full-blown panic attack. By the time the elevator doors opened, I broke out in a cold sweat and was gripping my stomach.

It didn't help that it was Chase who was standing in front of the elevator and not Kami.

"Shit," I muttered and backed farther into the elevator.

He slammed his palm against the sliding door, keeping it open. "What the fuck?" he growled.

I stared at him. Seeing him here—in his home, Kami's home—the realization of what I'd been doing and who I'd been doing it with was even more awful than I'd imagined it would be.

"I…um…"

"I knew you lied to me," he bit out. "And you've got two fucking seconds to explain why before I pick you up, take you straight to my room, and let Kami hear me fucking the shit out of you."

"Chase—"

"I mean it, Eva. Unless you want Kami to hear you screaming my name, you better start talking."

I blew out a shaky breath. "I'm pregnant," I blurted out. "I needed Kami."

His eyes went wide. "What?"

"Pregnant, Chase!" I cried out softly. "Baby inside of me!"

He stared at me. No longer angry, no longer anything. Just a blank-faced stare.

Then the strangest thing happened. Chase's eyes went soft. Chase didn't have soft eyes; he had cold eyes, blank eyes, calculating eyes, I'm-going-to-fuck-you-blind eyes, but never soft.

It changed his entire face. And so did the smile that followed. Not his shark smile, but an honest-to-God smile.

He looked...human.

I stared at him, not knowing what to say or do, wondering what the hell he was so happy about. Then I froze because I realized Chase was happy. *Chase. Happy.* And he was happy because I was pregnant. This revelation brought me up short, and my world resumed spinning.

"Eva," he whispered, reaching for me. "I—"

"Evie!" Kami screamed, running up behind Chase. He immediately moved away from the elevator door, and I stepped into their foyer and caught a velour-sweatsuit-covered Kami as she barreled into me.

"Where have you been?" she squealed, squeezing me tight.

"Busy with Frankie," I whispered, staring at Chase over her shoulder. Arms folded in front of his chest, he was leaning against an intricately carved pillar smack dab in the center of the foyer staring back at me. Smiling.

I closed my eyes and squeezed Kami back. "Missed you," I choked out.

"God, Evie, me, too. Devin, too."

She pulled away. "Devin!" she bellowed. "Aunt Evie is here!"

She turned back to me, grinning, and her mouth fell open. "Evie, what are you wearing?" she whispered.

I looked down. Crap. I had been dressed to meet Chase for lunch. I wasn't wearing any of the elaborate crap he bought me, but I wasn't wearing anything I would normally wear. Designer skinny jeans, artfully distressed, covered my legs; my tank top was a shimmery black silk that both clung and flowed. All of this was paired with Jimmy Choo strappy black sandals and my black rhinestone-covered Coach bag. I had blown my hair straight, and then feathered it. I had a shit ton of makeup on and more jewelry than I had ever worn in my life, all of it expensive and chic. It wasn't me, whoever me was, and she knew it. We both had to wear uniforms to school, but I always found a way to make mine my own. And even though I wore a designer evening gown to prom, I paired it with my Chucks and didn't do a damn thing to my hair. It was still wet from my shower when the limo picked up Frankie and me.

I turned bright red as she continued to gape at me.

"I think she looks stunning," Chase said, his voice low, his eyes blazing. A surge of desire shot through me. I wanted his hands on me. I wanted the pain, pleasure, and humiliation he brought me, and I wanted it now; I was starting to breathe heavier just thinking about it. He saw this, and he smiled his shark smile.

"No one cares what you think!" Kami snapped. She narrowed her eyes at me. "What's going on?" she demanded.

I swallowed thickly. "I had a meeting with the D.A. this morning. Frankie's bullshit, you know? I didn't want to look like biker trash."

Sheesh. Lying to Kami made me feel filthy. Disgusting. I had never lied to her before, not once in twenty-five years of friendship.

This seemed to placate her, but she still looked suspicious. "You've never cared before, and you've never looked like trash because you aren't trash."

I opened my mouth, another lie on the tip of my tongue, but was saved from having to dig my hole deeper when Devin barreled into the room much the same way his mother had.

"Aunt Evie!" he screamed as I bent down to engulf him in a squeezing hug. I buried my face in his sweet-smelling neck and fought the urge to cry. I had been avoiding both Kami and Devin—two people I loved more than anything—for this bullshit with Chase.

"You look so pretty," he said, giving me a cute kiss on my cheek.

"Thanks, baby," I whispered. "And you look very, very handsome."

"Amazing, isn't it?" Chase sneered. "How my very handsome son looks nothing like his mother or his father but more resembles Mrs. Gonzalez, our housekeeper."

My eyes shot to Chase. It wasn't any secret Devin wasn't his. Devin was dark. Both he and Kami were light. Devin had black hair, dark features, and tanned skin that had nothing to do with sun exposure. He was taller and broader than any other four-year-old I'd ever met. He looked every bit his father's son.

His father...Cox.

Kami glared at Chase. Thankfully, Devin seemed oblivious as always to Chase's digs.

"Kind of hard to have a child that looks like you," she hissed softly, "when your wife refuses to fuck you."

He shrugged. "As much fun as it was to fuck a dead fish, I've since found much better. Much, much better."

I closed my eyes. I had to get out of here.

Giving Devin another big hug, I stood. "Let's do lunch tomorrow. And some shopping," I suggested to Kami. "There's a new thrift store in SoHo that Snickers said has a boatload of mint condition vinyls." I tried to smile. "You know I have to hit that up."

"Who's Snickers?" Devin asked.

"One of Papa Fox's friends from the club," Kami said. "All he eats are Snickers bars."

"What lovely names they all have," Chase muttered.

"Evie, lunch and shopping tomorrow sounds perfect, but I want today, too. I was just about to drop Devin downstairs for a playdate. I'll only be a minute, and then we can go get pedicures. My treat. Sound good?"

"OK," I whispered, glancing at Chase, knowing he was going to be pissed at me.

Kami glanced over at Chase, then back at me, and her eyes narrowed.

"One minute, don't leave," she said, grabbing Devin's hand.

The elevator doors closed behind them.

"Cancel with Kami," he demanded. "Go straight to the Waldorf."

"God, you're an asshole," I hissed.

I found myself pressed up against the elevator as Chase's erection ground against me. I sucked in a breath.

"You want me," he said coldly.

God, I did. I wanted him badly. Right here, right now.

"Go, Eva. I'll be there shortly."

Thirty minutes later, I was at the Waldorf begging Chase to fuck me.

Chapter  THIRTEEN

Deuce watched Eva tear out of Kami's building looking like a brunette version of Kami—the hair, the clothes, the makeup, and she'd dropped a good twenty pounds. What had happened in the three months since he'd seen her last?

He came to Manhattan for two reasons. One, he had a lead on Eva's hit; two, he wanted to see Eva; three, he wanted to see Eva; and four, he had to fucking see Eva, or he was going to go insane. So more than two reasons.

Three days ago, accompanied by Mick and Cox, he pulled out of midday Manhattan traffic into the Silver Demons MC parking lot. He had just removed his helmet when he saw some pretty-boy asshole step out of the front doors of the club, accompanied by Eva and Preacher.

He signaled his boys to remain where they were as he watched the three of them interact. Preacher stuck his hand out and shook the pretty boy's hand, and then retreated into the club.

The pretty boy focused on Eva, and his chest went tight. He'd seen that look before; it's the look a man gets when he's looking at something he wants inside of.

Gripping Eva's chin, the pretty boy backed her up against the club doors.

Cox's hand came down on his shoulder. "Breathe, Prez. She's not exactly fightin' him off."

No, she wasn't. She had her arms wrapped around his neck, gripping him, while the fucker gnawed on her face and groped her backside like he was digging for change. None of this made sense to him. She ran away from him to help Frankie, but how she was going to accomplish that by fucking some uptown douchebag was beyond him.

Something was up. Something he was pretty sure he wasn't going to like.

"Mick," he hissed. "Find out who the fuck that is."

His VP's eyes met his. Mick thought his relationship with Eva was fucked-up, and he made no bones about telling him.

They stared at each other. Mick gave first. "On it, Prez," he said quietly.

The pretty boy strolled arrogantly down the walk and slid inside a sleek silver Aston Martin DB9. When he pulled out into traffic, Mick's Harley pulled out behind him, and they both disappeared into the mess of New York City traffic.

Eva sat down on the front steps, slumped forward, and buried her face in her hands.

Fuck him. Something was way off.

"Somethin' goin' down here, Prez," Cox muttered. "Your girl's not lookin' too good."

"I get that," he growled. "And she's not my girl. Not sure she ever fuckin' was."

"Load of fuckin' crap," Cox said. "Seen the way you two look at each other. Like no one else in the world exists."

He cut his eyes at his RC. "You a fuckin' poet?"

Cox shrugged. "If that's what it takes to get laid, then I'm a fuckin' poet. Other times, I'm a fuckin' accountant. Or a plumber. Sometime's a man's gotta do what a man's gotta do."

Cox pretending to be an accountant with all his piercings and tattoos was just about the funniest thing he had ever heard.

"Come on, Prez. Let's go to Queens." Cox slapped him on the back. "We came here for a reason. And that fuckin' reason is to keep that woman of yours breathin'."

They went to Queens. They tortured and killed two independent gravediggers to get the information they needed. Then they crossed the Hudson and took out the hit. The asshole had a file on Eva as thick as a phone book—full of photos, addresses, and schedules. Despite not needing to bury her unless Frankie kicked it, the digger was thorough and ready at the drop of a hat to get his job done.

The digger had been paid to kill her; he didn't know Eva from a hole in the wall, but Deuce knew her and he loved her. Because of this love, instead of giving the asshole a merciful death, he prolonged the pain and let him bleed for a good long time before finally stopping his heart. It didn't make him feel any better about the pretty boy with his tongue shoved down Eva's throat, but it relieved some pent-up aggression.

Until he found out who the pretty boy was. Then all that aggression came back tenfold.

So he followed her. He watched her run out of Kami's building and hail a cab. He followed her to the Waldorf Astoria and watched her wave to the doormen like she fucking knew them and disappeared inside. Not even ten minutes later, he watched Chase pull up in his DB9, toss his keys to the valet, and stride through the doors.

He wanted to kill something. No, he wanted to kill Chase.

Instead, he waited. He waited all day and all night and neither of them came out.

At dawn, when the sun was cresting, Eva came walking through the front doors looking half-asleep, pale, and disheveled. A doorman moved quickly, ready to hail her a cab, but he didn't give her the option. His Harley roared to life; he gunned it straight across four lanes of traffic and came to a rubber-burning, tire-squealing stop directly in front of her.

Her mouth fell open.

"Get the fuck on," he growled. "I won't tell you twice."

Her mouth worked soundlessly for several moments, and just as he was getting really impatient and angry, she burst into tears and threw herself into his arms.

Fuck.

Flipping off the gaping doormen, he held her for a long time just breathing her in, knowing she'd just fucked another guy, smelling him and the sex they had on her, and feeling like crushing skulls with his bare hands because of it. But he kept it reeled in because she was in his arms, she was seeking comfort from him, and she needed him, so whatever the fuck she'd been doing while they'd been apart didn't matter unless she started doing it again. And since he was going to put Chase to ground the minute he got a chance, he figured there was no chance of that happening anyway.

"Get on, Eva," he said. "I'm taking you home, and then I'm taking you home with me."

She surprised the fuck out of him. She got on without a word, without an ounce of fight, and no attitude tossed his way. This scared him more than the tears and more than her selling her pussy to save Crazy Frankie. If his girl was broken, someone sure as fuck was going to die for that.

Preacher met them in the hallway of the club; Cox and Mick were by his side. He took one look at his daughter's red eyes and puffy, blotchy face, and lost it.

"What the fuck?" Preacher shouted. "What happened?"

When her old man tried to touch her, she shrank away from him and buried her face in his armpit. Not his first choice of a hiding place seeing as he just spent twenty-four hours in the same clothing, but she didn't seem to care, so he didn't move her and just held her tight.

Preacher looked bewildered. The man really didn't have a clue something was wrong with his daughter.

"What's goin' on?" Preacher demanded.

"I don't know," he said. "Where's her fuckin' room?"

"You think I'm gonna let you take my daughter up to her fuckin' room? I haven't fuckin' forgotten what you did when she was just a kid."

"Daddy!" Eva whirled around, glaring. "I've been fucking Deuce since I was eighteen! I wanted to fuck him when I was sixteen! Maybe I even wanted him when I was twelve, too! Who knows! What I do know is I have been in love with him since I was five! So get over it! And don't you dare shoot him, or I'll shoot you!"

Cox slapped his hand over his mouth and turned away. Mick rolled his eyes.

Preacher's jaw dropped.

Oh…shit. At least he knew her fire was still burning bright, but still…oh, shit. He didn't have a good track record dealing with his bitch's fathers. For some reason, they never liked him, and the one in front of him had already shot him twice.

"Don't fuckin' shoot me again," he growled. "I didn't do shit to her when she was twelve. That shit when she was sixteen, that wasn't my fault. I was shitfaced, and she was jerkin' herself off on my fuckin' belt buckle, and her tits were bouncin' in my face, and what the fuck, I'm only fucking human. I blame her tits for the whole fuckin' thing. But every time I fucked her she was fuckin' legal. So no fuckin' shootin'. This time I'll shoot back."

"Tact, Prez," Cox muttered. "You fuckin' need some."

Both Eva and her old man were gaping at him.

"Did you seriously just say all of that to my daddy?"

He looked down at her. "What? You're the fuckin' dumbass who brought it up. It's the fuckin' truth anyway."

"The fuckin' truth," Preacher muttered, "is I already knew she was a willin' participant, you fuckin' idiot. Doesn't change the fact that you took advantage of a sixteen-year-old girl."

"Daddy," Eva hissed. "How old was my mother when you knocked her up?"

Preacher's eyes shot to his daughter. "Deuce is forty-eight, Eva! I'm fifty-five! Don't that seem a little fucked-up to you?"

"How old, Daddy?" she demanded.

"Six-fuckin'-teen," he said darkly, glaring at her.

Damn. Looked like his old man and Preacher had some shit in common. At least he didn't belong to that fucking club. That was something. Sorta.

"Yeah," she shot back. "And how old were you?"

"Eva!"

"Daddy!"

"I was twenty-four," he snarled.

She folded her arms across her chest and cocked her hip out. "Huh," she said. "Interesting."

"Yeah," he shot back. "Fuckin' interesting. Your old man was a fuckin' idiot who fell in love with a junkie runaway who took off runnin' scared after she gave birth to you! Real fuckin' interesting! Didn't get to spend nearly enough time lovin' her, treatin' her to all the shit her parents never gave her, and all the women since her have been fuckin' bed warmers, nothin' more! Excuse the fuck outta me for not wantin' that kinda shit for my baby!"

Preacher's eyes had gone glossy halfway through his revelation, and now tears were flowing freely down his cheeks. Everyone stared. Preacher didn't cry. Preacher killed in cold blood. But there it was.

"Didn't matter 'cause I fucked you up anyway, baby girl," Preacher rasped. "Didn't see how bad Frankie was 'til it was too late. Trapped you in that shit without even knowin' it. Shoulda got him help a long time ago. Shoulda gotten you away from him. Shoulda done fuckin' somethin'."

"Doesn't matter," she whispered. "He's not getting out anytime soon, and he's getting the help he needs."

This made Mick stomp off down the hallway. His boys wanted Frankie dead. He wanted Frankie dead, but Eva and Preacher loved Frankie. Deuce got that. You can't turn feelings on and off like a fucking light. He knew. He tried. He tried to love his wife, and he tried to stop loving Eva. Neither worked.

That said, Frankie still needed to go to ground.

"Eva!" Hurricane Kami came bursting through the front doors. Kami shoved him out of her way, grabbed Eva by her upper arms, and started screaming.

"You fucking idiot! Why didn't you tell me what he was doing? For God's sake, Eva, you didn't have to fuck him! Do you know how much dirt I have on that skanky asshole? Tons, Eva, tons! I would have broken him down in time!"

"Frankie didn't have time!" Eva screamed back. "Chase wouldn't meet with me until Frankie got put in solitary!"

Deuce saw red. The asshole didn't just play on her love for Frankie; he outright cornered her with her love for Frankie.

Preacher's gaze darted back and forth between Kami and his daughter. "Eva, what the fuck did Kami just say?"

They both ignored him.

"Oh, Evie," Kami cried. "I'm going to kill him! You are too good and too sweet, and a man like Chase didn't deserve a taste of that kind of beautiful!"

If she kept saying shit like that about his woman, maybe he could learn to like Kami.

"How did you find out?" Eva whispered.

Kami let out a frustrated breath. "He came home like twenty minutes ago informing me that our marriage was over." She snorted. "Can you believe him? I was like, 'What marriage?' and started laughing at him. He got pissed, told me about you, told me you guys were together, told me you were having his baby, but left Frankie out of it. Only I knew, I just knew, you would never touch him without a good reason! And, I knew that reason was Frankie! Avoiding me for months, the clothes, Evie, the makeup, the Jimmy fucking Choos…I am not stupid!"

"I'm gonna ask one more time, Eva," Preacher growled. "What the fuck is Kami talking about?"

He stared at Eva.

She was pregnant.

His woman was pregnant. And it wasn't his.

All eyes were on Eva, but she only had eyes for him, and damn her fucking eyes, but he couldn't look away. He couldn't even blink.

"I'm sorry," she whispered.

He blinked.

"Kami?" Cox said quietly, his voice unusually low. His head swiveled to his RC.

Kami, noticing Cox for the first time, shrieked and scrambled backward. That's when he saw the little boy she was shoving behind her. Eva jumped beside her, and they created a wall.

"Wait," Kami whispered, holding her palms up. "You don't understand."

Confused, he looked at Cox's furious expression, then back at the little boy who was scared out of his mind, peeking out between Kami and Eva's legs.

Understanding dawned. Little shit looked just like the bigger shit.

Fuck. This was going to get ugly. There were two things in the world Cox truly cared about. The club. And his daughter. If he had known he had a son, the kid would have been on that list, too.

"What don't I understand?" Cox hissed. "I don't understand that there's a fuckin' kid standing behind you 'bout four fuckin' years old who looks just like me? I don't understand that I fucked his mother thirty ways from fuckin' Sunday the last time I fuckin' saw her, which was when, bitch? Five fuckin' years ago? Is that what I don't understand?"

Preacher stepped in front of Kami. "You're talkin' shit 'bout the boy's mother right in front of him, which is bad enough. But that mother is family and so is the boy, and talkin' shit to my family does not happen in my fuckin' club."

"Fuck off, Demon," Cox spat. "In case you haven't noticed, that's my fuckin' kid!"

"Yeah, asshole, I fuckin' noticed. Hard not to when he looks just like ya."

"Would everyone shut the fuck up?" Kami screamed. "He doesn't know about you! All you're doing is scaring the crap out of him!"

Preacher shoved between Kami and Eva and scooped up the little boy.

"Once I get Devin upstairs and out of fuckin' earshot from you lot of assholes, you can resume fuckin' screamin' at one another." He looked at Eva. "Me and you, baby girl, are gonna be havin' words. If what I think happened actually happened, I'm gonna get real trigger twitchy."

Nobody said a word until Preacher disappeared into the stairwell. Once he was gone, Cox exploded.

"This is so fucked, bitch! Hiding a man's kid from him! Really fuckin' fucked!"

"You crazy fuck!" Kami screamed. "You live in Montana. You're married. You already have a kid! I live in New York, and I'm married! What was I supposed to do?"

"What you were s'posed to do, bitch, was tell me you fuckin' shit out my kid!"

"You're disgusting!" Kami hissed. "A dirty, disgusting biker whore!"

Cox's eyes bugged out of his head. "Bitch, you think I'm fuckin' disgusting? Were you or were you not the same fuckin' whore who was ridin' my cock bareback, shovin' your fuckin' tits in my mouth, begging me to bite harder, while Ripper drilled into your fuckin' ass?"

Eva went screaming crazy and lunged. Cursing, he tried to grab her, but the crazy bitch faked right and then went left, managing to coldcock Cox in the jaw just before he caught her and hauled her backward.

"You're fuckin' dead, bitch!" Cox shouted.

Deuce snapped. Shoving Eva off to the side, he spun around, grabbed Cox by his shirt, and slammed him into a wall. "Bitch is pregnant, and you're gonna threaten her? You're gonna fuckin' threaten my fuckin' pregnant woman?"

"Oh, Evie," Kami wailed, forgetting entirely about a very homicidal Cox. She threw her arms around Eva, and together they sank down to the floor in a tangle of brown and blonde hair.

He released Cox and slumped back against the wall. He hadn't slept in over twenty-four hours, and there was too much crazy going on around him to deal with on no sleep.

"Settled this shit in my head already," Cox hissed. "I'm takin' my kid home."

"You're not taking my son away from me!" Kami cried.

Cox glared at her. "Then you best pack your shit and find a fuckin' place to live in Montana."

Kami scrambled to her feet. "Montana!" she shrieked. "Devin is not going to Montana!"

Deuce wasn't quick enough to grab Cox before he got up in Kami's face. "Bitch," he hissed, "I want to know my fuckin' kid. You already stole four fuckin' years from me. You're not stealin' any more."

Kami's lower lip trembled. "You don't understand," she whispered. "Until Devin, my entire life was spent doing what I was told, and then finding ways to fill up the empty space in between. The drugs and drinking and the sex—all of it—was me not knowing what to do with myself, not knowing where I belonged. The moment Devin was placed in my arms everything clicked into place, and suddenly, I knew exactly what I was meant to do and where I belonged. I can't let you take him from me."

Her voice grew shrill. "I can't let you take the only person in the world besides Evie that has ever meant anything to me!"

Eva burst into a fresh bout of tears. Sighing, convinced he was the only sane person left in the world, Deuce pulled her to him and started rubbing her back.

Cox turned away from Kami. "Shit," he muttered. "Shit. Shit. Fuckin' shit."

He turned back around and took Kami's hand in his. "Woman, I wouldn't have taken him from you; we woulda worked somethin' out, back-and-forth bullshit. I'd never take my boy from his mama."

Kami burst into tears, and her knees buckled. Cox caught her before she crumpled to the floor, scooped her up in his arms, and took off down the hall. Deuce watched him lean down and kiss Kami's forehead before he made a left, and they were out of sight.

He decided to start back up where he left off. "Where's your room, Eva?"

"I'm sorry," she whispered.

His nostrils flared. Jesus Christ, all he wanted to do was get this bitch to her room and take care of her.

"For fuck's sake, what the fuck are you sorry for?"

"The motel," she whispered. "I wasn't thinking, and I didn't put a condom on you before I…and you didn't pull out…" she trailed off.

He stared at her.

"You tellin' me that's my kid inside you? Not that fuckin' pretty boy's?"

"No," she said, dropping her eyes. "I'm telling you I'm sorry because I don't know whose kid is inside me."

I had never planned to tell Deuce I was pregnant, therefore, I had never envisioned what his reaction was going to be. Whatever reactions I had dreamed up during the three seconds it took me to tell him that the baby might be his, the reaction he had was not one I would have ever dreamed up.

"Can you walk?"

Huh?

"What?"

"Can you walk?" he repeated. "Or do you need me to carry you?"

I blinked. "Carry me?"

"Yeah, babe. Carry you to the shower."

Oh God, he was trying to take care of me. How could a man be so perfect for me and yet so wrong for me all at the same time?

"I'm disgusting," I whispered.

His eyebrow rose. "Yeah, babe, that's why I'm tryin' to get you in the shower."

"No!" I cried. "I mean I'm disgusting! I'm a whore!"

Deuce's face went rock hard. "Fuckin' listen to me. Up until you started askin' favors usin' your pussy as payment, you'd been with only two men. Me and Frankie. You're not a fuckin' whore. You're a fuckin' idiot."

I gaped at him.

"Yeah, babe, an idiot. You've been takin' care of that crazy fuckwad so damn long you think it's your fuckin' destiny. Chase knew that; he saw an opening, and he fuckin' took it. And because he took it, he's gonna fuckin' die. But, babe, you're not a whore—farthest thing from it."

I swallowed hard. "I'm still disgusting," I whispered.

His eyes flashed with anger. "Goddammit, Eva! What the fuck did I just—"

"I liked it!" I blurted out. "I don't even like Chase all that much, but I liked fucking him and stuff…because I'm disgusting! I did things with him…" My voice cracked, and I swallowed hard.

"Disgusting things…and I liked them, and I liked that it was him doing them," I finished in a small voice.

Deuce took a deep breath, and then blew it out slowly. This was it. In about two seconds, he was going to tell me exactly how disgusting I was, and then I would never see him again.

"Eva," he growled. I braced myself.

"You're bein' an idiot again."

"Excuse me?" I whispered.

"You heard me. You're bein' an idiot. But I get why you're bein' an idiot. You'd never fucked someone just to fuck 'em. So I'm gonna lay this out for you, babe. You don't gotta like someone to like fuckin' 'em. You can even hate their fuckin' guts and still like fuckin' 'em. Sometimes that's the best kinda fuckin'. Angry, crazy, fucked-up fuckin'. You got nothin' to be ashamed of, darlin'.

"That said, it don't mean I'm not fuckin' pissed as hell that you've been in another man's bed and enjoyin' it, that you might got a kid inside you that ain't mine, and that you've been runnin' from me for eight fuckin' years now. I know I'm a fuckin' bastard with a bad temper, and I don't fuckin' deserve you, but shit, Eva, if you woulda stayed put, I woulda done better by you than you've had. You feel me?"

I stared at him. And fell in love with him all over again.

"I feel you," I whispered.

His eyes went soft. "Babe," he said gently, "I know that fuckin' look. Can't fuckin' tell me you might have my kid inside you, then look at me the way you're lookin' at me, and expect me to keep it reeled in."

I shook my head. "I can't do this anymore."

"What part, babe? You can't keep tryin' to save Frankie from himself? Or you can't keep fuckin' Chase? Or you can't keep pretendin' that this crazy shit between us is gonna go away just 'cause you keep runnin'?"

It was infuriating how well he knew me without even knowing me.

"All three," I snapped.

"That's good, babe, 'cause I can't do this anymore either."

I drew my brows together. "What can't you do?"

"I'm gettin' old, babe. Got grown-ass kids and gray fuckin' hair. Spent too much time married to a bitch I couldn't stand and too much time beatin' myself up for wishin' I was balls-deep in a bitch eighteen years younger than me. Add that shit together and that equals me being fuckin' miserable for a long fuckin' time. So yeah, I can't do this anymore. Can't fuckin' live without you. Want you on my bike and in my bed. Want my kids inside you. Want you by my side, babe, for as long as I got left."

By his side.

"By your side?" I whispered.

His hand went to my neck and tugged on the chain around it. For a moment, I thought he was going to break his father's necklace again. Instead, he tugged it out of my shirt and held it up in front of my face. The medallion spun around. "You think I just like decoratin' ya?"

I sucked in air.

It wasn't his father's. It looked exactly the same as his father's, except the back of this one read DEUCE.

My chin began to tremble. "I thought…I-I thought you'd put your father's necklace back on me."

He shook his head. "Told you, you shoulda never been wearing that. You shoulda been wearin' mine."

Sheesh. I was going to cry again.

"Fuckin' listen, Eva, and listen good. Words are shit, and I ain't good with them anyway. So here's the fuckin' truth for you—straight up. I'm forty-eight years old, gonna be forty-nine all too soon, and I damn well know a good thing when I see it. And, babe, all I've ever been able to fuckin' see is you. Not many chances a man has in his lifetime to do right, to earn the love of a good woman, and to get a taste of true freedom. And, babe, for me, you're all fuckin' three. Have been for a good while now."

He dropped my necklace, cupped my cheeks, and tilted my head back.

"Whatever this shit is between us, it's always been there, and it's always gonna be there. I'm shit-fuckin' tired of tryin' to ignore it. I'll try to do right by you, Eva. You'd be the first, but I'll fuckin' try my damnedest. And, baby, true freedom is the open road, the wind on your face, and a good woman on the back of your bike, holdin' you tight like you're her reason for breathin' because she sure as fuck is yours."

My mouth fell open. Didn't he just tell me he wasn't good with words, and then he went and said all that to me? I was floored. Shocked to my core. I wasn't wrong about him after all.

"Deuce," I whispered, "you love me."

He eyes went skyward, and he snorted. "Babe. Yeah. Long time now."

Deuce watched her go liquid. Every part of her just went soft. Fuck, he loved that look. That look told him that he was her whole fucking world.

"OK," she whispered. "No more running."

He breathed in a ragged breath of relief.

"Jesus, babe," he muttered as he ran his knuckles down her cheek. "'Bout fuckin' time. Now, where's your fuckin' room?"

Chapter FOURTEEN

Deuce, accompanied by Cox, walked onto the thirty-fifth floor of Martello Tower, into the law offices of Fredericks, Henderson, and Stonewall, and stopped in front of a very pretty, very young, wide-eyed receptionist.

"Do you have an appointment?" she asked.

"Yeah," Cox muttered. He pulled an envelope out of his back pocket and slapped it down on the desk. "A thirty-fuckin'-thousand-dollar appointment, which buys us you keepin' your mouth shut and not callin' security. You feel me?"

Her mouth fell open, and she stared down at the envelope. "Thirty thousand dollars?"

"Yup."

"Legal?"

"It's not tagged, darlin'."

She jumped out of her chair and spun around. They both stared as her skirt-clad ass went up in the air as she bent down and rummaged through a file cabinet. She resurfaced with a purse and sweater and snatched up the envelope.

"Thank you," she said breathlessly. "I hate Mr. Henderson! He is the worst boss I have ever had! I'm so going back to bartending!"

She let out an excited shriek, flashed them a killer grin, and ran out of the office.

They looked at each other. "That was easy," Cox said.

"She forgot her photos," he said, pointing at her desk.

Shrugging, they headed past reception and straight into Chase's office.

He glanced up from his laptop.

Deuce stepped forward. "Eva Fox," he growled.

Chase glanced between him and Cox and stuck on Cox. His eyes went wide. "Jesus," he muttered. "It's about time you came and picked up your kid. Wasn't sure how much longer I could stomach pretending the little spic was mine."

Cox's fists clenched.

"Eva Fox," Deuce reminded him.

Chase glanced back at him. "I'm a little busy right now. Do you mind coming back another time? Maybe making an appointment?"

Cox sat down on a leather armchair and put his feet up on Chase's desk. "We'll wait."

"Yeah," Deuce said, spotting a photograph of Eva. He picked it up off the desk. "You take your fuckin' time."

Her high school graduation. She was wearing her gown, holding her cap in her hand and grinning, looking like she didn't have a care in the world. His mouth went dry looking at it. That photo had been taken right before he had her in that alleyway and made her his forever.

"Beautiful, isn't she?" Chase murmured.

Yeah, she fucking was, but he wasn't going to mince words. He had come here for a reason, and it wasn't to discuss how beautiful his woman was.

"Thought you only had to worry 'bout Frankie Deluva, yeah? And since Deluva's locked up tight, you thought you had nothin' to worry 'bout."

Chase smirked. "I take it I was wrong?"

"Yeah, asshat," Cox said. "You were fuckin' wrong."

Chase pointed his index finger between him and Cox and grinned. "Are you both here defending Mrs. Fox-Deluva's honor? Because if that's the case, I'm sorry to tell you, but I'm pretty certain I fucked it all out of her."

"Sorry, slick," Deuce said to Chase. "Eva's got fire inside her you ain't never touched."

"Considering I've touched every possible part of her there is to touch, including her womb, I'm inclined to disagree with you."

His nostrils flared.

"Oh," Chase arrogantly continued, "didn't you know? Funny thing about condoms. They don't work very well when you break them beforehand. So as far as Eva's fire is concerned, I think I've cornered the market."

"Funny thing 'bout condoms," he growled. "They don't work very well when you don't use them at all."

Deuce watched, satisfied, as Chase lost his grin and anger flickered in his eyes.

"Oh, didn't ya know," he said, "I've been cornerin' that fuckin' market 'bout twelve years now."

Cox leaned forward and plucked a framed photo off the desk. "Goddamn, Kami looks slammin' in a bikini," he drawled. "Like her better naked, though. And ridin' my face screamin' my fuckin' name."

Chase shrugged. "You think Kami screams, you should hear Eva."

Holy shit, he wanted to kill this asshole.

Chase folded his arms across his chest and leaned back in his desk chair. "That baby is mine," he said evenly. "I made sure of it."

Gritting his teeth, he counted to ten before he did something that would land him in a cell next to Frankie. While he was counting, he stared at the picture of Eva. Why did this asshole have a picture of Eva from her high school graduation? Unless…

He looked back at Chase. Fucker was a cruel bastard, but if he just wanted a taste of Eva, he wouldn't have tried to get her pregnant. He wouldn't have her photo on his desk, a photo taken twelve years ago, no less, and he wouldn't give a shit who else she was fucking.

Jesus Christ…

"I know what Eva sounds like when she's screamin'," Deuce said quietly, waiting for the reaction he knew would come.

"Know what it feels like to be buried deep inside, her sweet pussy squeezin' my shit so fuckin' hard it hurts."

Chase's face went tight.

"Best part—and you should know this since you're fuckin' her—is when she's comin' and screamin' she loves me and—"

Chase lunged forward in his chair, and his fists came down on his desk. "Shut the fuck up!"

Yeah, Chase Henderson loved Eva Fox.

"Funny thing 'bout Eva," Cox said. "Prez don't ever shut up 'bout her. We quit tryin' to make him a long fuckin' time ago. Always talkin' 'bout her big titties and tight pussy—"

"Get out," Chase hissed. "Or I'm calling security."

"Don't worry, kid," Deuce said. "We're gettin' the fuck out. Came up here to feel you out, see what the fuck your game was. See if I needed to take you to ground, but I get it now, know exactly what you're about. You ain't got no game. You just want my woman, plain and simple. Wanted her for a long time now. Wanted her so bad you were desperate enough to settle for fee-for-service fuckin' instead of love."

Chase's jaw locked up tight.

"I ain't got shit to worry 'bout. Eva's never gonna look at you as anything more than a ride she got off on."

"GET! OUT!"

Grinning, Deuce lifted his chin at Cox, and they headed for the door. Not a moment later, after they had closed Chase's door behind them, something smashed against it, rattling the walls.

"We're not gonna kill 'im?" Cox asked.

"Trust me," he said. "This is much fuckin' worse. Boy is in a world of hurt. Been hurtin' for a long time now. We just sharpened the fuckin' blade a little. He'll bury himself in no time…that is, if Frankie doesn't find out and do it first."

Cox nodded. "Sweet."

Once they were inside the elevator, he grabbed Cox by his neck and slammed him into the wall. "You ever fuckin' talk 'bout Eva's tits or pussy again, I will fuckin'—"

"Prez!" Cox said, laughing. "That was all for show. Chill the fuck out."

Freshly showered and sipping a tall glass of ginger ale, I was sitting in my beanbag chair, watching Kami and Devin curled up in my bed sleeping, and hoping like hell Devin wasn't going to need counseling from the events of the day.

Because I sure did.

My bedroom door clicked and opened slowly. Cox walked in first, followed by Deuce. Cox's gaze flickered over me before landing on Kami and Devin. There was possession in his eyes. He wasn't giving up his kid—no way in hell. I wasn't sure what that meant for Kami, but I was going to find out.

"Cox," I whispered. He turned.

"I'm not sure what your plans are, but Kami and Devin are a package deal. You try to fuck that up, and you're going to go up against a wall of Demons. We clear?"

Deuce's lips twitched, but Cox remained impassive. "Yeah, Foxy," he whispered. "We're clear. You don't gotta worry 'bout your girl. Had some time to cool off. Figure some shit out."

Cox walked over to my bed and sat down beside Kami. "Bitch," he whispered in her ear, "wake the fuck up."

Kami blinked sleepily, saw Cox looming over her, and let out a shriek.

Cox slapped his hand over her mouth. "You crazy? My kid is sleepin'."

Kami's pretty blue eyes narrowed, and she mumbled something nasty-sounding against Cox's hand.

"Just met your fuckin' husband, and sure as fuck don't want my kid near that asshole ever again, 'specially don't want him callin' that motherfucker daddy." He gently pushed a lock of hair out of Kami's eyes. "And bitch, you're not goin' back to him. Not ever."

Kami visibly relaxed and sank back into my pillow. Cox removed his hand.

"Gonna lay it out for you, babe," he continued. "Not about to take my boy away from his mama. So we can work somethin' out. I gotta get to know him first, want him to feel safe with me, and then we can talk 'bout him goin' back and forth, yeah?

"Or you can pack up your fuckin' shit and haul your bony ass down to Montana, and I'll help you get a place. Maybe shit could happen between us, maybe not 'cause you're fuckin' crazy, but no way in hell you're ever goin' near Ripper. Basically, bitch, you will promise me right the fuck now that you will be stayin' away from Ripper from now 'til fuckin' forever."

Shocked, I glanced at Deuce. He was looking at the ceiling, praying for patience maybe.

"What about your wife?" Kami hissed. "Will you be staying away from her?"

"I'll take care of it," Cox hissed back.

She snorted. "And how will you be taking care of that?"

"Not your concern."

Kami jackknifed into a sitting position. "You expect me to pack up my life, uproot my son, move to a town where 'Super Sluts' is the only salon in sight, just so some *shit* may or may not happen between us? You might be fine as hell and fuck like a god, but sorry, I don't think so."

Cox grabbed Kami's upper arms and jerked her forward. Nose to nose, they glared at each other.

"I'm gonna be brutally honest with you. Not one woman has ever worked me like you do. Not one and I've fucked a lot of women. Pissed me off every time you split when I still wanted more. Now you got my kid, and you still look slammin', and I still want more. You come to Montana, and we'll see if this shit works. If it does, I'll leave my wife; if it doesn't, I'm not fuckin' leavin' her. Don't wanna do my own laundry, and sure as shit don't wanna be payin' alimony."

"Oh my God," Kami breathed. "You are the biggest asshole I have ever met."

"And you're a damn crazy, seriously spoiled bitch."

I'm still not sure who moved first, maybe they moved at the same time. One second they were glaring, and the next they were kissing. And wrestling. Wrestle kissing?

They rolled off the bed in a heap, Kami reaching for Cox's belt while he tore open her shirt.

I ran for Devin since neither of his parents were taking into account that their four-year-old was mere feet from them.

"Jesus, you're fuckin' perfect," Cox rasped.

"Shut up," Kami hissed. "And fuck me!"

Deuce held the door for me while I carried Devin out of the room.

Last thing I heard before Deuce closed the door was Cox groaning loudly, "Oh, fuck yeah, bitch, your crazy ass is comin' home with me."

"No, I'm not!"

I shook my head. What a difference a day makes.

"You ready to go home, darlin'?"

I looked over at Deuce. He was staring at the little boy in my arms.

"Yeah," I said softly. "I'm ready."

He looked up and smiled. "That's good, babe. Real fuckin' good."

Deuce turned onto the interstate. Wearing his helmet, Eva sat behind him, her thighs cradling his hips, her arms encircling his waist, her cheek pressed between his leather-clad shoulder blades. It felt good. Right. It felt like a fuck of a long time coming, but it was here now, and he could finally breathe easy.

Extending his arm straight out, palm facing down, he signaled his boys to slow down. Then he put his arm up in the air and extended his index finger. The boys slowed and went single file in order of their rank: Deuce, Mick, and then Cox bringing up the rear.

They headed home.

Chapter
FIFTEEN

"I'm not going in there."

Deuce folded his thick arms across his wide chest. "You gonna sleep out under the stars?"

I shrugged. "Since I'm not going in there, yeah."

Closing his eyes, he took a couple of deep breaths. I knew I was wearing down his last nerve, but honestly, I couldn't find a shred of give-a-damn. He had good intentions, yes, but he wasn't listening to me and didn't care how I felt about any of this. I had just up and left behind everything I'd ever known for him, and he was expecting me to move in with him and his kids. His grown-up kids. His grown-up kids I'd never met!

From what I could see, he had a beautiful home. It was a two-story rustic Montana cabin, widespread, with a wraparound porch and a backyard that went on for miles. It was off the beaten path—no neighbors, no traffic, no nothing. Just Deuce. And his two grown kids.

Holy crap. I had to get far, far away.

Was there a bus stop in the mountains? I didn't remember seeing any. In fact, I don't think I saw any buses either. Or people. Or anything at all actually. But there had to be a bus stop, right? If there's a road, more than likely a bus will show up eventually…right?

"Reel it in, Eva," Deuce growled. "How far you think you're gonna get? You don't even know where the fuck you are."

"This is kidnapping!" I yelled. "And stop reading my mind!"

"Fuck me," he muttered. "Are you always this crazy?"

"Yes!" I screamed. "Which is why you need to take me to an airport or a bus station or any sort of civilization and let me go home!"

He ignored me. "I don't remember you bein' this crazy."

"You want to know why you don't remember me being this crazy? Because out of the twenty-five years we've known each other, we can count on our fingers and toes how many days of that we've spent together. And some of those days weren't even full days!"

"Eva," he said, exasperated. "You've spent four days on the back of my bike and sleepin' in a tent, pukin' your fuckin' guts out. You look like shit, you smell like shit, and I'm willin' to bet you'd love to sleep in a real bed. So how's 'bout you and I continue this fuckin' bullshit inside?"

I was praying for serenity, praying for the strength not to rip his throat out, when I heard the most awful noise in the entire world.

"Dad?"

A miniature Deuce sauntered down the driveway. I stared at him. He was nearly as tall as his father, not quite as well-built, but still impressive for an eighteen-year-old. His hair was long and blond and pulled back in a man bun, and when he flashed me his lady-killer grin, it was Deuce at Rikers all over again. But he didn't have his father's eyes. While Deuce's were frosty blue, mini Deuce's were brown.

Deuce pointed at his mini him. "Cage," he grunted. Then he pointed at me. "Eva."

Sheesh. He sounded like a Neanderthal. "Me man, you woman."

The mini Deuce grinned again and lifted his chin. "'Sup, Eva."

I buried my face in my hands. "Oh my God," I whined. "I need a bus station."

"Daddy!"

I peeked through my fingers at the screaming, giggling mass of blonde hair flying down the driveway. Dear God. This chick was a teenage diva. Skinny jeans and a sparkly pink tank top with furry pink boots, highlighted blonde hair, long and layered with perfectly side-swept bangs. Way too much eye makeup. This did not bode well for me.

I was not a diva. None of my clothing had ever been accused of being furry.

She launched herself at Deuce and wrapped her body around him. Since no one was looking at me, I decided to tiptoe slowly out of the driveway. How hard could it be to find a bus stop?

"Eva!" Deuce bellowed. "Don't you fuckin' dare!

I stopped and glanced over my shoulder. Deuce was storming toward me while both his kids looked on curiously.

So I did what any victim being forced to live with your man's grown children would do. I turned tail and ran like hell. True, I had no idea where I was going, but there was a road, and a road had to lead somewhere. If it didn't, how would people get anywhere?

Deuce's boots pounded heavy on the pavement behind me, growing closer and closer until he was close enough to grab me. I screamed and made a hard right off the road, jumped over a small ditch, and headed straight for the woods.

I didn't make it.

"Bitch, I know I wasn't fuckin' hallucinatin' when you said you were sick of runnin'," he growled.

"Fuck you," I hissed. "FUCK YOU!"

"That what you need, Eva? You need me to fuck you to remind you where you fuckin' belong?"

"Daddy?"

"Fuck," he muttered. "Go back to the house, Danny."

"I want to talk to Eva."

"House. Danny. Now."

"No, Daddy, I want to talk to her."

Sighing, Deuce set me down. I scrambled away from him, glaring. He glared right back.

"Hi," Danny said cheerfully. "Daddy told me all about you!"

Danny grinned at me. Sheesh, she was gorgeous. She had Deuce's eyes—icy blue and hypnotizing. But her face was her mother's, sweetheart features, delicate, and utterly beautiful.

"I thought you would be older," she said and giggled. "Daddy's age or maybe my mom's age. But you're so young."

"Fuck," Deuce muttered. "She's not that young."

I glared at him. "I'm thirty."

Danny burst out laughing. "She's like closer to my age than yours, Daddy! You're like fifty!"

Deuce looked to the sky and closed his eyes. "I'll be on the porch," he growled. "She runs again," he pointed at me, "you fuckin' yell."

He stalked off.

Deuce sat on his porch steps, his elbows on his knees, and his face in his palms. He was destined for a life of crazy.

"She's hot, Dad. Really fuckin' hot."

He turned his head toward his son. "Yeah," he muttered.

"Great fuckin' legs," Cage continued. "And her tits. Jesus, no fuckin' bra with tits that big... *fuck me.*"

He glared. If Cage didn't shut the fuck up, he was going to knock him out.

"You get done with her, pass her the fuck to me."

"Reel it in," he growled. "Or I'm gonna knock you the fuck out."

Cage stared at him. "Are you serious?"

"As tequila."

"Since when do you give a fuck if I tap club ass?"

"Since right fuckin' now. And she's not a club whore. Call her that again, and you're gonna be pissin' blood for a fuckin' minute."

Cage burst out laughing. "Oh shit," he gasped, holding his stomach still laughing. "You fuckin' like this one."

Like? That didn't even begin to cover how he felt about that crazy bitch.

He grabbed his whore of a son by the front of his T-shirt and yanked him across the step until they were nose to nose. "You're fuckin' young. You think ridin' and pussy are all that fuckin' matters. I get it. I've been there, but you're gonna learn real fuckin' quick to respect women, whores, good girls, old fuckin' ladies—all of 'em—or I'm gonna bury you. You feel me?"

"Yeah, Dad," he said quietly. "Sorry."

He shoved him back and looked toward the woods. Still no sign of Eva or his daughter.

"Dad?"

"Yeah?"

"She the reason you're pissed off all the time?"

"Yeah."

"She the reason you left Mom?"

"Yeah."

"You love her?"

"Yeah."

There was a long pause.

"Cool."

"…yeah."

"Dad?"

"Jesus, Cage. What?"

"Does this mean I can have at Miranda?"

Christ.

"Yeah, you fuckin' hornball. Have at it."

"Cool."

Danny and I walked back to the house—me, silent with my arms wrapped around my middle and her, a bouncing blonde ball of teenage girl, telling me all about her summer break from school. She was sixteen—the same age I was when I first kissed her father and fell hard for him—and it all felt supremely awkward.

As we reached the end of the driveway, I could see Deuce and Cage sitting on the porch steps. Cage was leaning back on the railing smoking a cigarette; Deuce was doing a face-plant in his palms. My heart clenched; he was upset.

When he spotted us, Cage kicked Deuce in the calf. Deuce's head jerked left, his face tight with anger, and Cage reared back, pointing at me. Our eyes locked.

"Danny," Cage yelled, getting to his feet. "Help me make dinner!"

Danny touched my arm. "You good?"

"Yeah," I muttered.

"He would never hurt you," she whispered.

I looked down at her. "Yeah, baby, I know."

She grinned, and I cringed. The girl didn't just have his eyes; she had his heart-stopping grin.

"Daddy calls me baby," she whispered. Then, with a hop and skip, she ran off. She and Cage disappeared inside the house, leaving Deuce and me staring at each other.

Oh, Lord, help me. I couldn't do this. And yet, I was walking straight toward him.

I stopped in front of him. "Look, I can't do—hey! What the hell?"

Deuce grabbed my waist and pulled me on his lap. "Fuckin' hell, bitch," he said hoarsely. "You make me fuckin' insane."

I let out a long, shuddering sigh and sank into his body. His arms tightened around me.

"You're not leavin', Eva."

I was. But I didn't tell him that. Instead, I told him how unbelievably bad he smelled.

"Yeah, babe. So do you."

Deuce's home was incredible. An honest-to-God log cabin dream home. The inside had been decorated rustic chic. When you first walked in, you were greeted with a two-story foyer complete with a handmade wooden chandelier. The entire first floor was an open plan. The only divider was the sprawling staircase that led to the second-floor balcony.

To the left of the foyer was a living area separated from the family area only by furniture. The furniture was top-of-the-line, not at all lived-in, and reminded me of Chase. The family area was more my thing—beat-up wide-seated couches, a thick, furry throw rug, an enormous flat screen, and every video game console a teenage boy could dream of. Photos of Deuce and his boys, of his kids, of his different motorcycles over the years covered the width of two walls. To the right of the foyer was an enormous kitchen and dining area. The kitchen was nearly identical to the one at his clubhouse. Black-and-chrome appliances and black-and-white marble counters. The dining set was exquisite, with solid, cherry-stained oak and high-back ladder chairs fitted with forest green cushions.

Up the sprawling staircase and across from the balcony were five bedrooms and three bathrooms, not including the master bedroom, which had an all-inclusive bathroom with a Jacuzzi for a bathtub and a shower big enough to fit a family of ten, complete with benches and multiple showerheads. Deuce's bedroom was just as ridiculous. Although sparsely decorated, what was there was not at all how I pictured Deuce's bedroom. A long dresser with a large vanity mirror and a matching stool lined one wall. A Tiffany lamp hung off to the side. On the opposite wall were two vertically tall dressers. The bed was a four-poster California king with black silk bedding and too many pillows to count. And there were mirrors everywhere, even on the ceiling.

I stared at Deuce, who shrugged and muttered, "Christine."

Cage's bedroom was typical of a teenage boy. Dark sheets and dark curtains. Posters of motorcycles and naked women posing with motorcycles and stolen street signs lined the walls. The floor was carpeted with clothing and sneakers, his bed was a mess, and dirty dishes were piled high on his dresser.

Danny's was of the utmost girly-girl variety. Everything was either pink or purple, or pink and purple and fuzzy. The second I stepped inside, I felt like I'd walked into Candy Land and instantly retreated to safety.

When my tour was complete, Deuce brought me back to his bedroom, pointed me toward the dresser with the vanity, and ordered me to unpack. I scowled at him. "I'm not staying," I told him. "Therefore, I am not unpacking."

"Fuckin' hell," he muttered. Grabbing my arm, he dragged me into the adjoining bathroom and started the shower. Then he stripped.

When he was standing butt naked in front of me, I stared at the tattoo of his wife, a half sleeve of her face. I had seen it before, but had never given it much thought. Until now. Until I was here in her home with her husband and her two children.

"Don't fuckin' go there, Eva," he growled. I narrowed my eyes. How did he always know what I was thinking?

Muttering something about crazy women, Deuce crossed the bathroom and pushed me up against the ceramic-tiled wall. He yanked my T-shirt over my head and tossed it in the garbage can. Had his wife picked out the garbage can? Was her toothbrush in here somewhere?

I was momentarily distracted from my musings when I felt Deuce's hands on me. Deuce's mouth on me.

"There it is," he murmured around a mouthful of nipple. "There you fuckin' are, Eva. Gotta keep fuckin' you to remind you where you belong. I got no problem with it."

Deuce carried me into the shower, his hands gripping my backside, and his mouth feasting on my neck.

"Fuck," he kept muttering over and over again like a mantra. "So fuckin' sweet," he murmured, nuzzling against my neck. "Fuckin' beautiful and sweet and crazy…and fuckin' mine."

I swallowed hard.

Fuckin' mine.

God, the things this man did to me, the things he made me feel.

"That baby, Eva, it's mine. You feel me?"

My breath caught. "I feel you," I whispered.

His hand dipped down between us, and he slipped first one, then two fingers inside of me. Gripping his shoulders, I let my mind go blank and gave myself over and into the care of Deuce and his magic fingers. It wasn't hard to do.

"You feel me now, darlin'?" he growled.

I didn't answer. I couldn't. But yeah, I felt him. Everywhere.

"You plan on patching shit up with your old man?"

Deuce was in his bathroom brushing his teeth, watching a towel-clad Eva sitting on his bed, biting her nails, looking like she was going to bolt at any second. He'd set the house alarm for this reason. She didn't know the code, so if she tried to open the door or even a fucking window, he'd know. And he'd haul her ass back to bed.

"You're always calling my daddy an old man," she called out. "But you're almost as old as him."

She thought he was old? He spit a mouthful of toothpaste into the sink.

"What are you trying to say, darlin'?"

She shrugged. "Just wondering when you're going to start needing Viagra, too."

He froze.

What?

What the fuck?

Throwing his toothbrush across the room, he stalked out of the bathroom and headed straight for her. He placed a hand on either side of her and leaned down, forcing her to lie on her back.

"Did I not just finish workin' you over?"

The crazy woman pressed her lips together. She was laughing at him. Laughing!

Without preamble, he flipped her on her stomach, yanked her ass up in the air, and sank inside of her. Christ, she was wet. She'd baited him. He shook his head. She was crazy and sex-crazed.

"How'm I doin', you little brat?" He grunted. "You gettin' what you need?"

Panting, she shook her head. "Nope. I think you might need to go faster."

His nostrils flared, and he brought his hand down hard on her backside.

She burst out laughing. "Again," she giggled.

Christ.

"You want it raw, you promise me you're gonna stay and try this shit with me."

She pulled away, flipped onto her back, and spread herself open for him. He pushed inside of her again. Their eyes caught and locked.

"I promise," she whispered.

"That's good, babe," he said. "Real fuckin' good."

Chapter  SIXTEEN

"I'm fat," I whined, staring at my ginormous belly.

Deuce, sitting on the edge of the bed pulling his boots on, looked over his shoulder. "Yup."

I sat up in bed, or rather, I wiggled myself up. "Did you just call me fat?"

"Yup."

Oh my God. He was so infuriatingly honest! I hated it!

"I'm not fat!" I cried. "I'm nearly eight months pregnant!"

He stood up and grabbed his deodorant from the top of his dresser. "Yeah, babe, I know. But that baby ain't in your ass."

My mouth fell open. "Did you just call my ass fat?"

In the middle of tying his hair back, he turned around. "Yup."

"I hate you," I hissed. "If I could get up on my own, I would kick your ass!"

He grinned. "Not gonna lie, babe. Your ass got fuckin' fat. Don't really care though 'cause I got big fat hands, so it's all good."

I threw my pillow at him. Laughing, he ran out of the room.

"Where are you going?" I yelled.

"The club!" The front door slammed.

Huffing, I lay back down and pulled the covers up over my head. I was so bored, which was probably why my ass got fat. Deuce kept true to his word and was treating me well—when he was home. Which most days and most nights, he wasn't. Two months ago, I went into premature labor, went to the hospital, and was given magnesium sulfate to slow my contractions. It worked, and the labor was stopped, but I was given strict instructions to stay off my feet as much as possible, to stay away from stressful situations, and to refrain from sexual intercourse.

After that, Deuce stopped sleeping at home. He was always at the club. And I was not allowed at the club unless he brought me there, which was pretty much never.

I wasn't stupid. I knew he was sleeping with other women. Only I didn't know what to do about it. He had laid it out for me, told me he would try, and I told him I would try. So I was trying, but trying to maintain a relationship with someone who was never around was incredibly difficult.

There were a few times I had been breaths away from throwing these things in his face, but then I would remember that he had never promised me an exclusive relationship, nor had he promised me he would be home on a regular basis.

It was official. I was an old lady. And it was awful. I had gone from being a vital part of my club with strong ties to all my boys to this. To nothing.

In the meantime, I hung out with Danny when she wasn't at school. I hung out with Danny and Cage when Cage was home and not at the club, which was a lot less frequent than his father. And I developed a pretty good relationship with both of them. Cage and I became friends, and Danny pretty much decided I was her role model. I thought this was a bad idea, but I didn't mention it because, in all honesty, I thought it was a cute bad idea.

I had access to Deuce's pickup, but there was nowhere to go. Miles City, Montana, had a population of roughly nine thousand people and consisted of a few streets with various shops and restaurants and a whole lot of empty land. The residents didn't seem to mind this. As long as they had clothes on their backs, food in their bellies, and a post office, they were good.

I wasn't.

I'd been born and raised in New York City.

New York City. Eight million people. A power city, a cultural capital, the most linguistically diverse city in the world, a hodgepodge of commerce, finance, media, art, fashion, research, technology, education, and entertainment.

Sighing, I curled up on my side. I missed my city. I missed my father and Kami and Devin. I missed my boys.

But I loved Deuce. And I promised him.

It was late when Deuce pulled into his garage. He shut down his bike and headed inside. The kitchen was his first priority, second was Eva. He hadn't been home in four days, and he was itching to touch her. He couldn't fuck her, something about the baby, but he was solving that problem, usually with Miranda, but Miranda wasn't Eva. None of those whores came close to working him the way Eva could. He couldn't be around her without wanting her and her mouth, and as sweet as it was, it wasn't enough. He wanted inside her. He'd wanted inside her since the Demon barbeque fourteen years ago.

Fucking hell, he was hard just thinking about her.

Bitch made him crazy.

He grabbed a beer and was about to head upstairs, had one foot on the first step, when the sound of incessant female giggling brought him up short. It was a school night, and Danny shouldn't be up at one in the morning. Eva knew this.

Narrowing his eyes, he went left, through the living room, and into the family room. Eva, Danny, and Cage were packed on the loveseat together, their eyes glued to the television. Danny took up the left corner, Cage had the right, his arm slung over the back of the couch, and Eva was curled up in the space between his arm and torso. Cage's fingers were running distractedly through her hair, and her arm was slung over his belly. A dark blue woolen blanket covered the three of them.

He stared. What the fuck was going on?

"Oh my God!" Danny cried, bouncing up and down in her seat. "She's really going to make him a vampire!"

"No way," Eva said. "She won't. She can't. That is just so wrong."

"She could make me a vampire," Cage muttered. "She's so fuckin' hot."

Eva burst out laughing. "You'd give up your life for a nice pair of tits, huh?"

If he wasn't so pissed, he would have laughed. He'd been shot twice for a nice pair of tits.

Cage looked down at Eva and grinned. "For those tits, babe, hell yeah. For yours, too."

Eva snorted.

"Pig," Danny muttered.

"Yep."

"You can be a pig," Eva said, laughing. "As long as you keep rubbing my feet every day." She sighed happily. "Pure heaven, Cage."

Cage's grin turned into a soft smile. "Anything for you, gorgeous."

His fists clenched. Rubbing her fucking feet? Every day? Gorgeous?

"Ha!" Eva shouted, slapping at Danny's arm. "I told you she wouldn't do it!"

"Whatever," Danny muttered with a smile on her lips. "She should have. Eventually, he's going to get old. If I were her, I would have immortalized all that hotness."

He stormed into the room and stopped directly in front of the television.

"Daddy, move," Danny said, trying to look around him.

He didn't.

"Danielle West," he growled, "I wanna know why you're not in bed."

He watched his daughter fold her arms over her chest and scowl at him.

"Today and tomorrow are parent-teacher conferences," Eva said quietly. "No school."

He narrowed his eyes. She was still curled up around his kid. Right in front of him.

"Eva," he barked. "Kitchen."

"Here, babe," Cage said. He shifted his body out from under hers and slipped an arm around her back to help her up. She tottered for a minute, and then both her hands went to her swollen belly.

"Shit," Cage muttered. "Are you having contractions again? Or is it the salt thing?"

"Oh!" Danny cried, jumping to her feet. "Do you need your pills?"

Salt thing? Pills? What the fuck?

"Eva," he growled, growing more agitated by the second. "Get in the fuckin' kitchen!"

"Dad!" Cage yelled. "Shut the fuck up! She's fuckin' sick! Blood pressure's off the charts. Her OB has her coming in nearly every day to check on her!"

What? What and what and huh?

"Why do you know this shit?" he demanded.

"Better question," Cage shot back. "Why the fuck don't you?"

It was either deck his only son or break something, so he whipped his beer bottle across the room. It slammed into the stone fireplace and shattered in a spray of beer.

"Answer me!" he roared. "Why the fuck do you know this shit? And why the fuck were you holdin' her?"

Cage's lip curled. "Who do you think takes her to her doctor's appointments and the fuckin' hospital? Who do you think has to help her in and out of bed and in the fuckin' shower? Sure as fuck ain't you."

His nostrils flared. "You help her in the fuckin' shower?" he hissed.

"Yeah, Daddy," Danny said quietly. "You're never home, and I can't help her all the time. Her doctor said she should be off her feet, and we gotta keep her salt intake low and calm her down when the contractions start by havin' her take warm baths or rubbing her back. Most of the time, they're Braxton Hicks, but because she went into labor already the doctors are worried."

"And who the fuck you think is drivin' Danny to school?" Cage yelled. "And pickin' her up after cheerleadin' practice? And takin' her to fuckin' gymnastics? Mom's fuckin' workin' ten-hour shifts, Eva can't do it anymore, and you're not fuckin' around. That leaves me!"

With tears in her eyes, Eva moved slowly across the room and disappeared into the foyer. He had planned on following her, only Cage wasn't done running his mouth.

"You're doin' it again," he spat. "You're fuckin' everything up. You did it to Mom, and you're doin' it to Eva. You're never fuckin' home, you're leavin' her alone with no one to talk to and nothin' to do, and she's gonna leave, Dad, if you don't stop sleepin' at the club and fuckin' whores. And, fuck you, but I don't want her to leave and neither does Danny. Havin' her here has been fuckin' awesome; she's cool to talk with, she's fuckin' fun, and she makes shit feel good, better than it has in a long time. And you're fuckin' it all up 'cause you're a fuckin' selfish asshole!"

Danny moved to stand in front of Cage and took a protective stance. "Yeah, Daddy."

He had to take several deep breaths so he didn't end up saying something he didn't mean. Done breathing, he turned and left the room.

Deuce entered the kitchen shortly after I did. He walked right by me without as much as a glance my way and headed for the refrigerator. I bit my tongue. I had been biting my tongue a lot lately, but I couldn't fathom anything good coming out of a heart-to-heart when he just got into a fight with his kids.

Instead, I tried to think of something to talk to him about and kept coming up empty. I didn't have a clue what he'd been doing lately—not for work, not with his boys, nothing.

"I got served," I blurted out.

Empty-handed, he closed the refrigerator and turned around. "What?"

"Served," I repeated. "Chase wants a paternity test, and he's court-ordered me to have it done."

He blinked.

"When did that fuckin' asshole doctor say the conception date was?"

I took a step backward. "Deuce, why are—"

"When, Eva? Fuckin' when?"

"The end of June," I whispered. "But it's not always accurate."

"Really?" he sneered. "Is it not accurate 'cause it was the beginnin' of fuckin' June when we fucked?"

I stared up at him, speechless.

"Jumped from my fuckin' bed straight into Frankie's, jumped from Frankie's right back into mine, and then from mine straight to fuckin' Chase's bed! That fuckin' kid could be Frankie's, couldn't it?"

"Stop!" I cried. "You know it wasn't like that! You showed up, and you had Frankie locked up, and I was a wreck, and you were you, and I have never been able to be rational around you. I just wanted to be with you one more time! Chase was a mistake! I was trying to help Frankie, but then I was trying to hurt Frankie, and then I just wanted to hurt myself, and I was so fucked-up in the head. And I don't know, Deuce! I just don't know!"

"No, you never fuckin' did know shit, did ya? Didn't know your old man had cameras in his fuckin' stairwell. Didn't know Frankie wasn't just crazy but a fuckin' homicidal maniac. Didn't know Chase fuckin' loved you, didn't know he was hole-punchin' the fuckin' condoms so he could knock you up and keep you! Don't even fuckin' know who put that fuckin' bastard inside you!"

Chase was what? Oh my God. *OhmyGodohmyGodohmyGod…*

"Yeah," Deuce sneered. "Now you get it. Now when it's too fuckin' late. That's his fuckin' kid in you, and then he's gonna play that fuckin' card. And I fuckin' know you, shit starts to get hard, you get upset, you're gonna run."

"Where am I going to run to?" I demanded. "Since you know everything, you tell me where I am going to run to!"

"Back to Daddy," he said darkly. "Back to the fuckin' club. Back to where it's safe, and you don't gotta deal with your fuckin' life 'cause you got a whole shitload of men who'll deal with it for ya. And then you can keep tryin' to save Frankie 'cause that's all you've ever done with yourself, and you don't have a fuckin' clue what to do when you're not tryin' to save him. And you and Chase can get back to beatin' each other senseless, fuckin' each other in public and gettin' off on it, 'cause you both fuckin' hate yourselves and your fucked-up lives."

I felt my face get hot. I was angry, but I was also embarrassed. Deuce had just aired my dirty laundry in a house with an open floor plan. I had no doubt Danny and Cage had heard everything.

"Shoulda never fuckin' laid a hand on you," he spat.

My heart seized. "What?" I whispered.

"You heard me, bitch. I wish I never fuckin' touched you. Never fuckin' met you. You've done nothin' but fuck with my life."

As if he'd slapped me, I staggered backward, reaching for the countertop to steady myself.

"Deuce," I whispered. "Please take that back."

He didn't. He didn't say anything at all. Just turned away from me and left.

Chapter
SEVENTEEN

I stormed into the clubhouse on a mission. Deuce hadn't been home in over a week. He wouldn't answer his cell phone, and his boys were covering for him.

I made it to the back hall when Cox was suddenly in front of me, pushing me back.

"I'll get him for you, babe, just hold tight."

"Fuck off," I hissed, shoving him back. "I'm not stupid. I know what he's doing back there!"

Cox grimaced. "I let you in there, he'll kill me."

"Then write out your will because nothing short of a bullet is going to stop me from going in there."

"Foxy," he said quietly, "I can't let you back there."

I glared up at him. "Are you shitting me?"

"No, babe. He will take my cut if I let you back there."

"Fine, Cox, you wanna play with me? Things are going pretty good with you and Kami so far, right? Been going back and forth and seeing Devin, getting to know him? Been lying to his mother, telling her you left your wife and all sorts of other bullshit just so you can keep fucking her, right?"

Cox's face went tight. "Eva," he warned, "you can't—"

"Shut up," I hissed. "I can, and I will. I will tell her not only have you not left your wife, but that you are still fucking everything on two legs that comes your way. So, what's it gonna be, Cox? Are you going to let me back there, or are you going to lose Kami?"

Glaring at me, he moved out of my way and swept his arm to the side. "Go right ahead, you fuckin' bitch."

Deuce's door was locked, but the doorknob was cheap. Two solid fist drops to the top, and it busted. I kicked the door open, and Deuce's eyes flew open.

"Eva!" Miranda exclaimed, turning red. "You're here!"

Deuce was pushing out from underneath her, pulling himself up into a sitting position. His eyes were bloodshot and unfocused, courtesy of the empty bottle of Jack lying on the floor next to the bed.

"I'm not here," I informed her. "I just need to tell him something, and then I'm gone."

She started getting up, and I signaled her to stop. "You should stay," I told her. "After I'm done with him, he'll probably need to fuck you again."

"You stupid fuckin' bitch," Deuce growled. "Get the fuck outta my club."

That hurt worse than walking in on him and Miranda. If he truly loved me, I didn't understand why he didn't want me to be part of his life.

Miranda scrambled off the bed. "I'm...uh...I'm gonna go."

Without bothering to find her clothing, if she'd even had any to begin with, she took off down the hall.

"How the fuck did you get back here?" Deuce yelled.

I shrugged. "I'm a whore. I jumped a couple of beds."

Deuce was instantly sober and across the room. Gripping my bicep, he started dragging me out of his room and down the hallway. Butt naked.

"Since you're kicking me out, I'll make this quick," I told him. "I get why you're mad about Chase, but Frankie is different. I've loved Frankie for as long as I can remember."

Deuce's face went hard, and he started walking faster, forcing me to scramble just to keep up with him.

"We grew up together; we went through a lot together. He was always there for me, and I was always there for him. He lost everything at a very young age. He latched on to me as a child, and it was in no way sexual. It wasn't until later that he needed me for that as well."

Deuce yanked me to a stop. "Needed you for that?" he hissed. "Do you have any idea how fucked that sounds?"

"Yes!" I shot back. "But I loved him! I wanted to help him!"

"You're sick, babe." He started walking again, dragging me with him. "Frankie made you sick."

"Yeah," I yelled. "I know!"

"What do you fuckin' know?"

"I know I'm fucked-up. I know I've been fucked-up for a long time. I know I don't know the first thing about a normal relationship because fucked-up is all I've ever known, but I have been trying so hard to make us work! I also know that I am sick of your bullshit! You made me promises, and I left my entire life for you! And you bring me to the middle of nowhere and dump me in a house with your kids and expect me to be your old lady when you knew, *you fucking knew*, that was the last thing I wanted. So I let you treat me like a piece of fucking furniture who'd be right where you left me every time you decided to grace me with your presence because I promised you I wouldn't run. But I can't do it anymore!"

"Cox!" he bellowed, making me jump. A heartbeat later Cox appeared at the end of the hall.

Deuce shoved me forward. "Get her the fuck outta here. Make sure she gets home and stays there."

Cox didn't move. "Sorry, Prez. I'm not draggin' an angry pregnant bitch that just caught her man slammin' a whore anywhere. I like my fuckin' balls where they are."

I swiveled on Deuce. "Don't worry about it. I'm leaving. You have whores to attend to, and I have fucking life I'd like to start living!"

I whirled on Cox, and he took a step back.

"And you! I don't give a shit how you treat your wife. I don't care if you want to fuck every man, woman, and dog on the planet, but you keep fucking with my girl, and I will end it! You assholes love to spout off about brotherhood and the code of the road, but you never think about the trail of women you're leaving behind you, and I'll be fucking damned if one of those women is going to be Kami!"

"Jesus, Eva," he whispered. "What the fuck did I ever do to you?"

"Not me," I hissed. "Kami. She is not club ass, and I won't let you treat her like it!"

"GET THE FUCK OUT!" Deuce bellowed.

"I'M GOING!" I screamed.

I made it two steps outside the door when blinding hot pain shot through my lower back. More pain followed; my vision swam as my belly tightened painfully, and sharp stabbing sensations prickled across my midsection. My hands flew to my stomach. "No!" I cried. "Please, God, no!"

"Bitch caught you with your cock in Miranda and didn't even flinch."

Deuce glared across the bar at Cox. "Whose fuckin' fault is that?"

Cox glared right back. "Prez, she already knew what you were doin'. Bitch had your number before she even got here. Bitch has everyone's number. I'm startin' to think she knows us better than we know ourselves."

Blue threw back a shot and cleared his throat. "'Course, Foxy's got us tagged. She's a biker brat who grew up in a club full of brothers who fuckin' love her more than they love their old ladies."

"That's the fuckin' problem," he muttered. "Bitch doesn't know her place 'cause Preacher's a fuckin' idiot."

Blue shook his head. "Son, you are a fuckin' moron. You wanna know what I see? I see a girl who isn't just a girl, but a fuckin' prize, and why the fuck she chose an asshole like you to give that fuckin' prize to I haven't a fuckin' clue. Stupid if you ask me.

"But you're throwin' it all away 'cause you can't stop fuckin' whores and 'cause you're refusing to give her a piece of the club. Not a lot to ask, if you ask me, but since you ain't askin', I'll shut the fuck up and let you be a fuckin' moron."

He glared at Blue. If the bastard weren't so damn old, he would be in a world of hurt right now.

"You need to start bein' straight with yourself," Mick said quietly, speaking up for the first time. "You're not really mad at her; you're fuckin' jealous."

He looked around the bar at his somber-faced boys. "What the fuck?" he yelled. "Why are you all gangin' up on me?"

Mick shook his head. "Just givin' it to you straight, Prez. You need to man up and admit it. You're jealous of Frankie for gettin' her for all those years, for gettin' to marry her, for her undyin', misplaced loyalty to his crazy ass. You're jealous of Chase just 'cause he got a taste, and she liked what he was givin', and you're jealous of that fuckin' baby inside her 'cause you're thinkin' it might not be yours, and you want that kid so bad to be yours 'cause you want so bad to own that bitch that you ain't seein' shit straight.

"You've had a hard-on for Eva Fox for a long time now, and you're so used to either fuckin' her or fightin' with her or losin' her that you don't even realize you finally got her. That bitch loves you, has for a long time now. You're not the only one who's known her for a grip. I saw the way she was lookin' at you way back when in Chicago. She was just a kid then, but fuck me if she didn't think the world of ya."

Tap nodded. "He's right, Prez. Don't think you're gonna be gettin' another chance this time. She looks tired as hell, can see it on her face. I'm bettin' Frankie wore her down somethin' fierce with his bullshit. Only so much bein' shit on a woman can take before she just can't take it no more. Look at me. Tara left, split to Atlanta. Now she's shacked up with some computer programmer, who my baby girl is tellin' me is a big fat dork—her words, not mine. But I'm guessin' he couldn't fight a fly if he had to. But Tara wants him and not me 'cause I didn't treat her right, and he treats her like a goddamn queen."

He didn't know how to respond to that—mostly because it was all true—so he tossed back another shot instead. Mick smirked at him. Fucking asshole.

He wasn't doing right by Eva; he knew that. His old habits were dying hard. But he couldn't afford to go soft and get weak, and Eva made him soft and weak. Spending too much time with her and he'd end up gluing her to his side. He needed the space. He needed a clear head. Didn't want to drop the ball.

Shit.

He didn't know what to do. Half of him wanted her to go home, and the other half stopped breathing at the thought.

"PREZ!" Hands and arms covered in blood, ZZ came barreling across the room.

"Eva!" he said breathlessly. "She's not talkin'…eyes are closed…so much fuckin' blood…called an ambulance…"

He didn't hear the rest because he was running out the door.

Chapter  EIGHTEEN

Deuce sat in the hospital waiting room in the same position he'd been in for four days, elbows propped on his knees and face in his hands.

He fucked up a lot in his life, but he never fucked up this bad.

He'd gotten Eva so fucking upset she'd gone into labor six weeks early and nearly bled out doing it. Doctors had done an emergency C-section, and now there was a tiny baby girl in an incubator with tubes up her nose because she couldn't fucking breathe on her own, and a woman—*his woman*—who was refusing to speak to him because he was a fucked-up asshole who was out fucking other women when he had the one he wanted in his house, in his bed, and hanging with his kids.

"Prez?" Jase nudged him with his elbow.

"What?" he muttered.

"Kami's here."

He looked up and found a miniature Cox smiling at him. He smiled at Devin and looked higher. Devin's crazy mother was scowling at him. He scowled back.

"Chase is dead," she bit out angrily.

He blinked. OK. Well…that wasn't exactly bad news.

"So what?" he said. "Saves me the time."

Kami drew her brows together, looking less angry and more confused. "It wasn't you?" she said.

He jumped up and got in her face. "Bitch, you crazy? You don't fucking talk about that shit in public! Fact, *you* don't talk about that shit ever!"

"I'm sorry!" she yelled. "You'll have to forgive me! I tend not to think clearly when I find out my best friend almost lost her baby and her life, and not five minutes later I have the NYPD at my door informing me that my husband was tortured for hours, then gutted! Fuck, Deuce, they said his insides were strung around his Christmas tree! He was so mutilated they wouldn't even let me see his body!"

His blood ran cold. Turned into motherfucking ice.

"Ripper!" he barked.

Ripper was already on his feet, pulling out his cell phone. "On it, Prez," he said, heading for the exit.

"What's going on?" Kami demanded.

"Daddy!" Devin squealed and took off running.

"Shit," Tap muttered, nodding toward the hospital entrance. "Anna's with him."

Jase shrugged. "His own fault. Havin' babies all over the world."

"He's still with his wife?" Kami hissed.

It took Cox a millisecond to realize what he'd just walked in on. Deuce watched him have a millisecond of a freak-out before dropping down on one knee. He caught Devin as the kid launched himself at him.

"Hey, little man," he said gruffly, squeezing him tight.

"What the hell?" Anna shrieked.

Still holding Devin, Cox shot to his feet. "Not in front of my fuckin' kid, bitch."

Kami crossed the room and held out her arms to Cox. "I can see you still have things to *take care of*," she sneered. "So give me Devin while you do that."

Nostrils flaring, Cox handed him over.

"Go sit down over there, baby," she whispered, pointing to a chair across the room. Devin scurried off.

"You fucked this skinny blonde bitch?" Anna screeched. "You had a goddamn kid with her?"

Cox closed his eyes. "Jesus, Anna, get a fuckin' grip; we're in a hospital."

"Yeah!" she screamed. "And I just found out you are still fucking around on me!"

"Did you seriously just call me a bitch, you fucking bitch!" Kami shrieked.

Before this shit went full-blown soap opera, Deuce grabbed Cox and pulled him aside. "Chase is dead. His insides strung around a Christmas tree. Three fuckin' guesses who did it. Get one of your bitches out of here before there's a fuckin' cat fight in the hospital my fuckin' woman almost died in, and I'm just suggestin' that it might be Anna you wanna get rid of, seein' as Kami's Eva's girl. And the only way you'll get her outta here is a lot of kickin' and screamin', which will upset my fuckin' woman—and if you upset my woman, that's gonna end bad for you."

Sighing, Cox turned away. "On it, Prez," he muttered. "Tap."

"Prez?"

"Call all the boys. I want round-the-clock guard on Eva and my girls. Cage, too. Best make that discreet though."

"On it."

Ripper rejoined the group. One look at his boy's face, and he knew the news wasn't good.

"Frankie?" he asked.

Ripper nodded. "Killed three inmates last week, was gettin' transferred upstate because of it. During transport, he killed all four guards, and from what I heard, the way he did 'em in, shit wasn't pretty. A real fuckin' gore fest. He's been tagged for the Henderson hit, too. Law's gunnin' for him. He's runnin' scared. Or knowin' Frankie, he's runnin' happy. And no doubt he's gunnin' for Eva."

Kami's eyes went saucer-wide, and she threw herself at Ripper. "He's going to kill my Evie!" she cried.

"No, baby, not gonna happen," Ripper whispered soothingly, rubbing her back while he grinned over her head at Cox. Cox, who had since escorted his hysterical wife outside and returned alone, froze when he saw this.

"Keep fuckin' touchin' her, asshole, and you ain't gonna have hands!"

"Fuck off," Kami hissed. "Since you're still fucking your wife and probably half the state of Montana, I've decided I'm going to fuck Ripper!"

Ripper, who couldn't care less that Cox was two seconds from snapping his neck, kept rubbing Kami and grinning like a fool.

"You really want to make him jealous, Kami?" Jase said. "You could give me a try."

Scrubbing his hands over his face, Deuce left the group of idiots in the waiting area and headed for Eva's room.

Danny met him at the door. She was wearing her pink sweatsuit from three days ago and looked damn exhausted.

"No, Daddy. Bad idea."

He took a deep breath. "Bad shit goin' down, baby girl. I know she's hatin' me right now, but I gotta talk to her. 'Sides, you need to take a shower and get some sleep. Call your brother and go home."

Reluctantly, she stepped aside, and he entered the room, closing the door behind him. The dark curtains were drawn tightly; the room dark and shadowed. Eva was lying in bed on her side. She looked pale and weak, had dark circles around her eyes, and had an IV in her arm. When she saw him, she turned away.

"Go away," she whispered hoarsely.

His chest tightened. "Baby, I can't. We gotta talk."

He rounded her hospital bed so he could see her face, and she immediately rolled to her other side.

"No, we don't. Go away."

OK, different tactic.

"Eva. Chase is dead."

He watched her body go rigid.

"He was tortured," he continued. "Gutted. Insides strung up on his own Christmas tree."

Eva dragged herself into a sitting position, clutching her abdomen. "Where's Frankie?" she whispered.

"Off the grid."

"Oh my God. Chase…oh my God…this is all my fault…he didn't…I…*oh my God*—"

"Baby." He gripped her face and forced her to look at him. "Listen to me good. Chase knew what he was getting into when he made that deal with you. He knew Frankie personally, and he worked Frankie's cases. He knew exactly how fucked in the head Frankie is and what he is capable of. Thing is, he wanted you so bad he didn't care."

A tear rolled down her cheek. "He didn't deserve that. I mean, no one deserves that, but Chase really didn't deserve that," she whispered. "He could be a jerk, but he wasn't a bad person. He just wanted to be loved; he wanted a family to love and to love him…he just didn't know how…Oh God, Chase…*Oh God*…"

She was grieving; he got that, but the last thing he wanted was to hear her cry for an asshole she had fucked and had feelings for.

Feeling the jealousy start to creep up and the anger that followed, he sat down beside Eva, took her mouth, and kissed her hard.

She didn't fight him, and they shared a long, slow kiss, full of wet lips and greedy tongues. When he pulled away, Eva pressed her forehead against his and sighed into his mouth.

"How is she?" she whispered.

He cleared his head. The baby—she was talking about the baby. "She's still not breathin' on her own, babe."

Biting her lip, she nodded. "It's not your fault," she whispered.

Yeah, it was. He opened his mouth to protest, but she placed her finger over his lips.

"It was a difficult pregnancy. It's not your fault."

His chest compressed, and he sucked in air. He didn't deserve her. He never had. He never would.

"I named her," she said softly. "Ivy Olivia West. Ivy because it's sort of still Christmastime, and Olivia after—"

"My mom," he said hoarsely, feeling like the biggest piece of shit in the world.

"Deuce?"

"Yeah, babe?"

"The birth certificate. What do you want me to do?"

"Nothin'," he whispered. "I'll fill it out. She's my kid."

She locked on to his eyes, sucking him in, holding him still, and making him so fucking crazy. Always making him crazy.

"Deuce?"

"Yeah?"

"No more women."

Fuck.

"Yeah, babe, I know. I've been fuckin' up."

"You get angry at me, and you want to take it out on pussy, you take it out on mine. It won't matter how mad I am; I will never deny you." She gave a shaky laugh that made his chest ache. He'd fucking hurt his woman real bad.

"Eva, baby," he said softly, "there's not gonna be any more women. Already moved Miranda out and cut all ties. I promised you I'd fuckin' earn you, and it's 'bout time I started doin' that."

She let out a shuddery sigh that only made him feel worse.

"I love you, Deuce," she whispered. "So, so much."

He stared at her, she stared at him, and he knew exactly why his boys had railed at him. She did love him. He was her world. He knew because he could see it in her big gray eyes. Suddenly, the past didn't fucking matter anymore.

She wasn't going to run, and he was going to treat her like the goddamn queen she was.

Chapter  NINETEEN

For the first time in a long time, Deuce knew true peace.

Three months went by, and Ivy was discharged.

Eva turned half his room at the club into a nursery.

Then the crazy bitch gave Danny her own room at the club and helped her decorate the fucking thing, too. Pink and purple as far as the eye could see. He flipped his fucking shit. Put a steel door on her room with a sliding deadbolt. Put bars on her window. Lined all his boys up and told them straight up his baby girl was off-fucking-limits. Told them if any of them looked at her the wrong way, they were going to ground.

Not one of them so much as looked at her. In fact, they stopped talking to her altogether.

Shit moved forward.

Life got good. Real fucking good.

Kami and Devin moved to Montana to be near Eva and Ivy. Not Cox. Kami swore up and down Cox had nothing to do with her decision. Deuce might have believed her if she hadn't been in Cox's lap while she was spouting her bullshit.

He turned forty-nine.

Cox left his wife and moved in with Kami.

Danny got a boyfriend.

Danny's boyfriend broke up with her, and Deuce swore he had nothing to do with that.

Cox finalized his divorce. He put a diamond ring on Kami's finger. She didn't like it and bought herself a bigger, more expensive one. And matching earrings. He thought he heard Cox muttering about taking away her Internet access—something about shoes that cost several thousand dollars.

Devin turned five.

Cox bought him a dirt bike, and Kami beat the crap out of him with a cooking pot.

Eva turned thirty-one.

Kami kicked Cox out—something about not liking the way he'd been looking at a supermarket cashier. He was more interested in how she managed to get Cox into a supermarket.

The boys had a new tag made for him, the back of which read FOXY. He managed to punch three of them in the face before they all turned tail and ran. Then he put it on.

And grinned.

Summer was good to the club. Lots of business. Lots of coin rolling in. Two of his boys got married. The club voted in three new brothers.

Eva's ass deflated—not that he cared. He'd take Eva any which way he could get her. Thin, curvy, juicy as hell. A fucking blimp. What the fuck ever. It had never been her body that kept him tied to her. Shit with Eva went a hell of a lot deeper than looks. Although those tits of hers...and those lips...

And God knows those fucking eyes made him damn crazy.

Cox and Kami got married; she let him move back in.

Ivy turned one. She took one look at her Hello Kitty birthday cake, Danny's idea, and did a face-plant dead center. A picture of her covered in cake and frosting—her white-flecked blue eyes glittering, grinning her old man's grin—was sitting front and center on his desk.

He started planning something big. Something real fucking special for his woman.

Then one summer day it all blew to smithereens.

Chapter
TWENTY

Ivy, Deuce, and I walked hand in hand through the club's large backyard. Country music was blaring through several strategically placed speakers. Three large grills were already lit and cooking up hot dogs, hamburgers, and steaks as bikers and their wives, girlfriends, and children were milling around, drinking beer or soda, talking animatedly with each other.

Smiling.

Dancing.

Happy.

Deuce squeezed my hand. "Babe, go get busy with woman shit; I gotta talk to Ripper."

Before I called him any one of the assortment of names I had stashed away for all of his chauvinistic bullshit, I hurried off to a long table displaying several different varieties of macaroni salad, chips and dips, pretzels, and assorted veggies. Dorothy stood behind the table, wearing a black apron over her cute pink sundress, dishing out food.

I kicked off my sandals and went to help her.

"Hey," I whispered, nudging her with my hip. "You OK?"

Biting her bottom lip, she shook her head. "I'm never OK when I have to watch him with her."

I followed her line of sight to Jase, his wife, Chrissy, and their three kids. Thirteen years he had been messing with Dorothy; she was thirty-three now, and he still hadn't made good on any of the promises he'd made her. She'd left her husband for him; her daughter was sixteen, headed for college next fall, and she was going to be all alone. It was none of my business, but that didn't mean I had to like it.

"Take a break," I suggested. "I got this covered."

Her eyes went wide. "You're Deuce's old lady."

I shrugged. "So? I'm pretty sure that doesn't mean I can't serve noodles."

Shaking her head, but smiling, she untied her apron and handed it to me. "Thanks," she whispered and ran off. Jase turned away from Chrissy and watched her flee the barbeque and disappear inside the clubhouse. Frowning, he whispered something in Chrissy's ear—who nodded and smiled—and took off after Dorothy.

"Eva?"

I turned back to the table and found Cox's ex-wife, Anna, standing in front of me. She'd cut her long black hair short; it looked good.

"Hey," I said. "Dropping Mary Catherine off?"

She nodded and pointed to her preteen daughter who was laughing, chasing after Devin.

"Food?" I lifted up a plate in offering.

She wrinkled up her nose. "No thanks. I'm trying to lose weight."

I looked her over, wondering where she needed to lose weight.

"Hi, Eva! Anna!" Chrissy sauntered over. She was gorgeous. Tall, lithe, big perky breasts, long auburn hair. With her perfect tan and perfectly shaped and symmetrical features, she was an all-American wet dream. She was everything Dorothy wasn't. Hell, she was everything I wasn't. Good thing I didn't give a crap.

"Chrissy," Anna said, greeting her.

"Are you two coming to yoga tomorrow?" Chrissy asked, bouncing up and down in her cutoff jean shorts and tight white tank top, drawing the attention of every biker within thirty feet. Even Deuce.

I glared at him. He flashed me a mouth-watering grin before turning around and resuming his conversation.

"Yep," I said. Chrissy and her yoga classes had been my saving grace. I had lost all my pregnancy weight and then some.

"Yep," Anna said. "God knows I need it."

I shook my head. Anna had gone a little nuts after Cox left her.

"Awesome!" Chrissy cried and started bouncing again.

"Where's Dorothy?" ZZ bellowed from across the lawn, trying to be heard over the music.

I raised my palms in an I-don't-know gesture and yelled back, "What do you need?"

"Lighter fluid!"

I gave him a thumbs-up and headed inside.

I was halfway down the hall of bedrooms when I heard loud moaning coming from Jase's room. I headed that way, knowing exactly what I was going to find.

Sure enough, with his pants around his ankles, Jase had Dorothy pinned up against the wall, her dress pushed up to her waist.

"I fuckin' love you," he rasped. "You don't even know, D. You don't even fuckin' know."

Dorothy, whose face was buried in Jase's neck, whimpered.

Quietly, I reached around the door to press the lock button, and then silently pulled it closed, testing it to make sure it was indeed locked. Chrissy did not need to walk in on that.

Dorothy didn't deserve to be led on, either.

But it was typical. And there was nothing I could do.

A short time later Dorothy returned to the barbeque, looking flushed. Together, we watched Jase leave the clubhouse and head back to Chrissy. Chrissy curled herself around him while he stared at Dorothy, promising her with his eyes all sorts of things I knew he would never make good on.

"He's finally going to leave her," she whispered, her eyes on Jase.

I pressed my lips together and looked down at the serving spoon in my hands. He was never going to leave Chrissy; he loved her in his own fucked-up way. He loved Dorothy, too. He had whittled his female admirers down to just the two of them and had no plans on leaving either.

Thankfully, Deuce appeared beside me, saving me from having to respond to her.

He looked quizzically between us, and then followed Dorothy's gaze to Jase and frowned.

"D," he said in a low voice. She glanced over and blushed.

"Sorry," she whispered.

"Can't have you pissin' off my old ladies and makin' shit hard for my boys, D."

"I know," she whispered. "I'll go if you want."

I dragged him a good distance away. "It's his fault," I hissed. "He followed her inside and did 'you know what'!"

Deuce raised an eyebrow. "You know what?" he repeated, smirking.

I folded my arms across my chest, and his gaze zeroed in on the cleavage that had just popped out of my deep purple sundress.

"Can we go do 'you know what'?" he asked, grinning.

I rolled my eyes. "No."

"Please?"

I fought my smile and lost. He ran his knuckles down my cheek.

"Got you a present," he said softly.

"A big, sweaty man present?" I asked.

Deuce grinned. "That, too. Come on."

He grabbed my hand, led me inside the club, past the bedrooms, through the living area, and pushed open the front doors.

"All yours, babe."

I blinked rapidly. Then I forgot how to blink and just gaped at the priceless beauty in front of me.

"No," I whispered.

"Babe. Yeah."

Solid cast aluminum wheels, a beefy front fork, and a wide-bodied fuel tank. Twin shocks tucked neatly out of sight, the rigid-mounted Twin Cam 96B engine, the chrome over/under dual exhaust, and the five-gallon fuel tank.

I was in shock.

"Boys who did the custom work gave me a whole lotta shit 'bout those sparkles, darlin'. You fuckin' owe me."

It wasn't as if he had the entire bike custom sparkled—just the seat—and I absolutely loved it.

"I can't believe you remembered," I breathed, running my hand over my bike. My perfect, perfect bike.

"Cutest kid I ever met. And at Rikers, no less. Talkin' 'bout sparkly Fat Boys and pink fuckin' helmets with skulls on them and tellin' me straight up you were gonna be queen of an MC. That was your dream, babe. I'm your man. You feelin' me?"

Oh my God. He'd made me queen. Because he was my man and that was my dream. My man made my dream come true.

He got me my sparkly Fat Boy.

And my pink helmet with skulls on it.

I turned, grinning so wide it hurt, and poked him in the chest. "You love me."

He snorted.

"Babe. Yeah."

I launched myself at him. Gripping my waist, he swung me up and into his arms. Our mouths crashed together, and we kissed the way we always kissed—

desperate, hungry, full of such crazed intensity that if bottled could power an entire city.

Sheesh. He so loved me. Just…sheesh.

"Hey," I said softly and cupped his cheek.

"Yeah?"

"What about your dream?"

His face went dimples. "I'm lookin' at it, darlin'."

Oh. Crap. My heart felt near bursting. I was absolutely done for. This man owned me, body and soul, and everything in between.

"I wanna go do 'you know what' now," I whispered.

"That's good, babe," he whispered back. "Real fuckin' good."

We fell onto our bed in a tangle, kissing feverishly, tearing at each other's clothing. "Love you," I breathed, "so, so much."

He pushed the straps of my dress down my shoulders and spread kisses along my collarbone. His mouth traveled lower with his hands pulling my dress down as he went. I threaded my fingers through his hair, moaning and begging him for more.

Using the tip of his tongue, he traced the scar from my C-section.

"Fuckin' love you, baby," he rasped.

Then he got to his feet and tugged my underwear off. Lifting my legs, I rubbed my grass-stained feet over his bare torso and giggled.

Grinning, he unzipped his jeans. "You want it hard?" he asked gruffly.

I bit my lip and shook my head. "I want it slow, baby."

His eyes went soft. "Fuck," he murmured. "I just wanna look at you, babe. I just wanna stand here and look at you until I can convince myself you're really fuckin' here, and you're not goin' nowhere, and you really want me."

I closed my eyes, letting his words sink inside of me.

"Get the fuck off her, *motherfucker*, before I blow a hole through your fuckin' skull!"

My eyes flew open. I knew that voice.

Frankie appeared from behind Deuce and moved to his side, pressing the barrel of a gun into Deuce's temple. He was a mess. Filthy. His hair was greasy, his beard was long and unkempt, and his clothing was full of holes and covered in stains.

"Horseman!" Frankie bellowed. "I said back the fuck up!"

Nostrils flaring, his expression murderous, Deuce zipped up his jeans and backed slowly away. I hurriedly pushed myself into a sitting position and pulled my dress up.

"Don't fuckin' move, cunt," Frankie hissed at me. Turning, he tossed a pair of handcuffs at Deuce, who caught them one-handed.

"Cuff yourself to the radiator," he demanded.

Deuce stared at him. "No fuckin' way," he growled.

"No?" Frankie grabbed a fistful of my hair and yanked me across the bed. The barrel of his gun felt cool against my neck. "You want her to die?"

Shaking with fury, Deuce bent down beside the radiator under our bedroom window, clasped a cuff around one of the steel bars and the other around his right wrist.

Frankie turned back to me, grinning.

"Been watchin' you, baby," he said. "Been watchin' you a long fuckin' time now." He leaned over the bed and got up in my face.

"Been watchin' you fuck this asshole!"

Trembling, I stared into Frankie's dark eyes. "You killed Chase. You butchered him."

"Yeah," he sneered, standing up straight. He shook his head and laughed. "Fucker screamed like a girl, too."

I felt the acidic burn of bile rise in the back of my throat.

"You didn't think I knew, did ya? But I did. Every time he'd come to fuckin' talk to me, I saw it in his eyes. Him thinkin' he was pullin' one over on me. Thinkin' he could get away with fuckin' my wife."

"I did it for you," I whispered.

Still gripping my hair, Frankie yanked me to my knees and slapped me across the face. "You fuckin' the Horseman for me, too?"

Holding my cheek, I stared up at him.

"Frankie," I whispered, "please don't do this."

"Get on your fuckin' stomach, bitch," Frankie snarled, releasing my hair and shoving me down. "Gonna show you and this fuckin' asshole who really fuckin' owns ya."

Deuce made a strangled noise in the back of his throat, and my eyes shot to him. He was six feet four inches and two hundred and fifty pounds of murderous rage. He pulled on the handcuffs so hard his hand was bleeding. His body was strung bowstring tight, his veins were bulging out of his arms and neck, and his eyes were bugging out of his skull. He was vibrating—literally vibrating—with hate.

Trembling, trying to blink back the tears burning in my eyes for Deuce's sake, I shifted onto my stomach and turned my head to the side, keeping my gaze on Deuce.

"Been gettin' sloppy fuckin' seconds from this fuckin' asshole for too fuckin' long," Frankie muttered as he shoved my dress up and spread my legs apart. "That's gonna fuckin' stop today."

I heard his belt buckle open, the slide of his zipper, then I felt his weight, and he began pushing inside of me. I bit my lip to keep from crying and kept my eyes on Deuce.

His eyes never once left mine. He kept me with him and held me tight inside his eyes, where it was safe and warm and no one could hurt me.

Deuce had been beaten within an inch of his life.

He had been strangled, stabbed, and shot.

He had shot, stabbed, strangled, beaten, and killed.

He'd been hurt, scared, mad, angry as fuck, and homicidally inclined.

Fuck, he had been so fucking pissed off he had his old man killed. His own flesh and blood.

But never, NEVER, had he felt like this.

There wasn't a word powerful enough to describe what he was feeling or to convey what was happening inside of him. It was beyond words and surpassed all emotions.

It was living death.

He was living through motherfucking death.

His eyes never left Eva's. As long as he held her gaze, she remained impassive, a little lost even, as if she had detached from her body and was taking shelter inside his. It was all he could fucking give her, and it wasn't even close to enough. This should never have happened. He'd gotten lax thinking Frankie wasn't a threat anymore. This was his fault, and Eva was paying for it. He was paying for it.

Frankie wasn't hurting her, not physically. Emotionally, mentally, yeah—but physically, he was being gentle, touching her with the sure knowledge of a man who knew how to pleasure his woman, knew what she liked, what would make her come, kissing her bared skin, stroking her relentlessly, and making it nearly impossible for her to control her body's reaction to what he was doing.

Worse, this wasn't new to her. Frankie had raped her before; he was sure of it. His Eva had become accustomed to forced sex, had taught herself to make the best of it, to fucking enjoy it because she'd known Frankie wasn't ever going to let her go.

It was killing him. Every dip of his mattress, every one of Frankie's grunts, and every harsh intake of breath and whimper from Eva…was killing him.

Frankie said he'd been watching them. He knew just how much he loved Eva. And he knew that this would kill him—slowly—day after day, week after week, year after fucking year.

Chase had gotten off easy.

In his peripheral vision, he saw Frankie get up on his knees and lift Eva's hips. His hand snaked around her waist and dipped between her thighs. Eva lost her battle. Her breath caught and her eyes rolled back, even as tears streamed down her face. Her legs quaking, she went face first into the pillow, crying out softly through her orgasm. Frankie followed her down, groaning loudly, his body jerking.

Then Frankie turned to him. And grinned.

Living death.

He cried for the first time in forty-four years. He cried exactly three silent tears. But for him, it was a fucking waterfall.

Chapter
TWENTY-ONE

6:38 p.m.

Deuce blinked up at Cox.

"Prez?" Cox whispered hoarsely, staring at his cuffed hand.

"My girls?" he asked numbly. "Ivy, Danny?"

"With Kami," Cox whispered. "Where's Foxy?"

"Gone," he said brokenly. "Frankie."

Cox dropped to his knees and tested the cuffs. As if he hadn't already. As if he wasn't missing most of the skin on his hand and hadn't broken all his fingers trying to get out of it. But his hands were too fucking big. So now he was cuffed to a radiator with a skinless broken hand.

"Gotta get Freebird," Cox said. "He's the only one who can pick cuffs quickly."

Deuce nodded.

Cox paused at the door. "Deuce," he said quietly, "we're gonna get her back."

He didn't look at him.

"He's a dead man, Prez."

No. Frankie wasn't a dead man. *Frankie was a dead man.*

11:11 p.m.

Frankie's entire body twitched violently, something that always happened before he went into a violent rage. I stayed where I was, sitting on the motel bed, watching him closely.

"Can't take much more, Eva. You fuckin' Chase broke me, and then you start fuckin' the Horseman bastard AGAIN. You have his fuckin' baby, and I swear to you I almost killed you a million times. Comin' out of his fuckin' club, playin' with his fuckin' kids in the yard, ridin' on the back of his fuckin' bike. I stood in a line behind you at the bank, holding a knife to the base of your fuckin' spine, ready to kill you and your bastard baby. But I couldn't fuckin' do it! I couldn't hurt you! AND IT FUCKIN' BROKE ME, EVA!"

"Baby," I whispered, trying hard not to think about Frankie killing my daughter. "The cops know you killed Chase. They're looking for you."

He gave me a look that suggested I was the crazy one in the room. "Babe. Who the fuck cares 'bout the cops?"

Suddenly, his eyes bugged out. "You liked fuckin' him, didn't you, bitch? You liked rich boy cock!"

"No," I whispered, swallowing hard. "It's what he wanted in return for getting you out."

Frankie laughed. "Glad I made him eat his own cock. Fuckin' deserved it."

Unable to get the imagery of what he had done to Chase out of my head, my stomach lurched, and I began to gag. Frankie sat down beside me and rubbed circles on my back.

"That's what he did, baby," Frankie whispered, and I could hear the smile on his face. "Gagged and screamed."

My stomach emptied.

9:03 a.m.

Deuce stared at his fucked-up hand. The doctors at the ER couldn't give him a cast because of the lack of skin. They had to set each bone and individually splint his fingers, then they treated and wrapped his skinless hand, and put the whole fucking mess in a sling.

Now he was back at the club, drinking a bottle of scotch, watching Danny play peekaboo with Ivy. He and his boys had searched for hours for any sign of Frankie or Eva and had come up empty. They had no choice but to involve the cops, who hadn't turned up jack shit.

The FBI was going to show up any minute now.

Deuce knew Frankie wasn't going to go back to prison. Men like him would rather die than be behind bars. And this particular man was so fucked in the head, he was going to take Eva down with him. So she could be with him forever.

Fucking hell.

He was going to lose her to Frankie. Again. This time for good.

"Deuce," Kami said, sitting down beside him. "You need anything for the pain?"

He needed Eva. She was *all* he fucking needed. She was all he had ever needed.

"No," he croaked.

She wrapped her skinny arms around him, and he let her hold him because he knew she was hurting just as bad as he was. And truthfully, he needed the fucking comfort.

ZZ looked over from behind the bar and the stacked security monitors there. "Prez. Feds are here."

Ripper stepped out of the hallway. "Prez, go ahead and let 'em in. Boys got shit locked up tight."

He lifted his chin in ZZ's direction. "Get the kids outta here and let the assholes in."

9:07 a.m.

I pulled on my restraints, wincing as the rope chafed painfully against my skin. I was on my stomach, all four of my limbs were tied together behind my back. Frankie had even gone so far as to connect my wrists to my ankles and stuff a pillowcase in my mouth.

All of this just so he could feel safe leaving me here while he went for food.

He didn't trust me, and when Frankie didn't trust someone, it never ended well.

With a lot of maneuvering and an incredible amount of pain, I was able to roll onto my side to relieve the pressure on my lungs and stomach.

I should have listened to Deuce a long time ago. Frankie was beyond saving. This was who he was—who he had always been. Who he would always be.

I had to end this once and for all.

9:14 a.m.

"So what you're trying to tell us, Mr. West, is that despite your state-of-the-art security system, Franklin Deluva was still able to enter your club entirely unnoticed?"

Deuce scowled at Agent Ricardo Quintanilla. He was a short, fat, and bald Mexican who wore clothing a size too small for him. He'd had to deal with him before—many, many times—serving warrants and doing impromptu searches at the club. He had a new partner—a sexy little blonde bitch with a tight ass, big perky tits, and bad attitude. Half his boys were eyeing her like she was a piece of fucking cake. He wanted to stab her in the eye with a screwdriver.

"He musta cased the place for a while," Ripper said, glaring down at Quintanilla. "Knew what cameras to avoid."

Quintanilla surveyed Ripper's face and grimaced. "Deluva's handiwork, I assume," he said, gesturing his cell phone toward Ripper's face. "Seen it before. Only those unlucky bastards were all dead."

"Fuckin' great," Deuce growled. "Let's just keep sittin' 'round here chattin' about the fucks Frankie buried while he starts choppin' up my fuckin' woman."

"Mmmmmmmm," the blonde bitch hummed, tapping her pen against her lips. "Don't you mean Franklin Deluva's woman or maybe Chase Henderson's woman?"

She turned in a circle, doing a survey of the room and all the people in it. "Have you all had Mrs. Fox-Deluva? Is she everyone's woman?"

He shot up off the couch and then Ripper and Jase were on him, pushing him back down.

"Say something else, bitch!" he roared, struggling against his boys. "And you won't live to see another day!"

"Are you threatening a federal agent, Mr. West?" she said. "I'm simply suggesting your woman may have gone willingly with her husband."

"Marie!" Quintanilla bellowed.

"Willingly?" he roared. "He made me watch him rape her! Do you fuckin' get that? I was chained to a fuckin' radiator watchin' my woman gettin' slammed by a fuckin' psychopath, and I couldn't do shit about it!"

He heard a shriek that could have been either Danny or Kami or both. The rest of the club went silent.

Cox sucked in a breath. "Prez," he whispered.

He ignored him. "Listen to me, Agent Cunt," he hissed. "I'm way past threatenin' you. I'm straight ready to fuckin' bury you, so you best hope my boys don't let me go."

"Don't let him go," Quintanilla said dryly. He turned to his partner. "Get the fuck outside."

11:55 a.m.

I wolfed down my cheeseburger and fries. It had been forever since I'd last eaten, and I was starving. Frankie was watching me from the corner of the room near the door, a bottle of vodka between his legs and a blank stare on his face.

"Can I have some?" I whispered, pointing at the half-empty bottle.

He glanced down at the bottle and then back to me, nodding.

I slid off the bed and slowly walked toward him. Stopping a few inches from his feet, I sat down and reached for the bottle. I had just wrapped my fingers around the neck when Frankie's hand clamped down over mine.

I looked up.

A tear slid down Frankie's cheek. "Eva," he whispered, "can't sleep, baby, can't fuckin' sleep. It's been weeks and weeks and weeks…"

My heart skipped.

"Baby," I said, reaching for him. "Come here."

Scrambling to his knees, he engulfed me in his arms and buried his face in my neck. Trembling, my heart breaking, I stroked his hair and his back.

"Remember my prom?" I whispered. "Remember dancing on the roof afterward? We danced and laughed until the sun came up. It was one of the best nights of my life, baby."

His large body sagged against mine, and he started sobbing.

"Oh God, baby, no." I pulled his head up, so I could see his face. "Frankie," I breathed, wiping his tears off his cheeks. "You don't have to cry anymore. I'm here now. I'm never leaving you, never again, baby."

"You can't," he rasped. "I can't sleep without you, and I can't breathe, baby. I can't fuckin' breathe. I feel sick to my stomach all the time."

"Shh," I soothed, stroking his cheeks while battling my own tears. "Make love to me, baby. Let me show you how much I love you."

The familiar taste of his tears mixed with vodka flooded my mouth, and I let myself go for a little while, tasting Frankie for the very last time. His hands traveled my body, pushing my dress straps off my shoulders and my dress down to my waist.

"Eva," he breathed, cupping my breasts. "My Eva."

"Yes," I whispered. "I'm yours. Forever."

I pushed his back up against the wall and went for his belt buckle. He sat down and lifted his hips so I could slide his jeans down his legs. Holding me close, he rocked me backward and covered me with his body.

"I love you," I cried softly, grabbing his backside and taking him inside of me. "I've loved you for as long as I can remember."

"Fuck, baby," he groaned. "I love you, I fuckin' love you, I love you so fuckin' much."

With every thrust, he proclaimed his love for me, moving faster and harder each time.

I reached beside me for Frankie's jeans and the serrated blade he kept sheathed on his belt.

"Harder, baby," I whispered, needing him distracted. "Give me all that love."

Frankie buried his face in my neck, his tears drenching my hair as his body began slamming into mine.

Gripping the handle of the dagger, I slid it out of its covering.

When I felt him stiffen, felt his orgasm, I ran my hand through his hair and gently tugged. "Look at me, baby."

He blinked up at me.

"I'm never going to leave you again, baby. You're with me always now," I whispered, tears streaming down my face. "No more nightmares."

He smiled at me, his lost-little-boy smile. "You've always made them go away."

I brushed my lips across his.

Then I sank the blade into the side of his neck, and with all my strength I wrenched it sideways and twisted.

1:32 p.m.

"We've got a hit," Quintanilla said, holding his cell phone to his ear. "Local uniforms spotted Deluva outside a motel a few towns over."

Deuce didn't ask any questions. He just kept praying.

"Tell them to hold off," Quintanilla said. "Deluva is undoubtedly armed, extremely dangerous, unstable as all hell, and he's got a hostage. I'm going to call a team in right now."

Quintanilla's eyes went wide and locked on him. He felt his stomach lurch.

She was not dead. She could not be dead. No. God, please God, don't let her be dead.

"When?" Quintanilla demanded.

Fuck. Fuck him. Fucking Christ. He couldn't deal. He couldn't. His kids couldn't deal. Kami and Devin couldn't deal. His boys couldn't deal. This could not happen.

Quintanilla hung up. "Deluva's dead."

He shot to his feet. "Eva?"

"Hysterical, but unharmed."

A violent shudder of relief tore through him.

"How'd they take him down?" Tap asked.

Quintanilla pressed his lips together and made a smacking sound. He looked around the club as if debating whether to share what he knew.

He sighed noisily. "They didn't. The woman did. Nearly severed his head clean off with a dagger. She came walking out of the room holding it, half-naked and covered in blood."

Kami fell to her knees screaming at the top of her lungs. Cox dropped down beside her and pulled her into his arms.

"Fuck…" Cox looked up at him, his boy's horrified expression mirroring how he felt. "Prez," he whispered. "Foxy…"

He sat back down and buried his face in his good hand. Mick's arm came around his shoulders and squeezed. "She's OK, Prez. She's alive."

"She's alive," he said hoarsely. "But I can tell you right fuckin' now, she sure as shit ain't OK."

Chapter
TWENTY-TWO

The Demons buried Frankie on a cloudy Tuesday, wearing his cut and my engagement ring and wedding ring on his pinkie finger. Deuce stayed by my side, holding me up when I would have collapsed. I was overwhelmed with grief and regret, swamped with guilt, and at the same time, relief so great I felt dizzy from it.

I hoped in death Frankie found the peace he never could find in life.

I stayed a long time after the service ended and the crowd disbanded. I talked to Frankie for a while and cried for a while.

Before I left, I traced his name on his tombstone. "Sweet dreams, baby," I whispered. "Always."

Before we headed home, Kami and I visited Chase's grave. Hand in hand, we sat down in the grass and leaned back against his tombstone. Sharing a $75,000 bottle of whiskey, we held each other and cried. We cried for very different reasons, but for Chase all the same. As fucked-up as both our relationships with him were, he had been loved. He'd just been too fucked-up to realize it.

Then Kami, Cox, Deuce, and I went home to our kids and our club, and the healing began.

Deuce was in a bad way. Worse off than anyone else. For a long time, he wouldn't touch me—couldn't touch me. He blamed himself for everything. It was his fault Frankie hadn't been found. It was his fault Frankie had been able to break inside the club, his fault that Frankie had forced himself on me, and his fault that I'd been the one to kill him.

But it wasn't. None of it was. It was Frankie's fault—all of it. This I had a hard time accepting as well. At first, I placed blame on myself, for letting my relationship with Frankie get to the point it had.

But I got there…alongside my family and my friends and my club…I got there.

Getting Deuce there was another matter altogether.

But we got through it. Together. It didn't happen overnight, and it wasn't easy.

Nothing worth doing ever is.

And love is worth everything.

EPILOGUE

Deuce scowled at his father-in-law. "You're older than me," he grumbled.

Preacher snorted. "Both in our fifties. Only difference is you got yourself a beautiful younger woman to keep you young, and all I got is a club full of stupid shitheads who think bathing is optional and farting is an art form."

They both looked to where Eva was standing and talking with Kami, a very pregnant Dorothy, Mick and his wife Adriana, and Danny and…ZZ, whose fucking arm was slung over his daughter's shoulders. His fists clenched, but he kept it reeled in. He promised Eva he wouldn't kick the shit out of him again. Danny was twenty-one years old, and Eva had said ZZ was head over heels for her. She kept reminding him that ZZ had never fallen into the same patterns the rest of his boys had. He didn't drink excessively, he didn't have a quick temper, he never disrespected a woman, and he didn't do whores.

Still…he really fucking hated it. Really. Fucking really.

He gritted his teeth and looked back at his wife.

She was thirty-five and fucking gorgeous. Her body was sleek and toned—thanks to yoga four times a week—but she still had her curves, so he was happy and didn't give a shit if she felt the need to twist her body into a pretzel and look damn ridiculous doing it.

Her dark hair was newly cut and hung halfway down her back in soft waves; she had bangs now, long and swept to the side—Danny's doing. She was wearing a pair of jeans he was sure were older than he was and looked it, and her old Led Zeppelin tee that showed her star-covered belly. No bra.

God, he loved her.

His tag around her neck was gleaming in the sunlight. Her iPod was shoved in her back pocket with her earbuds hanging halfway down her jeans. On her feet, pink Chucks. And even though he couldn't see it from this distance, on her left ring finger was the ring he put on her the day he married her—a thin platinum band inscribed with their names.

DEUCE & FOXY.

He watched her turn around and bend over to pick up Cox's and Kami's one-year-old son, Diesel, and saw his name—DEUCE—tattooed right above her ass in large, scrolling script. It had been his birthday present last year, and he'd been fucking her on her knees ever since.

"Fuck," he muttered.

Preacher glanced at him.

"Just thankin' God," he said, shaking his head, "for that fuckin' woman."

Preacher grinned.

"Never forget the day she came bouncin' into my fucked-up life, shakin' pigtails, singin' Janis, wearin' Chucks, sharin' peanuts, and straight up stole any decency I had left—which wasn't a whole lot—but she fuckin' took it, and I've been hers ever since."

Preacher's eyes glossed over. "Good thing I went up the river same time as your old man," he said, his voice breaking. "If you hadn't…if Frankie woulda—"

He clapped Preacher on the back. "Fuckin' yeah," he said roughly. "Don't I know it."

"Hi, Daddy!" Ivy yelled, running past them. "Hi, Grandpa!"

"Hiya, beautiful girl," Preacher said smiling.

"Get back here, you crazy little shit!" Cage bellowed, streaking across the lawn after her. "And give me my keys!"

Her blonde pigtails bouncing, her pink Chucks kicking up dirt, Ivy laughed her evil little laugh and kept running. Cage shot past her, circling around her. Ivy skidded to a stop; Cage faked right; Ivy whipped to her left, and Cage grabbed her. Swung her right off her feet and up through the air.

"Gotcha!" he said, tossing her up in the air and catching her. She shrieked and giggled and screamed until he set her down.

"Ivy Olivia West!" Eva yelled. "Give your brother his keys!"

Bending down in front of her, Cage rocked back on his heels and held out his hand.

"Here," she muttered, slapping the keys into his outstretched hand. Cage's hand closed around hers, and he pulled her forward into a bear hug.

"Love you, you crazy little shit," he growled. "Couldn't have asked for a better sister. 'Cause, ya know, Danny's kinda bitchy."

Danny flipped Cage off.

Ivy grinned. Cage grinned.

Deuce closed his eyes.

He stuck out his hand.

"Name's Deuce, sweetheart. My old man here is Reaper. It was nice talkin' with ya."

She put her tiny hand in his, and he squeezed.

"Eva," she whispered. "That's my name, and it was so, so great to meet you, too."

He smiled.

She smiled.

The rest is fuckin' history.

THE END